# THE SHINING COMPANY

*Vaguely, I was aware, to left and right, of riders crashing through the burning stockades – through and over in a score of places. I was aware of yelling faces and flamelight on the swinging blades of axes and the long straight Saxon knives, and the narrow heads of our own spears.*

Young Prosper is a shieldbearer for The Shining Company, a brotherhood of warriors chosen to defend the northern tribes of Britain from a Saxon invasion. With Conn, his bodyservant, Prosper leaves the valleys of home, to join a war of wits and weapons against the strong Saxon swords of the opposition.

# Rosemary Sutcliff

**Rosemary Sutcliff** was born in 1920, in Surrey, and spent her childhood travelling with her father. At two, a rheumatic disease had left her crippled for life and her schooldays began late and finished at fourteen because of, as she said, 'My entire lack of interest in being educated'. Reading Rudyard Kipling led her into a feeling for history, and perhaps her lack of mobility gave her a faultless eye for minute detail, and an interest in the outcasts of society.

She planned to be a painter, but at Art School found the physical demands of painting difficult and turned to writing. In 1950 her first book, *The Chronicles of Robin Hood*, was published. A series of magnificent books, often set in Roman Britain or the Dark Ages followed.

She won many honours, including the Carnegie Medal for *The Lantern Bearers* in 1959; the Boston *Globe-Horn Book* award in 1972; the Other Award in 1978; the OBE in 1975 and the CBE in 1991. By her death in 1992 she had written over forty books, the last of which was *The Shining Company*, a stunning tale of fellowship and betrayal.

In a letter to her publisher dated 29 November 1990, Rosemary Sutcliff explained why she wrote this book:

'For years and years, when reading for other stories, I kept finding mention of the Gododdin, and got gradu ally more fascinated, then I came on Professor Jackson's translation and read the whole thing and knew that it was the background for one of my kind of books. Soon after, I was in Edinburgh attending the launch of my 'Bonnie Dundee' and thought what a good chance to do some on-the-spot research into 6th Century Dyn Eidin. Spent most of 3 days in Edinburgh University Library and such like places, gathered a mountain of tradition but discovered that there was no archeological trace of human habitation before Medieval times! I decided to go ahead all the same, because I was sure there *must* be truth of some sort behind the tradition.

'. . . And *then*, this very summer, the summer that "Company" was published, a "Dig" mixed up with building a tunnel for military vehicles in the Castle, found traces and lots of them, of Iron Age, Roman period and post-Roman occupation!

'. . . Think of those modern young soldiers with their armoured vehicles and so on, to say nothing of the Lone Piper on the battlements at the end of the Edinburgh Tattoo (who I always have felt must be calling up ghosts), all living and training and having their being on the same chunk of rock but in a different layer of time, as my 300 young men training for that Kamikaze style attack on Catterick, around 1400 years ago!'

# THE SHINING COMPANY

## – *Rosemary Sutcliff* –

RANDOM HOUSE
MODERN CLASSICS

A Random House Modern Classic

Published by Random House Children's Books
20 Vauxhall Bridge Road, London SW1V 2SA

A division of Random House UK Ltd
London Melbourne Sydney Auckland
Johannesburg and agencies throughout the world

1 3 5 7 9 10 8 6 4 2

First published in Great Britain by The Bodley Head
1990

This edition 1994

Set by Pure Tech Corporation, Pondicherry, India
Printed and bound in Great Britain
by Clays Ltd St Ives plc

RANDOM HOUSE UK Limited Reg. No. 954009

ISBN 0 09 936621 5

# A Dedication

'This is the Gododdin, Aneirin sang it.'

So spoke forth Aneirin, Chief of Bards to the King of Dyn Eidin, when he made his great song of the men who went to Catraeth. But of course he sang only of the Three Hundred, the Companions with gold torques about their necks, not of the shieldbearers who rode at their heels. Yet we also were young, with the hearts high and the life sweet within us, and our homes left behind.

# Contents

# Contents

# – 1 –

# The Brown Boy

I am – I was – Prosper, second son to Gerontius, lord
of three cantrefs between Nant Ffrancon and the sea,
of a half-ruined villa that must have been a palace in
its day, of a hundred spears and many horses. My
father had little caring for me, keeping what heart's-
warmth he had for Owain my elder brother. Old Nurse
said that was because I was long-boned and tawny-fair
like my mother who died in giving me life, whereas
Owain was dark and thick-set like himself and most of
the people in the valley. But truth to tell, I did not feel
much lack. I had the other boys of the kindred to laugh
and fight with; I had Luned, only a few months older
than me, and I had Conn.

It was my twelfth name-day when my father gave me
Conn for a body servant.

I was with Tydeus my tutor in the schoolroom, trying
to read Herodotus' account of the three hundred Spartans at Thermopylae, when one of the house servants
came to call me to the study. A bar of watery sunlight
from the window slanted across the unrolled parchment on the table, throwing up the two lines of poetry
that seemed to stand clear from the rest.

> Tell them in Sparta, you who read,
> That we obeyed their orders and are dead.

I did not think much about it at the time, as I got up
and went hopefully to answer my father's summons.

But I remember now . . .

A few moments later I was standing just within the study doorway, staring at the newcomer; a boy of about my own age, brown of skin and hair and eyes, who stood and stared back at me without lowering his head. I was angry and disappointed, for I had hoped for one of Gwen's pups. She had had five, and my father could easily have spared one from the hunting pack. Also I knew that the boy was not a true gift. He would remain my father's property like all the other bondfolk about the place; and I was only being given the use of him, because now that I was twelve I could not, as my father had just pointed out, expect Old Nurse to go on seeing that I had clean tunics and the like. But that was not all: my father would have made a shrewd merchant if he had not been born to the chieftaincy, and prided himself on his eye for good stock and his ability to pick out a bargain where other men saw only damaged goods. And the boy in front of me was most assuredly damaged goods, standing crooked with his left knee swathed to the size of a pudding in filthy rags.

'It is an old hurt too long neglected; but it will mend,' said my father. 'He is your responsibility now. Take him down to the monastery for Brother Pebwyr to see it.'

It was the first fine day after a week of spring storms, and I could think of better things to do with it than trail my new and unwanted body servant down to the holy brother for tending, when Old Nurse could have seen to it just as well. But my father's eye was on me; and when he gave an order, whether it was to his son or the least among his bondfolk, he was used to being obeyed.

'Yes, my father,' I said, and to the boy, 'Come, you.' And swung on my heel and headed for the outer court and the track down the valley. And as I went, I heard the new servant's feet padding behind me, the steps uneven because of his knee.

The sound followed me, proud and uncomplaining as a hound at my heels, through the clustered living-places of the kindred and down-stream past the mill among its alder trees and the smithy where Loban, my father's smith, was at work on an axehead, and in through the monastery orchard where the brown-robed brothers were busy among the bee skeps under the apple trees, to the gate of the monastery itself. I was well used to the huddle of farm buildings and thatched sleeping bothies about the small wattle church, and usually I would have stopped for a word with Brother Iorwin who was lime-washing the granary wall, or to scratch the back of the Prior's breeding sow who lay in a sunny patch surrounded by eleven contented piglets. But that day I had no thought but to get what I had come for over and done with as quickly as might be; and I headed straight through, without pausing, for the bothy on the far side, where Brother Pebwyr the Infirmarer brewed his evil-smelling salves and potions and doctored the hurts and sicknesses of all the people of the valley.

He was there now, boiling something over a small bright charcoal fire at the end of the crowded and brown-shadowed workplace. Whatever it was it must have been at a critical stage, for he did not even look up as we came in through the low doorway, only jerked his head towards the bench just inside.

I flung myself down on it, groaning inwardly for my wasted name-day, and would have left my new body servant standing, but the thought came to me that it might not be a good idea, not on that knee. It might not help the healing: and the sooner it healed the sooner he would cease being a nuisance and begin to be of some use. 'Sit,' I said, and jerked a thumb at the other end of the bench.

He sat, sticking his left leg awkwardly out in front of him, and stared through the doorway to where the first swallows were darting and swooping in the sunshine.

The brew in the pot came to the boil and Brother Pebwyr threw in broad-leaved herbs from the pile beside him. There was a hiss like fiery serpents, and another smell was added to the heady reek of spices and simples that already filled the place, and the pot went off the boil. Brother Pebwyr brought it up again three times, very slowly, then drew it to the side of the fire. 'It can see to itself for a while, now,' he said, and looked up for the first time.

'God's greeting to you, my son, and who is this that you bring with you?'

'My new servant,' I told him. 'My father handed him over to me this morning. But he has some kind of hurt on his knee, and so I bring him to you.'

The Infirmarer nodded. 'So, then let us be looking what is to be done.'

He came out from his crowding shadows and squatted down beside the boy and began to loosen the knot of the clumsy bandages. He was a snub-faced little man with not much more shape to him than an egg, but he had the kind of hands that should belong to a harper, and he used them just as surely as he loosed the stained and stiffened rags. 'What name do they call you by?' he asked, seeming to have forgotten me entirely.

'Conn,' said the brown boy, sounding as though his mouth were dry.

And I looked round at him, somehow surprised. I had been so taken up with disappointment at being given a body servant when I wanted a hound pup, that I had never even thought about him having a name, let alone thought to ask it.

Brother Pebwyr said, 'Then, Conn, sit very still, and I will hurt you as little as may be,' and he began to ease back the makeshift bandage.

I had got up so as not to be in his way, but I stood watching, somehow not able to look away, and I saw the crusts and the angry hole and the surrounding pale puffiness of an old abscess that had maybe started to heal and then broken down again, and my belly cringed a little.

'How did this come about?' Brother Pebwyr asked.

'A mule kicked me.' The dryness and the careful levelness were still in Conn's voice.

'So – and how long ago?'

'Two months – maybe three.'

'That is too long, but now we will start the mending.' The little man got up, rubbing his own knees – like a lot of the older brethren he had pains in them when there was rain about – too much kneeling, I suppose – and hobbled away into the shadows beyond the brazier and began to gather up things that lurked there. In a while he came back with fresh bandage linen and water from the big crock in the corner, and squatting down again began to bathe the place. When the bathing was over, he poured in a few drops of yellowish liquid from a small sinister looking flask. Conn drew in his breath through shut teeth but made no other sound. And Brother Pebwyr spread thick dark salve on a pad of linen and bound it over the old hurt.

'There,' he said by and by, gathering up the tools of his craft. 'All's over for one day.'

'Am I to send him back tomorrow?' I asked. At least the boy knew the way now, and could bring himself down.

But the Infirmarer shook his head. 'I have other ills to tend. Give him over to the Old Nurse tomorrow, she has as much skill as I in the healing of wounds. Bring him to me once, when the healing is complete, and so all will be well in Christ's name.'

A short while later, with Conn again padding hound-wise behind me, I was heading back through the monks' orchard, on to the old chariot tract that led homeward up the valley. It is strange how it lies clear in my mind even now, every detail of that day. The great head of Yr Widdfa away beyond the lesser hills that closed the valley, rising into the drifting spring sky, still wearing its mane of last winter's snow; the alders above the mill already hazed with thin first leaf, and my father's mares in the in-pastures beginning to show the weight of their unborn foals, and I remember too tipping back my head and seeing the broad out-thrust shoulder of the high moors that seemed almost to close the valley, and the blunt turf hummocks of old defences against the sky, where the long-past chieftains of my line had had their strong-hold before ever the Legions came and they moved down out of the clouds to the comfort of the valley floor and built themselves our great villa-house in the Roman style.

The old track led up between the thatched house-places of the kindred straight to the timber gate that was broad enough to let in piled grain carts and driven cattle at tribute time, and the gate stood open as always in time of peace. But I turned aside into our own orchard, heading for the rear of the house. For at this time of day, and now that the weather had cleared, Old Nurse would have brought out her sewing or whatever tasks were to hand, to sit on the colonnade steps in the sunshine, where she could keep her eye on all that passed in the outer court.

Old Nurse was so old that her memories went back far enough to join with men whose own memories touched the time when the Legions had scarcely left Britain, and she had spoken in her youth with men who had spoken with Arthur Pendragon, him that among his own hills was still called Artos the Bear. At least, that was Old Nurse's story. She was almost as good a storyteller as my father's harper. But she was as curious as a squirrel, and though I knew that I would have to tell her every detail of Conn and his injured knee and Brother Pebwyr's leeching of it, tomorrow, I was in no mood for it just now. So I made for the little postern gate behind the bath house, meaning to take a short cut across the herb garden to my own sleeping quarters, and so found myself having to tell most of it to Luned instead.

Luned, my kinswoman, had been brought up under our roof since her parents had died of the fever that comes sometimes in the spring after a mild wet winter, and neither of us could remember a time when we had not been together, so that it was almost as though we were brother and sister. She was squatting on her heels where the wood-violets grew thick under the thorn hedge, searching among the heart-shaped leaves when we came in through the postern. I whistled, and she looked round and saw us, then got to her feet and came running, thrusting the dark wings of hair back from her face as she came.

'There is fresh salmon out of the weir for supper,' she said. At winter's end, after the months of dried and salted stuff, that made good hearing, but her eyes were going over my shoulder. 'That is the new servant? Old Nurse was telling me –'

'Old Nurse talks too much!' I said.

'Why? It is not a secret, is it? Everybody knows that Uncle has bought a boy from the traders to be your body servant.' She looked him up and down with interest – it was not every day that one saw a new face, even a servant's face, in the valley – and her gaze found Brother Pebwyr's bandage. 'He has a hurt knee.'

'He was kicked on it by a mule three months ago, and the place hasn't healed properly. That's why Father got him cheap.'

'Poor boy,' she said, and her voice softened. We had been talking about him as though he were a horse or an arm-ring, as though he were not there at all, but now she spoke to him direct, 'Have you a name, boy?'

He nodded.

'Then what is it?'

'Conn. They used to call me Conn.'

'That's not a name of our people. Where are you from?'

'From Eriu, before the man-traders came.' He spoke steadily, but his voice had a raw edge to it, and I turned to look at him. That was two things I had learned about my new body servant, and neither of them I had found out for myself. For a moment that gave me an odd twinge of something uncomfortable, shame, I suppose, but it was gone again almost, though not quite, before I was aware of it.

Luned changed the subject in the quick glancing way she had, like a minnow in shallow water. 'I hoped there would be violets after the rain, but I can't find any.'

And Conn answered her, 'There will be violets soon, now that the fine weather has come, little mistress.' It was the first time I had heard him speak, except in answer to a question.

The three of us went on towards the inner court together, walking like hunters in single file – for the path between the rosemary bushes was too narrow for two to walk abreast – with Luned in the middle and Conn walking stiff-legged in his new tight bandage, bringing up the rear.

The next morning I took Conn in search of Old Nurse. Probably he could have found her on his own, by that time, but I knew Old Nurse. If you wanted her to do anything for you, it was best to go yourself and ask, with courtesy and humility. We found her at last in one of the storerooms, checking the cloth of the last year's clip and scolding one of the maids for a fault that she had found in the weaving. I explained all things to her, and she abandoned the wool and the weeping maid and, grumbling under her breath about never being able to finish one job before the next needed doing, she led us off to the little room, close to the herb garden, where she kept her own remedies and dealt with all the ills of the household that were not bad enough for Brother Pebwyr.

She clucked like a hen at sight of Conn's knee when she had the bandages off, and set to work on it with her sleeves thrust up. The old abscess looked much as it had yesterday, though it was certainly not in quite such a mess. My stomach cringed again, and I would

have taken myself off and left them to it. But something held me there. She was not rough, but she was in
a hurry, and her hands had not the calm sureness of
Brother Pebwyr's, also she seemed in an unaccount-
ably ill temper, and I had an odd feeling that to leave
my servant alone in her hands would be too much like
abandoning him. So, grudgingly, I remained standing
by and watching the work go forward.

'Well, don't be standing there like a salmon with the
gapes,' she said at last, knotting off the fresh bandage,
when all was done. 'Take him away until tomorrow, I've
enough work waiting to be done: too much for a body
that's head aches as sore as mine does.' And she sneezed
and rubbed her nose with the back of her hand.

On the green edge of daylight next morning, I woke to
find Conn, come up from the old slaves' quarters
where he slept, standing in the doorway waiting for me
to open my eyes.

'The old nurse said I am to bring you the clean tunic
that she washed for you,' he said, when he saw that I
was awake.

I flung back the warm sheepskin rugs and struggled
up, yawning. The morning still had a chill to it, and I
grabbed the tunic he held out to me and pulled on the
warm folds of saffron wool, and demanded my belt.
He looked about him in the light of the sinking night-
lamp and picked up the broad strap with its bronze
buckle from where it lay on the clothes chest. As he
turned with it, the skirt of his tunic swung out, and I
glimpsed the paleness of bandage linen under it.

'Did she seem to be in a sweeter temper this morning?' I asked.

He shook his head. 'I'd not be knowing, master. She's taken to her bed with the head cold that was brewing yesterday. One of the women gave me your tunic and the message.'

And that left the problem of who was going to dress Conn's knee. Not that there was any problem really: plenty of other servants could do it. Only – Conn was a stranger. The bondfolk of the villa were not over-welcoming to strangers and newcomers . . . I could send him back to Brother Pebwyr, of course, but that seemed somehow a poor-spirited thing to do. I hankered after the Infirmarer's good opinion, I suppose, and had a feeling, without knowing quite why, that if I did that, he would think the less of me. Maybe it would not matter leaving it for one day? Or, of course, I could do it myself. I had helped Cu, my father's hound-master, doctor a sick or injured hound before now: there had been the time last year when Gelert, who was young and foolish, had got his flank laid open by a boar's tusk, and Cu and I had saved him when everybody else was saying that a knife across his throat was the most sensible thing. But that had been different; a hound I knew and loved, a new clean wound . . . At the thought of the pulpy mass under Conn's knee my belly still turned a little – and anyhow I had other and better things to do with the first days of spring. Conn was still standing in front of me, holding out my belt. I took it from him and put it on. 'Go back and get the things she used yesterday from Old Nurse.'

He looked at me, questioningly, and I realized that we had not in fact mentioned his knee that morning, and he had no idea what I was talking about. 'Your knee. Someone's got to do it. Best be me.'

'I am thinking I can do it myself,' he said.

I dragged the strap tight through its bronze buckle. 'Don't be stupid, nobody can do that kind of thing properly themselves. Get the stuff from Old Nurse, and don't forget some warm water, and take it down to the bath house. That will be the best place to do it.'

And when he had departed on his errand, I went out into the growing light and headed for the bath house myself.

There would be no one there at that hour of the morning, though I could hear voices and sounds of movement from kitchen quarters and stable court, the whole villa waking to life and the new day all around me. It was really only Luned and the women of the household and very occasionally my father who used the bath house now, and then only the plunge-bath, for the hypocausts that had heated the sweating chamber in the high and far off days had long since fallen into ill repair. When the bath house was in use pails of hot water would be carried in, and thick linen towels, and there would be a great coming and going. The rest of the time it mouldered quietly, my brother and I and men of the household much preferring to do our bathing in the stream. But the bath house would, as I had said, be a good place to deal with Conn's knee; plenty of space and nothing to get fouled and less likelihood of onlookers. If I was going to do the thing, I had no wish for people coming to see what I was doing or telling me that I was doing it wrong.

I pushed the door open and went in. The cool damp smell of the place met me, and the faint whisper of moving water leaking in at one end of the plunge-bath and out at the other, and the flutter of bird wings overhead when the first house martins had returned to their nests in the roof. I sat down on the stone bench and waited, fidgeting, until I heard Conn's uneven footsteps on the cobbles outside. It seemed a long time and I told him so.

He set down the things he carried on the end of the bench. 'It took a while to get the things from Old Nurse. She was threatening to get out of her bed, too.'

'Well, now that you *are* here, pull that stool into the doorway where there's light to see by, and sit down,' I told him. The water he had brought with him in a covered bowl was still too hot. I took it over to the carved lion-mask whose trickle fed the plunge-bath, and poured cold water into it till I judged it cool enough, collected the big bronze rinsing basin from the corner, and came back to the doorway where Conn was sitting rigid, staring out into the early sunshine, just as he had sat in Brother Pebwyr's doorway two days ago.

I squatted on to my heels beside him and set to work trying to remember exactly what Old Nurse had done the day before. The wad of linen was stuck again, but not so badly as before. I eased it away with care and concentration. If I must do the thing at all I would do it to the best that was in me. I bathed the place and poured in a few drops of barley spirit, Conn drawing in his breath at the bite of it but making no other sound. I spread the salve with its strong smell of yarrow and feverfew on to a fresh wad and bound it in place. The bandage looked a bit clumsy when I knotted it off, but I thought that it would hold. I sat there for a few moments looking at it, aware suddenly of the shadows of the house martins darting to and fro. I remember that clearly. The odd thing is that I do not remember feeling sick at all.

'I am thinking that it will hold well enough,' said Conn, bending his knee a little, in much the same tone in which he had told Luned that there would be violets soon.

I looked up to tell him that I did not need *him* to tell me if my work would pass, and found his quiet brown gaze steady on my face. For a few moments we looked at each other, really looked, I suppose, eye to eye, for the first time. And oddly, it was not the look of one who had had a thing done to him and one who had done it, but of two who had done something, shared something, between them. And suddenly we were grinning at each other.

I gathered up the salves and spare bandage linen, and flung the stained dressing into a corner for someone to clean up later, while Conn poured the dirty water into the drainage channel. And together we went out into the morning, leaving the doorway open to the darting house martins behind us.

That night Conn spread his rug across the doorway of my sleeping cell, and slept there according to the custom for a body slave or an armour bearer, or as a favourite hound for that matter.

# The Archangel Dagger

It was young summer, dapple-shade in the valley woods and the hawthorn flowers already fading before we paid the clearing visit to Brother Pebwyr.

'So. It is finished and well finished,' he said, looking at the purplish scar below Conn's knee where the old abscess had been. 'Away with both of you and trouble me no more.'

I never did tell him that for three days it had been I and not Old Nurse who had tended the place. It seemed a long time ago and not very important any more. But I mind the sense of holiday that was now on me, I think on both of us, as we made our way down through the monastery apple trees.

Maybe it was because of that sense of holiday that we turned aside from the homeward track and the school-room where Tydeus would be waiting for me, and went instead to watch Loban at work in his smithy. Maybe it was because the Fates who weave the lives of mortal men were already setting up their loom for us . . .

Loban was an old man, beginning to be hunched by the long years at his work; all shoulders and no legs, but he must always have been small and meagre, and I had often wondered how he had managed to swing the great sledgehammer in his young days when he was learning his trade. He was a Master Smith now, with men under him to call him lord, and seldom set his own hand to a horseshoe or even a plough-share, keeping his skills for fine weapons and the like; his tool was the light hand-hammer that rang like a bell all up and down the valley.

But when we came towards the low-browed smithy that sprawled like a sleeping hound under the alder trees, the hand-hammer was silent and Loban himself was sitting on the bench before the door, working on something small laid across his knee, and deep in talk with the travelling merchant who had claimed guest-right for himself and his men in our hall the night before. Phanes of Syracuse, he called himself.

The Master Smith turned the thing on his leather-aproned knee, and I saw that it was a dagger, and guessed that the merchant must have brought it down to have something done to it. Normally Loban would have left that kind of small repair job to one of his underlings; it must be that the merchant was an old friend, or the dagger had something special about it to make it worthy of his attention.

I drew nearer to look, Conn just behind me as usual, and saw that indeed the dagger was not like any that ever I had seen before. The slim bluish blade on which the light through the alder leaves played like water, the like of *that* I had seen before among Loban's finest blades; but the hilt was strange to me. The hilt was a wonder. Of chiselled silver, the grip shaped like a human figure – no, not human, not mortal, that is, a fierce and austere male archangel clad in its own close-folded wings, the head with its gilded halo forming the pommel, the feet strong planted on the cross-piece.

Loban looked up as my shadow fell across his work, and said, 'If you are minded to watch, then sit you and watch, but do not you be standing there stealing my daylight from me.'

I muttered an apology and squatted down on to my heels. Looking up at the owner of the dagger I found him watching me with a glint of amusement in his eyes. Strange eyes, bee-brown, with somehow a look of dry winds and sunshine and far places behind them. 'This is not such a dagger ever I have seen before,' I said. 'Where does it come from?'

'From Constantinople.' His tongue had a twang to it that I knew was Greek because Tydeus my tutor had it also. 'I bought it from a friend of mine in the Emperor's bodyguard who was . . . somewhat light in his purse at the time, having wagered too heavily on the Greens at the races on a day when the Blues had all the luck.'

Something, a sort of fellow-feeling I suppose, stirred within me for the man of the Emperor's bodyguard who had found himself so short of money that he had had to sell this dagger which must surely have been his most treasured possession.

'If he was a friend,' I asked (I had not meant it to sound quite so accusing) 'could you not have bought something else from him?'

Phanes of Syracuse shook his head. 'Nothing of sufficient value. Nothing that would teach him such a useful lesson. Don't take it to heart – coming and going as I do along the roads and seaways of the world, there's a good chance that I shall come sailing up the Golden Horn once more on a day when the luck of the race-course has been with the Greens.'

I only half understood, but the words had magic in them, the sound of incantation and harpsong, and I understood clearly enough that I wanted to hear more.

'Tell about Constantinople,' I demanded, and settled more comfortably on to my haunches as one does when listening to a story.

The merchant's brown wind-burned face creased into a deeper smile. I suppose he had met boys eager for travellers' tales often enough before.

'So. I tell you about Constantinople, the Golden City,' he said, and sitting forward, elbows on knees, he began.

I listened, sometimes watching the archangel dagger as Loban turned it to and fro on his knees renewing the worn silver wires that bound the crossguard, sometimes watching the merchant's face, where it seemed almost that I could see the distance and the far off places, behind his eyes. Something of Constantinople I knew already from other travelling merchants. I knew that it was a city at the far end of the world, and had its name from the Emperor Constantine who had set up his capital there when the old world-striding Roman Empire was split in two; and that it was still the capital of the eastern half, the one remaining half since Rome herself had long ago fallen to the barbarians. But this was different. Maybe the man was a master-storyteller; maybe it was to do with the dagger itself, fiercely beautiful and so alien to my own world, that had come from the other end of the earth and like enough would one day be going back to the far country that it came from; maybe it was the two things coming together and gaining potency from each other . . . some kind of magic was weaving itself within me; an awakening magic, so that for the first time I knew, really knew, not just with my head but in my heart's core, that there was another world beyond the mountains; not the world of legend and faery of which the harpers sang, but a real world of living people, in which one of the Emperor's bodyguard was at that moment lacking his best dagger because he had wagered more than he could afford on a horse race, just as I lacked my enamelled belt-buckle because I had wagered Colwen of the kindred that I would reach the top of the oak tree by the ford before he did.

When the repair work was finished and the voice of the merchant fell silent, I woke up, as though I had been dreaming, and found my own world not quite the same as it had been before.

Beside me, Conn squatted on one heel, his left leg stuck out in front of him because it still hurt to bend it right under. He was leaning forward, his gaze fixed almost hungrily on the dagger. And somehow I knew that he had been sitting like that all the while.

'There it is, as good as though it came fresh from the hand of its maker-smith,' Loban said, handing it back to its present owner.

Conn's gaze moved with it. 'What makes it like that?'

The merchant thought that he meant the hilt, and answered patiently – it must have seemed a foolish question – 'The craftsman made it so, out of silver and his own skill.'

Conn shook his head like a horse beset by gadflies. 'Na, na, the blade. What makes the blade so that the light slips on it like the stripes in a river current?'

Loban took up the question. 'See now, for a good blade, one that will not betray its man in battle, rods of hard and soft iron must be heated and braided together. Then is the blade folded over and hammered flat again, and maybe yet again, many times for the very finest blades.' He had taken the dagger back into his own hand and was showing the way of it. 'So the hard and soft iron are mingled without blending, before the blade is hammered up to its finished form and tempered, and ground to an edge that shall draw blood from the wind. So comes the pattern, like oil and water that mingle but do not mix. Yet it is the strength of the blade for without the hard iron the blade would bend in battle, and without soft iron it would break.' The tip of one horny finger traced out the streaks of the metal as he spoke, 'It's the strength of the blade, which is the aim of all this, the beauty is by the way. The beauty is by the grace of God.'

Conn put out a finger also, and touched the blade, following the wave pattern very gently, as though he were exploring a mystery.

'And you – you also have fashioned blades like this?' he said.

And still faintly dream-bound as I was, I realized that something was happening which was not a good idea.

'We must be on our way,' I said, pulling my legs under me. 'I promised Luned I would take her to see Maia's new foal. She is not allowed in the stable court on her own.' I got to my feet, Conn following with the slowness of regret. 'It has been a good hour,' I added by way of thanks to the two men still sitting companionably on the bench. And set off home, with Conn like a loyal but unwilling hound at my heels.

We passed the mill and came to the place where the track crossed the stream, and paused as we often did to watch the flickering minnows in the clear mead-coloured depth below the ford. And watching the minnows, under the ripple pattern of the water surface, Conn said carefully, 'If I were to go down to

the smithy, just while you were at your lessons with
Tydeus – if I were to ask him, would you be thinking
that Loban might teach me to be a smith?'

'No,' I said.

There was a silence filled with the suck and ripple of
the water over the stones, and somewhere away down
the stream, a cuckoo calling. Then, 'Why not?' Conn
asked. 'I would work for him in payment.'

'Don't you know?' I felt for the moment that I wanted
to hit him for making me say it. 'My father would never
allow it. No bondman may learn to be a smith, or a
clerk, or a bard, because all these must be free men, and
so if a bondman comes by any of those skills –'

The words stuck in my throat, and the calling of the
down-valley cuckoo took on a note of mockery.

Conn went slowly white under the brown of his skin.
'He would become free,' he said. 'I am sorry. I did not
understand.'

'It was not me that made the law,' I told him angrily,
miserably.

Conn went on watching the minnows a few moments
longer. Then he looked up with his slow, grave smile.
'That I know,' he said, almost consolingly.

I tried to answer the smile, but my face felt tight. I
managed a crack of laughter instead. 'We could always
run for it, one night, and join the Emperor's bodyguard. Phanes said that there are men in it from all
across the world; any man who can call himself a
swordsman, Phanes said.'

'The trouble is that neither of us can call himself a
swordsman.' The trouble with Conn was that he never,
well hardly ever, winged off on any kind of flight of
fancy.

'Not yet.' It was a good flight, and I hung to it. 'But we could not go for a few years yet, anyway.'

And, 'That would give us time to learn,' Conn agreed. 'Meanwhile we must be moving, or the little mistress will be thinking that you have forgotten your promise.'

We went on our homeward way. But as we left the ford behind us, he was dragging his left leg a little as he still did when he was tired, or sore at heart.

# – 3 –
# The White Hart

Other word from the outside world came trickling into the valley through the months of that summer. Not from jewelled cities at the far ends of the Earth, but from beyond the mountains, all the same . . . Word of the northern kings and their kingdoms, Aidan of Dalriada, Gartnait, Lord of Caledonia, word out of Strathclyde and little Elmet; word of Mynyddog of the Gododdin, foremost of them all, who men called Mynyddog the Wealthy, Lord of Dyn Eidin of the Many Goldsmiths; all looking with anxious eyes towards the east, where the new Saxon kingdoms of Deira and Bernicia had begun to loom like gathering storm clouds.

For almost the lifetime of a man Bernicia had been only an offshoot of much stronger Deira, only a scatter of settlements along the coast. But in the first few years under their new king and warleader, Aethelfrith, they had been spreading and gaining strength. One day they would be as great as Deira – greater – one day the two might join warhosts; and when that day came, the storm clouds would spill over and come sweeping across the land.

'But if we – the kingdoms of Britain – also joined warhosts, couldn't we fling them back into the sea?' I remember asking Tydeus my tutor.

Tydeus looked up from the Herodotus unrolled on the schoolroom table, and said, 'Maybe, but it is a large "if". A lesson which my own Greek states found over hard in the learning.'

And when I asked much the same question of my father's harper as he walked under our apple trees seeking out a new song for supper, he said, 'I am thinking that on the day that the tribes learn to stand together instead of slitting each other's throats, the stars will fall out of the sky.'

'It was done before,' I said.

He drew a slow fall of notes from the little hand-harp he carried.

'Aye, in Arthur's time; Aidan and Gartnait and Mynyddog the Golden, they are not Arthur. Urien of Rheged tried it when your father and I were young, but Urien was slain – and that was not even the Saxons' doing, but the work of envy and hatred among his own kind. So Urien died and after him his son, and where is Rheged now?'

It was the kind of word that merchants and wandering harpers had brought into the valley for as long as I could remember, but it had not seemed quite real before. I have wondered, since, whether the threat really darkened and drew nearer that summer, or whether it was just that I was growing older, or whether the strange and beautiful dagger, coming from far away, had somehow pricked a hole in my familiar world and let in the world outside . . .

But from that summer on, I began to take more seriously the hours on the training ground below the settlement, where I learned horsemanship and running and wrestling and the skills of sword and shield and spear with the other boys of the kindred, feeling more of sense and purpose in them than ever I had done before.

Life in the valley went on as it had always done. Harvest followed seed time; hunting for fresh meat in the winter, when we mounted the wolfguard over the lambing pens and every full moon brought the threat of cattle raiders. Spring when the streams ran green with melt-water from the snows of Yr Widdfa. Autumn when they ran yellow with fallen birch leaves.

And so there came an evening a year and more after the merchant with the archangel dagger.

It was harvest time and so we were set free, me from my tutor and the training ground, Luned from Old Nurse and the skills of the women's quarters; and the three of us had been down-valley helping to get the harvest in. We came up slowly, scratching at our midge bites as we came, a mood of deep contentment on us, for it was not so easy for the three of us to be off together about our own affairs. We would have gone in by way of the stables and the stackyard, but the trampling of horses and the voices of men in the outer court drew us round that way instead, to see what was afoot.

My brother had been out hunting with a few boon companions – which might seem strange at harvest time when the rest of us were slaving in the fields, but the deer had been raiding the ripe corn. Now they were back, and with a couple of carcasses slung across the ponies' backs, but they seemed not best pleased, for all that.

Owain was giving tongue as he swung down from his weary horse, 'Not a sign of the brute. Well, he can be finding his own way home – or not, for all I care.'

'Lost a hound?' I asked one of our huntsmen, standing near.

'Aye,' he said.

'Which one?'

'Gelert.'

It would be Gelert, of course, born foolish and unfortunate.

The huntsman was turning away, but I grabbed his arm. 'Where?'

He paused and looked round at me, frowning. I think he was not happy himself at coming home with a hound missing out of the pack. 'If I knew that, maybe t'would have been easier to find him. We hunted down towards Coed Dhu and when the hunting was done and we came to whip in the hounds, he was not there. Maybe Gwyn ap Nudd took him to hunt the storm clouds with his own pack.' He laughed angrily, but made the sign against ill luck as he said it, and pulled his arm free and was gone.

I stood a moment thinking. Gelert had been special to me ever since I had helped Cu the houndmaster to get him over the bear's gash in his flank. Now, knowing him, he had probably run into trouble of some kind. I spoke over my shoulder to Conn, 'I'm away down to Coed Dhu.' And then, for the day had been long and it was near supper time, 'Go you and get us something to eat from the cookhouse, and come on after me.'

'Anyone who finds the brute can keep him,' Owain was shouting as I slid out through the crowded gateway and turned down-valley into the thickening of the evening light.

In a little I abandoned the track and turned up the left flank of the valley. I was on the edge of the scrubby birch cover beyond the intake land when Conn caught up with me, running lop-legged with barley bread and ewe milk cheese in a napkin. And we were hardly into the denser mazes of the woods when Luned came darting among the trees to join us, with her skirts kilted to her knee.

'Have you found him yet?' she demanded breathlessly.

'Does it look as though we had? We are scarcely into the woods yet,' I said, 'and you should not be here at all!'

'I came to help you find him. I know the woods as well as you.'

'But you're a girl,' I pointed out in exasperation. 'If you are out in the wild all night – and we well may be – Old Nurse will be angry and go to my father, and I shall be the one that's blamed, and I shall be the one that's beaten!'

'Three of us will be more like to find him than two,' Luned said. 'Is that not worth a beating?'

I hesitated, and she added in a swift piteous voice, 'You are not the only one to care what happens to Gelert.'

Conn stood looking from one to the other of us in the dusk, saying nothing. But I knew whose side he was on.

'Come then,' I said, and the three of us went on together, sharing out the bannock and cheese and eating as we went.

Behind us in the cleared land the light still lingered, but the shadows were gathering under the branches and as we thrust deeper and ancient oak and thorn took the place of birch and bird-cherry, the darkness crouched thick among the trees.

We pushed on steadily, following the shape of the land until we came to the place where the valley divided, and the northern cwm dropped steeply downward into the dark tide of the big tree country, the wildwood that flowed up there from the depth of the lowland forests, and the stream, parting from our own water, went down through Coed Dhu, the Black Wood. We followed the stream for a while, calling and whistling as we went, pausing from time to time to listen, but there was no answering bark; no sound but of our own making, faint brushing through the undergrowth, the snap of a dead stick underfoot, once a floundering crash as Conn fell through the rotten timber of a long fallen tree trunk into an ants' nest beneath. These, and the strange half-sounds that were the voice of the forest at night.

After a long while – it seemed a long while – with the Black Wood and the yew trees that gave it its name left behind us, we were in a part of the forest that was strange to us. Maybe in the daylight it would have been familiar enough but, now in the dark, it seemed not quite like any place where ever we had been before. We were not lost; we could have turned and found our way back easily enough, for somewhere away to our right was the whisper of falling water, which in these hills must lead back to our own young river; but none the less the wildwood had taken on a strangeness all about us, and I was glad not to be alone in it. We had been moving well spread out, though within call of each other, and the other two must have felt the same as I did, for without anything said we began to draw nearer together, and we were shoulder close once more when the wonder happened; the wonder in a way was the start of all that followed after . . .

The trees began to thin, and we came out on to the edge of a clearing; and in the same moment the harvest moon, which had been veiled by thunder-wrack, sailed out into a lake of clear sky. Ragged silver wings of cloud made the shores of the lake glimmer, and beyond the fringe of hazel and hawthorn that still lay between us and open ground, a milky mane of moonlight flowed over the clearing. Everything was very still; even the night-time sounds of the forest had fallen away, so that it was as though everything waited with held breath. For maybe three heartbeats of time the stillness endured, for we were downwind of the small herd of deer grazing on the far side. Though they must have heard us coming, there had been no high excited shouts of men on the hunting trail, no belling of hounds or echoing death-music of horns; and they lifted their heads to look in our direction seeming more curious than afraid. They had last summer's fawns with them, and one, over bold, even took a step or two in our direction. The doe called him back instantly, and as though her coughing call acted as some kind of danger signal, the whole herd took fright.

In an instant the clearing was full of movement and flickering shapes as the deer leapt away towards the shelter of the nearest trees. They crashed into the undergrowth as into water, sending up showers of leaves like spray, and were gone.

All save one. Just clear of the woodshore a big buck paused and half-turned to look back as though the habits and fears of the herd were not for him. Beyond him the dappled and ring-straked shadows of the trees closed in, but the moonlight fell full flood upon him, and showed him pure white.

There had been no word of a white hart anywhere in our hunting runs; maybe he had come in from some distant valley, driven out by his own herd because of his colour, or fleeing from the hunt, or – for a moment the thought came upon me that he was some creature out of ancient legend, such as the harpers sang of beside the fire on winter nights. He stood with his head back, poised and proud under the arching crown of antlers, seeming not so much to shine in the moonlight as to be fashioned of the same stuff as the moonlight itself. For a long breath-held moment we looked at each other. I'll swear we looked at each other, eyes into eyes as men look, and for that moment it was as though some enchantment held us all, humans and beast alike, within a perfect circle that had neither beginning nor end. And then the circle was broken by the desperate, mournful baying of a far-off hound. And the white hart turned and sprang away after the rest of the herd.

And now that we had the moonlight to see by, the forest grew familiar again, and we knew where we were.

'That's Gelert!' Conn said, as though there had been no break in our search. 'And something is wrong.'

'Come you,' I said, and next instant we were off running in the direction from which the sound had come, crashing through undergrowth that snatched at us with whippy branches and bramble-snarls, and calling as we ran.

The frantic sound, more howling than baying, came again from exactly the same quarter as before, downhill from us and still far off. Gelert was not moving, not coming to meet us. Maybe he could not move . . .

As the land dropped more steeply and the tree-tangle grew more dense, we could not run, but we pushed on with all the speed that we could make. I knew where we were now, but all the same I nearly pitched headlong when the land suddenly fell away from my feet. We were on the edge of one of those winter-bourns gouged deep out of the hillside by the melt-waters of Yr Widdfa; raging white-water in the winter rains or the melting snows, dry as old bones at this time of year. Hazel and hawthorn made a dragon-tangle along the lip of the sheer drop, and out of the darkness below came a frantic whining.

'Wait here,' I told the other two. 'Then you can help me if I need pulling up.'

'Let me go,' Conn said.

'Gelert is my dog,' I said, not noticing what I'd said until after the thing was spoken. Anyhow, we had none of us enough breath to argue. I found a place where a tree coming down in some past storm had pulled the bank away and made the slope easier, and dropped over the edge, finding a handhold among the bared roots, another on a hawthorn sapling growing between two rocks, and scrambled on down, the smell of moss and torn earth strong and heavy in my throat.

Below me, in the darkness of the overarching streamside tangle, something moved and gave a piteous whimper.

'Softly now, I come,' I called, groping for a foothold. I found the foothold, and it gave way with me, and I fell crashingly into the darkness.

The next thing I knew was a warm tongue licking my face as I hauled myself to my feet, and the living harshness of a hound's coat under my hand; and the anxious voices of Conn and Luned demanding, 'Is it well with you?' and 'Have you got him?' from surprisingly close overhead.

I gulped back some of the air that had been knocked out of me, and called up, 'Aye,' which answered both questions in one, for my chief concern just then was in finding how it was with Gelert. My feet slipping among the stones of the dry stream bed, I had my hands on his neck, exploring, and found the answer quickly enough. Gelert's broad studded collar was caught on the sharp spine of an alder root which had hooked through it, holding him captive. I mind talking to him as I set about getting him free. 'Easy now – easy now, Gelert the bold – sweff, sweff, old hero –'

I got the collar freed, while he thrust and whined against me like a puppy. And as I re-buckled the broad strap, I felt a kind of crusted stickiness on the side of his head. Close by, a blot of moonlight spilled through the branches, and I hauled him over to it, and saw a broken swelling still oozing between his left ear and eye.

He must have gone over the edge as I had nearly done, and knocked himself witless in the fall which explained why he had made no sound while the hunt was still in that part of the woods. I called the word up to the other two, then got Gelert turned to face the almost sheer side of the bank and gave him an upward heave to start him on his way. If I could get him up to where the tree roots began it should not be too difficult.

He sprang and scrambled upward maybe the height of a man, and fell back whining, then tried again. I was scrambling up beside him, shouting to him with all the breath I had, one hand twisted in his collar, 'Come up! Hup! Hup with you!' while with the other I clung to branch or tree root, my feet slipping on the raw earth as I hauled him after me. Conn and Luned had each hooked themselves over one of the jagged tree snarls on the lip of the gully and were reaching down to us. Luned's hand was suddenly beside mine on Gelert's collar, and Conn's was grabbing my other wrist, then the neckband of my tunic, dragging me upward. There was a space of slithering and kicking and heaving and gasping, and the four of us were sprawled side by side among the torn tree roots.

We lay there for a few moments getting our breath back. Then we got our shaking legs under us and set off for home, Gelert loping close beside me with my belt through his collar for a leash.

It was not until we were through into our own valley and up it to the edge of the cropland in the snail-shine of the sinking moon, that the earlier thing came back into our minds. It seemed that it came into all our minds at the same time, and we paused looking at each other.

'None of us must ever tell,' I ordered.

Conn shook his head, 'None of us ever will.'

'Because if we did, men would come and hunt him,' Luned said in a small clear voice. And, I mind, I was grateful to her, because that was true and made a sound sensible daylight reason for keeping the thing secret among ourselves. But we all three knew the deeper reason; the moment's shared and shining vision that was not for shouting from the roof-tops.

'Glad I am that the three of us saw him together,' she added after a little silence. And that was really all there was to say.

We started off once more, up the valley in the dusk of the sinking moon that would soon fade towards dawn. Already there was a thin fluting of waking birds among the stream-side alders.

I have wondered, since, that my father sent no searchers out after us; but Conn and I were well past thirteen, coming up towards manhood, and knew the forest as well as most of his huntsmen, and I suppose he reckoned that Luned would be safe enough with us. There seemed to be more lamplit windows, more torches at the corners of buildings than was usual in the time before dawn. A general air of wakefulness, but that was all.

The doorkeeper let us in, yawning and grumbling, and while Luned fell to the hen-wife scolding of Old Nurse, who had waited up for us, Conn and I with the weary hound trailing at our heels, stumbled off to our own sleeping place; and for what little remained of the night Gelert stretched out with Conn across the doorway of my sleeping cell.

I woke to find the morning sunlight making a square patch of brightness quivering with leaf-shadows on the wall beside my bed, and Conn shaking me. 'My lord your father says you are to come.'

I groaned, rubbing the sleep out of my eyes. 'In the stable court?' My father and Owain generally started the day in the stable court.

But Conn shook his head. 'Na. He is back in his chamber. The stable court was an hour ago. Gildas, who brought the message, said he was to let you sleep late.'

I wondered if that meant that my father was not so

very angry with us after all, if it meant that I was going to escape my beating; but I had not much hope. Well, now that I was awake, best not to keep him waiting. I flung back the sheepskin rug and plunged out of bed; Gelert, who had been sitting prick-eared in the door-way, got up and shook himself and came padding across the narrow cell to thrust his muzzle under my hand. I huddled on my tunic, raked my fingers through my hair – no time to look for the comb just now – and a few moments later I was heading along the colonnade towards my father's chamber at the far end of it. Conn would have followed, but I bade him bide where he was and keep Gelert with him.

'If there is to be a flogging, there should be two to stand before your father,' he said.

'There will not be two in any case,' I told him. 'My father will not beat you for what was my doing.'

'Because I am only a bondman and you are my master?' he said in that dry rough-edged voice he had at times. 'That is not justice.'

'It's an unjust world,' I told him. 'Hadn't you noticed? Bide here and I'll be back.'

He squatted down on his heels, scowling, his arm around Gelert's neck.

My father was sitting in his great chair with the lion feet, rubbing his chin with a lump of pumice stone. By the time that I remember, most of our people had taken to letting their beards grow, but my father still went clean-shaven in the Roman way, with razor and goose grease when need be, with pumice when the traders brought any. I saw his long supple dog-whip lying across the bedfoot beside him and my heart sank.

He looked up when I came in, then went back to work on his long chin. I mind the harsh sound that the pumice made.

I said hopefully, after a while, 'I have brought Gelert back.'

'So it has been told me,' my father said. 'Also that Luned was out in the forest the main part of the night.' He felt his chin with two fingers, then laid aside the pumice and got up, reaching for the dog-lash. He stood watching me and drawing it through his hands – dark and supple with use – while I freed the bronze neck-pin and pulled my tunic back from my shoulders.

I had my beating. Seven stinging cuts of the dog-whip. It was always seven, never more, never less; that was one of the things that made it frightening to be flogged by my father, that it was always done in cool blood. He never lost control of the situation, he never lost count . . . When he had finished, my shoulders felt as though they had been criss-crossed with hot brands, and it took me a few moments to get back my breath, which seemed to have been driven out of my body. Then I began to pull up my tunic, keeping my head down because I felt tears humiliatingly near. When I was a child I had yelled sometimes under the lash both because it hurt and because I hoped it might soften my father's heart; but I knew him better now, and it had long ago become a matter of honour to make no sound.

I was just fastening the neck-pin of my tunic when footsteps came along the colonnade and Owain appeared in the doorway.

'My father, I have done as you bade me about the red colt,' he began, but truly I think the red colt was an excuse. He stopped, seeing me there and pinning the neck of my tunic, and the whip still in our father's hands; and hitched his shoulder in mock sympathy. 'If I come in a bad time . . .'

'Nay, the thing is over,' my father said, and tossed the whip aside.

Owain turned his attention to me. 'It has been told me that you have found my hound and brought him in.'

'He was out beyond Coed Dhu.' My voice was under control by that time. 'He had gone over into the winter-gully and knocked himself silly, and his collar was caught up on an alder snag.'

'So, and where is he now?'

'In my sleeping cell, with Conn.'

'Then go you and fetch him – if our father is done with you.'

No word of thanks, just claiming his own.

I heard myself saying, 'Did you not mean what you said yestere'en, about anyone who found him being welcome to him?'

I had not known that it mattered so much; but suddenly, as I waited for the answer, my mouth felt dry.

Owain began to fidget with the long bronze tag on the end of his belt as he always did when he wanted to get out of something. He laughed a little. 'Why, as to that, a man may say something in passing moment –'

I have said that my father had little love for me, and that is true, but it is true also that I always had justice from him. He said to no one in particular, 'And regret it in the cool at next morning and seek to forget his promise? But of such a time it is always as well to remember who else heard the promise made, and may remember afterward.'

'I only said –' Owain began.

'In the outer court, with half the household and most of your own companions standing by,' mused my father, watching a yellow-speckled fly that had hovered in through the open door.

For a long moment, silence settled on us, broken only by the high wing-whine of the fly. My mouth grew drier yet.

Then Owain shrugged, 'Keep him then. He's little enough use for the hunting, anyway.'

'Now as to the red colt –' my father said, and I knew myself dismissed.

When I got back to my sleeping cell, Conn was still squatting in the doorway with his arm round Gelert's neck. They both looked up as I came along the colonnade, walking, I suppose, somewhat stiffly – it is surprising how stiff one's whole back gets after a flogging, even though the lash has fallen only across one's shoulders. 'You had your beating, then,' Conn said, recognizing the signs.

I nodded, and squatted down with them and took Gelert's battered head between my hands. He thrust towards me, his tail thumping on the floor behind him. 'I had my beating but I have Gelert too – my father made Owain hold to his promise!' I began to rub my thumbs into the soft warm hollows behind his ears, and the joyful triumph rose within me, and the pride that comes to every boy with the ownership of his first dog. 'Mine is the hound to me! Mine, mine! –'

'Meanwhile,' said Conn, leaning sideways to look between my shoulders, 'there is blood on your tunic. Come down to the stream and I'll wash your back for you.'

There was mist scarfing the stream banks, under the alder trees, and the sunlight lancing through it, and I mind now the blissful coldness of the water as Conn palmed it over the burning soreness of my back, while I bathed Gelert's wounded head at the same time; and the gladness upon us that was all one with the morning and the white hart in last night's moon-shot forest.

# – 4 –
# The Prince's Hunting

None of us ever spoke of what we had seen in the forest that night; but of course other people, a hunter, a charcoal burner, glimpsed the white hart, and the story got out all the same.

In due time it reached the Royal Hall of Urfai the King and my father's overlord, in Rhyfunnog, and came to the ear of Gorthyn the King's son, who it seemed cared for few things in life as he did for hunting. And so on an evening far into the autumn, a rider came to my father's gate, bringing word that the Prince Gorthyn and his companions would be following in three days, to hunt the white hart which had been seen in my father's valleys.

I was out in the horse runs when the messenger came, and got back to find the whole village ringing with the news. Feeling much as though someone had jabbed me in the belly, I gathered up Conn and Luned – the messenger was still in the house but there was no time to waste on him – and a short while later, leaving Gelert on guard at the foot of the ladder to warn us of any comers, the three of us were crouching together in the loft over the old chariot shed, facing each other in the half dark among store chests and ancient horse-gear stacked there.

'But can the Prince Gorthyn come hunting in your father's runs like this, unbidden?' Conn asked.

'Yes,' I told him, 'he can, because his father is the King, and our overlord.'

'Maybe the hounds will not find him – our white hart,' Luned suggested.

'Maybe not.' Oh, but the sense of Fate was on me, and I knew that they would.

'Then maybe he will go away.' She answered my silence as though I had spoken. 'Back to wherever he came from.'

'Why should he, when he has not, all this autumn?'

'I do not know, but he might.'

Conn said, 'Could we drive him off?'

'I wouldn't wager much on our chances of finding him, just like that,' I said. 'And from tomorrow's dawn the woods will be full of my father's foresters.'

Luned began to cry with soft desolation; and she was not much given to tears. 'We cannot just let him be killed – we can't.'

'Stop that!' I told her. 'I am trying to think, and it doesn't help.'

We were all trying to think, desperately searching to and fro for some way to save the white hart, laying hold of wilder and wilder ideas which, when brought out and looked at, turned out to be each more impossible than the last. And all the while I was trying to thrust away the hideous picture that kept forming in my head and getting in the way of my thinking; the picture of the proud and beautiful creature who was in some way ours, hunted and terrified, pulled down by the pack, his milky hide torn and bloodstained, the wounds at his throat . . . and all the while in my mind the terrible knowledge was growing steadily, that there was one thing, and only one thing, that I might be able to do. I flinched away from the knowledge, but I had to force myself back to it, as one forces a scared horse back to barriers it is afraid to jump.

'If all else fails,' I said at last, 'I can – I will – try to kill him myself. My new hunting bow is strong enough. If I go with the rest, keeping it hidden under my cloak –' I could not go on for the moment. There was a feeling of shock shared among the three of us; but I knew that the others had been seeing the same thing inside their heads. At least that would mean a quick, clean death for our white hart, save him from the last terror, and the tearing of the hounds.

Then Conn said, 'You will have to be with the Prince's party, and that will make it hard to get the chance. Lend me your bow, and I will do the thing.'

'You are not so skilled with the bow as I am,' I told him. It was true. I had tried to pass on my own skills to him, but bondmen do not get the weapon practice, whether for war or the hunting trail, that freemen get.

'The best thing of all,' Luned said in a small cold voice that had no trace of tears left in it, 'could be if we could hunt the Prince himself.'

'You little she-wolf!' I said, and we laughed, and left the seriousness behind us, and gathering ourselves together, scrambled down the loft ladder and went in search of supper.

When the King's son rode in with his hunting companions three evenings later, I stood with the armour-bearers and the younger sons in the outer court to take charge of their horses, while my father and Owain waited on the steps to give him formal welcome. I looked up at the Prince as I went to his horse's head, and saw a rather ugly young man with a bony laughing face under a thatch of hair that shone the colour of oat straw in the ragged torchlight, and found myself wanting to like him, like him enormously, which was something I had not bargained for. I looked away quickly, giving my whole attention to the horse, as he dropped from the saddle.

That night our Great Hall seemed fuller than I had ever known it before. Full not only of men, but of life, voices and firelight and harpsong, and the rich heavy smell of mountain mutton baked in the cookhouse and borne in on great chargers for the feeding of my father's guests. The high roofed hall had originally been the atrium of the villa-house, built further and further out at the back as the years went by to make a feasting place for the chieftain and his kindred; but Old Nurse was the only person who used the Roman name for it now. To everyone else it was the Hall, the Fire Hall, the Mead Hall, the Great Hall; and there, guests and household and kindred gathered on feast days and at times of rejoicing.

During the earlier part of that evening, while the main business of eating was going forward, I was too busy among the armourbearers and younger sons, carrying food and drink to the warriors at the tables down the sides of the hall, to look about me or think of anything much else. But by and by, when the nobles and the warriors had eaten their fill, I found myself among the rest of my kind, feasting on our own account at the lower end of the great chamber. I was sharing a bowl of savoury left-overs with one of the Prince's party, a boy not more than a couple of years older than myself, square-built and freckled, with two front teeth missing; and him too, I could have liked well enough if he had not been Gorthyn's armour-bearer. As it was, I took as little notice as one can take of someone sharing the same bowl, and stuffing myself with ragged lumps of dried salmon and honey-baked badger meat, I stared up the long hall, to where my father and brother and the Prince sat together at the high table, and Luned and the maidens of the kindred moved to and fro with the Greek wine jars only brought out for the most splendid occasions, and the harper sat with his crot on his knee, making it ready to sing.

The boy beside me fished a lump of meat from the bowl with his forefinger. 'That is good,' he said, licking the finger afterward; and then, turning to look at me, 'But it is not good to eat out of one bowl with a stranger, not knowing his name. That way you could find yourself eating with one of the Lordly People out of the Hollow Hills. *I* am Lleyn. What name do they call you by?'

'Prosper,' I said. 'Not one of the Lordly People.'

'Then heart-up, Prosper; we shall have a fine hunting tomorrow.'

I reached for a stray crust of bread and did not answer, but he pushed on, like a friendly puppy. 'What's amiss? Are you not of the hunting party?'

'Oh yes. I am of the hunting party,' I said, and became very busy with my crust in the food bowl, mopping up juices to avoid having to talk any more. But I was still very aware of Lleyn beside me, and a few moments later his sudden stillness made me look up to see the reason for it.

He was looking up at somebody standing quite close
by, his cheek still bulging with food he had forgotten
to swallow. And when I followed the line of his gaze, I
saw that Luned had come down the hall with a wine-
jar for the younger warriors gathered at the lower end
of the hearth-row.

'What maiden is that?' Lleyn mumbled.

'That is Luned,' I told him. 'My kinswoman.'

He swallowed his bulging mouthful and said more
clearly, 'Beautiful, she is.'

Something in the way he said it made me look at her
again, and for the first time I saw that she was. It was
not only her best saffron tunic and the little flower-
shaped gold drops in her ears – I had never seen her
with gold drops in her ears before – not even the
flamelight making tawny feathers in the dark heavy
braids of her hair. It was that she always had been,
only I had not noticed it before.

'My father the chieftain will be marrying her to
Owain, my brother, in a year or two,' I heard myself
saying – chiefly to warn the other boy off – but as soon
as the thing was spoken, I found that the thought made
a bad taste in my mouth, and I abandoned the mazer
bowl to Lleyn with what was left of the badger juices
still in it.

Late that night in my sleeping cell, I made sure that my
three best arrows were to hand, and checked yet again
that I could carry my strung bow unseen under my
cloak. I had shot up in the past few months, and stood
almost as tall as I do now, so that if I wore my cloak
with one corner trailing a little there was distance enough between shoulder and hem for the short

hunting bow to lie safely concealed – so long as I did my
hunting on foot; horseback would betray it instantly.
Luckily, it was not at all uncommon for the younglings
among the kindred to follow the hounds on foot.

Striding up and down and swirling the heavy folds
about me, I passed on the evening's discovery to Conn.
'Did you see Luned in the Fire Hall after supper? She
is beautiful.'

I mind Conn paused in folding away my best tunic
with the crimson stripe, and said, 'Have you only just
noticed that?' in a rather odd tone of voice, then put
the folded tunic in the clothes chest, and lowered the
lid, very softly.

Next morning at first light we set out on our hunting.
It was a cold dawn without colour as we headed
down-valley under a sky as clear and colourless as
crystal, the plover calling and wheeling over the bare
crop-lands. The grey hoar frost flew like spray from
the bushes and brambles of the woodshore as the
horses brushed through, and the hunting horns made
echoes from the steep hillside above us.

I had joined the huntsmen and foot-followers according to plan, and was loping along among the
hounds, I and Gelert together; but even so, I found
myself after a while not far from the Prince on his
raking sorrel mare, for in the early stretches of the
morning, horse and foot and leashed hounds were
mingled all together. And I was achingly aware all the
time of what I had hidden under my cloak, not only
because I was afraid every moment that the heel of the
bow or the thrust of the three arrows in my belt would
betray me, but also because of the thing that I might be

going to do with them. I had taken great pains with the
arrows, choosing my three best, making sure that their
feathers lay perfectly, that the iron heads were sharp
and polished, deadly and beautiful, the balance perfect, worthy of the great white hart; but oh, my belly
was sick within me at the thought of using them.

Presently the hounds picked up a scent. They were
unleashed, Gelert with the rest, and for a short while
criss-crossed to and fro, questing through the thickets.
Then they streaked away, adding the wild sweetness of
their own music to the notes of the hunting horns on
an uphill line to the ridge above Nant Ffrancon; and
after them men and horses skeining out like wild geese,
myself among them, running with the rest, and torn
between excitement and dread.

We killed twice that day, but caught neither sight nor
scent of the white hart, and as the day wore on and the
autumn sun came slanting further from the west, I
began to hope that despite the forester's report, the
beast had left our hunting runs.

But then, with the shadows already lengthening,
though sunset was as yet far away, Cabel, one of the
oldest and wisest of our hounds, flung up his head and
gave tongue. The pack were unleashed again, and after
a short time of casting about, were off on the new
scent; and again the hunt was up and away after them
like wild geese through the autumn skies. A few moments before, I had known that I was leg-weary and
that carrying a strung bow under my cloak all day had
chafed my forearm almost raw, and that if the hounds
found again there was quite simply nothing more that
I could do about it. But now, with the hound-music in
my ears and the horns crying through the autumn

woods, I forgot all that. I was running with the rest, panting along well up among the hounds, my heart banging high in my throat, and somewhere deep within me the certainty that this time it was the white hart that led us.

Ever since, I have remembered that hunting like something out of a wild dream.

I was running, running as it seemed the heart out of my breast, and hampered by the bow under my cloak, branches snatching at me, roots clawing at my feet, and always ahead of me the music of the hounds. By and by the land began to lift under us, and the trees thinned and fell back, the crowding damp-oaks giving place to birch as we drew up towards the open surge of the great hills; and the sky opened to us, turning wide and shining, the grey paleness of it barred with silver in the west.

We were labouring uphill towards the blunt crest of the near ridge when the music of the hounds strung out over the skyline ahead of us changed note to the eager baying that meant the quarry was in view. The horns were sounding along the ridge, mingled with the shouts of men urging their weary horses to a fresh burst of speed. Then as we swept over the crest, I saw him across the shadow-filled cwm below us, shining against the dun dead bracken of the hillside as he headed desperately for the next ridge; the white hart that we had come to kill.

The hounds were running strung-out and purposeful on a sight line, the hunt sweeping after, downhill – I remember now the chill of the mountain stream as we crashed through it, sending up the sheeted water as we went – then upward again on the steep further slope.

The hunt had split in two, the Prince and his party drawing ahead, our own people falling somewhat behind, the laws of hospitality and good manners demanding that to the guests should go the honour of the kill. But I had no time for courtesies just then. In familiar country a man on foot who knows the short cuts and the hindrances may keep up with mounted men who are strangers to it, especially if he be desperate enough. I was desperate enough and the strange feeling of being in a dream was on me, coming between me and my torn and spent body: and I was still with the Prince's party when at last, on the high hill shoulder where the great stones of Hound Tor broke through the frosty turf, we brought the white hart to bay.

For a dazzled moment, a kind of lightning flash of time that went on and on, I saw everything caught and unmoving: the black crouching shapes of the rocky outcrop and the wind-shaped hawthorn bushes, rust-red with autumn berries, and against the darkness of them, the white hart standing with heaving flanks, his shining hide dark-streaked with sweat, his proud antler-crowned head flung back in terror, as the yelling hounds closed in. Then as the frozen scene splintered into movement again and the hounds sprang forward, I realized that I had been counting on the cover of the trees to slink off by myself and free my bow and those three precious arrows. Here in the open with only the sparse hillscrub and the hunt all about me, I would be discovered before I could nock my first arrow to the bow. I tried, all the same, making to fling back the hampering folds of my cloak. And that was when I knew suddenly that even if I had the chance, *I could not do it*. That was a thing I was quite unprepared for. I remember breaking out in a sweat, the struggle and the powerlessness within me. Whether I should have broken through and done the thing in the end, I've no knowing, because in that splinter of time the miracle happened.

From out of the general tumult of men and hounds and horses, one voice rose clear. One of those trained voices that can reach across a battlefield and still make sense at the other end. 'Off! Off, I say – the hunting is over; call off the hounds!'

And somebody was urging his horse forward into the midst of the yelling pack, leaning low from the saddle to send his whiplash curling across their backs. Gorthyn, the Prince. Others of his company had joined him, and the horn was sounding again, not the *Death* but the *Recall*; and between the horn and the whiplash the hounds, unwilling, and bewildered by the strange turn of things, were falling back, doubling to and fro among themselves.

And suddenly there was no white hart standing at bay among the thorn trees and the dark stones. For an instant there was a flicker of white among the bushes dropping away over the further slope beyond the crest towards Nant Ffrancon, and then that too was gone.

Almost at that moment Gelert returned to me.

I was looking towards the Prince on his startled and fidgeting horse, and I did not see him come, and so had no time to brace myself for his joyful onslaught, and his forepaws took me on the shoulder unawares, pitching me over backward, my cloak flying wide and

the hidden bow and the arrows in my belt laid bare to
view.

I had a hand twisted in his collar and was struggling
back to my feet almost in the same instant, but it was
too late. One of our own huntsmen was upon me with
a muttered, 'Now what's to do, young master?' And I
think he would have had me clear out of the way; but
the boy Lleyn was upon me also, dropping from
his horse with a shout. Gelert, half-strangled with
my hand in his collar, had them both in check for
the moment with a deep sing-song snarling far down
in his throat; his hackles were up, and I knew that at
any move from me he would have been at the throat of
one or the other of them – which is why I stood very
still.

And with a brushing and trampling through the dead
bracken and half bare thorns, Gorthyn reined in his
horse almost on top of us, and sat looking down. His
face was enquiring, more than anything else, his thick
brows quirking upward towards the headband of fine
crimson leather that bound back his hair. 'It seems you
hunt after a different manner from the rest of us, this
day,' he said.

I went on standing still, and stared back at him.

He flicked a finger at my bow. 'Or – it seems a
foolish question – was that for me?' He asked it at
half-breath, for the thing was not for all men's hearing.

I shook my head, 'For the hart.'

'Why?'

'Better than to be pulled down by the hounds.'

The Prince looked at me consideringly for a few
moments; then he smiled. I have never known any
other man with a smile quite like Gorthyn's; it was not

over broad, but it had wings to it. 'So, Prosper, son of Gerontius, you too. And all because the creature has the magic of a milky hide. At least I am not the only moon-wit in your father's hunting runs.'

And I mind that as I stared up at him across his horse's neck, something, a kind of fealty, went out from me to him that I knew would not return to me again so long as life lasted, his or mine.

Then the thing was over. He gestured to the other two to stand back and let me be, and swung his horse to meet my father and the rest of the hunt as they came up. I bent to slip the leash through Gelert's collar, huddling my cloak close round me once more, somehow surprised, when I looked up again, to find the world unchanged. It should have been changed, somehow, a little, because I was Prince Gorthyn's man, but the change was only in me.

I do not think that my father ever came to know of my planned part in that day's hunting. Tuan, our huntsman, would never have betrayed me, nor, I knew, would Gorthyn, and Lleyn and the few others who had seen what happened were the Prince's men. But when we reached home long after torch-lighting time with the gralloched carcasses of the two roe deer slung across the backs of the hunting ponies, and no sign at all of the white hart, word of the Prince's strange hunting must have run from kennels to cook-house to bower almost before the horses were unsaddled; for I had barely reached my sleeping cell where Conn rose from his waiting corner without a word, and as I flung off my cloak and handed over bow and arrow and began to strip off my hunting leathers, Luned appeared in the doorway. She was clad in her saffron gown for feasting, but with her hair hanging loose and tangled, just as she had escaped from Old Nurse.

'Is it true?' she demanded breathlessly.

'Is what true?' I asked. I knew well enough, but I needed time.

'He called off the hounds?'

'Yes, it is true.'

Conn turned from stacking my bow in the corner. 'Why would he be doing that?' he asked in that cool dead-level voice of his.

I shook my head. 'I do not know. Maybe when he saw the white hart he felt the same as we did.'

'That makes him not at all like most princes,' Luned said.

'You having met so many? It makes him a man who would be good to follow.'

There was a moment's silence, then Luned flicked away from the subject in that minnow way of hers. 'Gwyn will not be pleased. He has made a song about the Prince's hunting and the slaying of the white hart. He was going to sing it tonight at the feasting.'

I pulled my best tunic with the crimson stripe over my head, and reached for my belt. 'Gwyn will just have to change the end of the song.'

Conn said doubtfully, 'I do not think that you can be changing the end of a song or a story like that, as though it were quite separate from the rest. I think the end of a story is part of it from the beginning.'

There were other songs sung in my father's hall that night, but whether Gwyn the Harper agreed with Conn or not, the song of the hunting of the white hart

was not one of them. What with weariness and one
thing and another, that is just about the only thing that
I remember about that night, at all. It is the next
morning that I remember, sharp-edged as a blade. The
first snow of the coming winter flurrying down from
Yr Widdfa; the horses brought trampling round from
the stable court, and the Prince and his companions
mounting for the homeward ride.

I had contrived to be the one to hold Gorthyn's
stirrup for him – not that he needed a stirrup holder,
being accustomed to mount by the steed leap like the
rest of us; but for any parting guest, especially one of
the royal house, the courtesies must be maintained. He
mounted, and I was looking up at him past his bent knee
as he thanked me. I mind the fine white flakes settling on
his oat-coloured thatch and the huddled shoulders of
his cloak, and the quick smile that gave wings to his
bony face. I smiled back, and heard myself asking the
thing that I had not meant to ask, not yet a-while, but
which had been in my heart to ask ever since last
evening.

'Lord Gorthyn, let me ride with you.'

His mouth straightened, but the smile was still there
behind his eyes, 'How old are you?'

'I shall be fourteen, come lambing time,' I said,
stretching the truth a little. After all, some lambs are
born late.

'Too young,' he said, gentling his fidgeting horse.

'Lleyn is not so much older.' I heard a snort of
mingled indignation and laughter just behind me.

'A year or two. And his father is one of my father's
household.'

I had not known how deeply I wanted the thing until I knew that I was not going to get it; and I suppose I must have shown the urgent longing in my face, for suddenly he leaned down towards me and said, 'Wait, and you also will be a year or two older.'

Then Luned came with the stirrup-cup and I had to step back and yield her my place. And with that, I knew that I must be content. But I knew also that I had been given a promise, and that Prince Gorthyn would not break it.

# – 5 –
# The Summons

Two years went by, and the half of another year; and on an evening in Mary month the four of us were together on the old fortress hill that had been the chief place of our clan before the Legions came, sprawled in the warm southern curve of the great turf rampart. From the crest of the bank, among the wind-shaped hawthorn bushes, one could look down like a wheeling falcon on the whole valley, the sprawling time-crumbled villa house and the huddle of the settlement in the loop of the stream, follow the chariot-track and the stream-bank alders down past the mill and the smithy to the monastery among its apple trees and beyond, away and away to where the forest closed in over the pasture and crop-lands, the valley spread out like the fingers of a hand, and the distances turned blue. But from where we sprawled in the sun-warmed grass at the bank foot, there was nothing to be seen but wind-feathered sky and a golden eagle circling with the evening sunlight under his wings; swinging his hunting-circles so high that it would be half of Gwynedd, not just our valley that he saw.

I was lying flat on my back, Gelert beside me with his hairy head on my chest, and I was playing with his ears, rubbing my thumbs into the warm hollows behind them in the way he liked best in all the world. Conn, who was seldom without something to do with his hands, lay propped on one elbow, whittling a bit of hawthorn wood he had gathered on his way up into something that looked as though it might be going to be a fieldmouse; and beside him Luned sat with her hands linked round her updrawn knees, watching what he did.

Three days ago, my brother Owain had been married, a marriage made between our father and a neighbouring chieftain for the strengthening of both clans. Owain had not been best pleased, for he scarcely knew the girl and would rather have chosen for himself. But it was the custom, and he had done no more than grumble a bit. To me the marriage seemed a matter for rejoicing, partly because I had been afraid all along that my father would marry him to Luned, and partly because turned sixteen and counting as a man, I had ridden with the bridegroom's companions to help him fetch home the bride. The feasting had been truly noble, but the sham fight, which had not been entirely sham – I had a fading black eye to prove it – when the time came to carry the squealing girl off from her father's hall, had been even better.

But looking at Luned now, the thought came to me that maybe it was not a happy thing for her, to have a new mistress come into the house – though indeed the Lady Nerys seemed such a mouse of a girl that I could not believe her coming would make much difference to anybody. And then another thought came treading on the heels of the first; that maybe she had wanted to be the new mistress, married to Owain herself. I had not known if she felt like that; we had grown up together almost all our lives, but it struck me suddenly how much I did not know of her. She had always been one who kept her secrets to herself.

I rolled over towards her, dislodging Gelert. 'Luned, now that she's here, what would you be thinking of Owain's new wife?'

She looked up from her watching, half surprised. 'Nerys? I dare say I shall like her well enough as time goes by. I have known her only two days.'

'You did not need two days to know that you liked Conn.' I do not know what made me say it, especially with Conn there; something in the way she had been watching his hands on the scrap of hawthorn wood, I suppose.

She said softly, 'But Conn is Conn. Nerys is only a girl like a feather cushion. She eats too much honey-cake and presently she will spend all her time having babies while Old Nurse runs the household as she always has done.'

It sounded a bit as though my guess might have been right. In which case I should shut my mouth and leave the thing there. But there was something, a feel of coming change, on me that spring evening in the warm curve of the old rampart where it seemed that nothing ever changed except the wind. A feeling out of no-where, that the thing should not be left hanging ragged, lest there be no other time . . .

I plucked up a grass stem to chew, and said round it, 'Luned, did you – have you ever thought that it might be you, married to Owain?'

She said, 'Yes. I did not think there was much danger, seeing that I have no dowry; but it was there, just a little fear. And, oh, the gladness is on me that now I need have no fear at all.'

'Then you didn't want at all –' I said after a moment, stupid with relief.

She laughed a little. 'Have I not said? Oh, Prosper, you sound so grave and solemn and – like an elder brother!'

For a moment I thought she was going to do onè of her silvery minnow changes of the subject. But then she left the laughter behind and said quite seriously, 'No, I did not want, I do not want, anything that breaks up the three of us being together.'

'Since Father does not want you for Owain, maybe he has it in mind to marry you to me,' I said chewing on my grass stem. 'That would keep the three of us together.'

Luned had returned to watching the hawthorn mouse in Conn's hands. She said, 'Yes, I could marry you or –' She checked, and a wave of colour flowed up from the neck of her tunic to the roots of her hair, and ebbed away leaving her creamy pale. 'I could marry you, and that would keep the three of us together.'

And in the same moment Conn's knife slipped and gashed his thumb. He snatched his hand away and sucked the ball of this thumb, while Luned said the kind and obvious things that women say at such times, 'Oh, you have cut yourself – let me look.'

He shook his head and held his hand out to her, 'It was only a nick. See – no more blood.' And the moment was over and past like the little wind siffling along the hill grasses.

The shadow of the western rampart was creeping far across the hill top, and hunger telling us that it was time to be turning homeward for the evening meal, when Gelert suddenly lifted his head, ears pricked, listening. We listened also. At first there was nothing to hear, and then, faint and far off on the very edge of hearing, I caught the triple of a horse's hooves on the valley track; and in the same instant the others had it too. There was nothing unusual in that; there were always men and horses on the track that led up-valley to my father's hall; but it was not so often that travellers came down-valley from the drove-road that led into it from the north, and the odd sense of coming change that had been on me earlier was on me still, making me alert to anything that did not follow the common pattern. I rolled over and scrambled up the steep green wave-lift of turf and through the cream-clotted hawthorn scrub along its crest, just as the horse and rider came into view, ant-small on the track that was no more than an unspooled linen thread, so far off and so far below that no sound of hooves could have reached us but for the wind in the right quarter and the odd trick of the surrounding hills just there, that gathered sound and tossed it upward.

Conn had come up beside me, and Gelert's head was against my thigh.

'Someone in a hurry,' I said.

The valley was brimming with shadows and, watching, we could scarce have made out the rider if it had not been for that faint triple of hoof-beats on the stony track, looping around the base of the fortress hill towards the stream, then up the last stretch between the house-places of the kindred and in through the gatehouse.

'It will be a late-come guest to the wedding,' Luned said, holding aside a hawthorn spray and peering down.

Conn laughed. 'Hungry as *we* are, and hurrying to his supper.'

'Maybe,' I said, suddenly in a hurry. 'Let us be on our way.'

As we came swooping down through the steep pasture behind the house, Tydeus my tutor came to meet us – I suppose someone had seen the way we went earlier in the day. As soon as we were within shouting distance he started shouting, thin and high like a gull, 'Prosper – your father bids you come to him in his study.'

I waved to show that we had heard him, and he stopped and stood waiting until we reached him. 'What's amiss?' I demanded when we came together.

'A messenger – nay, I know no more than that, but seemingly it concerns you.'

I reached my father's study – he always called it that, though it was as much an armoury and as much an estate office, with a sword chest and spears racked against one wall, and farm records stacked along the shelves where once the scrolls of a fine library had lain long before our time. My father was seated sideways to his writing table, and a man in a dusty cloak was standing by the window. He turned when I came in, and I saw that it was Lleyn.

For a moment I was angry with Tydeus for not having told me who it was; but then I realized that even if he had noticed the Prince's armourbearer he had probably not remembered him at all. I remembered, but that was another matter.

His weary freckled face broke into a grin. 'Prosper!'

'Lleyn!' I returned. 'What brings you into these parts? Is the Prince coming?'

'No. But I come as his messenger.' He held out a pair of tablets. I took them, seeing the crimson thread unbroken and the seal still in place; but glancing from one face to the other, I saw that he knew what was in them, and had told my father.

'I have your leave?' I said, and almost before my father gave it, snapped the thread and opened out the tablets, and turning to catch the light of the newly-kindled lamp, read the few words scratched on the wax.

'Prosper, son of Gerontius, the year or two are passed. If you are still of the same mind, ride with Lleyn, the bearer of this. He will bring you to me at Deva,' and underneath, the deeply scored signature, 'Gorthyn.'

My heart was beating hard and high in the base of my throat when I looked up. 'Do we ride tonight?'

Before Lleyn could answer, my father cut in, 'Not so fast! Lleyn, do you tell him what you have told me as to the purpose of this summons.'

Lleyn said, 'Mynyddog the Golden, King of the Gododdin, has summoned my Lord Gorthyn to attend upon him in his High Hall in Dyn Eidin, and not Gorthyn alone, it seems, but others, many others, from the kingdoms of the North and West.'

'And all, I think you told me, younger sons,' my father said.

'So it is said. Each of them attended by two mounted shieldbearers.'

'And for what purpose?'

'To attend upon Mynyddog at Dyn Eidin,' Lleyn repeated himself.

Clearly he knew nothing beyond that. But his eyes brightened as we looked at each other, and I make no doubt that the brightness was echoed in my own. The summons for younger sons, also for two shieldbearers to each warrior called to mind the Arrowhead, the old Celtic fighting unit, and surely could have only one meaning.

'In other words, you will be riding blind into whatever plans the Golden King may have for you,' my
father said, and then as I did not answer – there did not
seem to be anything, really, that needed saying – 'So be
it. You have my leave to go on this trail.'

I looked round at him in surprise. It had not,
until that moment, occurred to me that I needed his
leave. I had simply known from the moment that I
opened out the tablets, that I was going, in the natural
order of things, as day follows night, as night follows
day.

Next morning in the outer court, with the horses already brought round from the stables, I knelt to receive my father's blessing before mounting to ride
away. It was a morning of broken skies, a little thin
wind and a fine spitting rain.

I had already taken my leave of Luned more private-
ly in the orchard where the first white petals were
drifting down. Conn and I both. How it came about
that Conn was coming with me, I have never been sure;
there did not seem to have been any argument or
discussion, it seemed to be as much the natural way of
things as it was that I should follow the Prince. Even
my father had raised no objection, and Lleyn when he
saw the two of us in the courtyard, and the extra
horse, had only shrugged and said, 'Well, I dare say he
will not be the only one.'

Luned had made no protest either, back there among
the apple trees. Her eyes had looked huge and very
dark, but they would have looked like that if I had
been riding alone. I had given Gelert into her keeping.
'Keep Gelert for me, let him hunt with the pack but

don't let him be housed in the kennels or he'll forget all his manners before I come back.'

'He shall sleep in my chamber,' she said, and took the leash from my hand. He was quite used to that, but when I went to rub his head, he whimpered and licked my thumb, looking up at me with puzzled eyes as though he knew that something strange was in the wind.

I had kissed Luned, then; the first time ever I had kissed her, like a brother, yet not altogether like a brother, with Conn standing by. I do not know whether he kissed her too; I turned away to the gate leaving them for the moment behind me. But I do know that he had had yesterday's hawthorn mouse in his hand, and I never saw it again.

There was quite a gathering on the colonnade steps to see us ride away; my father and Owain, and the plump little bride in tears – tears would always come easy to that one – Old Nurse, also, and others of the household, and Tydeus with a drip on the end of his long nose. I had asked Tydeus once what he should do when his days of tutoring me were over, and he had said, 'Rejoice! And go down to the monastery and ask the Father Abbot to shave the front of my head, and have peace and a modicum of intelligent conversation with Brother Pebwyr in my old age.' But I suppose he had a certain fondness for me, after all. I looked once towards the dark gape of the house door behind, half hoping to see Luned and Gelert one more time, but she must have taken him to her chamber and bided with him knowing that left alone he would have howled.

I flung up a hand to them all in farewell and turned my mare in behind Lleyn's as he headed for the gatehouse, Conn bringing up the rear with the pack horse. We clattered through and swung on to the track that led down-valley past the mill and the smithy and the monastery, away to join the world beyond the mountains.

Towards evening four days later, with the last of the mountains behind us, we came riding down the grass-grown track between leaning and fallen gravestones that had once been the paved military road from the west into Deva, the City of Legions.

The city gate still stood, though the city it guarded was a fallen ruin cloaked with brambles and the green tide of springtime among the sodden wreck of last year's bracken and willow herb; here and there a tottering house patched up and lived in, women spinning in door-ways, children and dogs at play. Here and there a cluster of thatched bothies sheltering within the man-high walls of a public building, the basilica, Lleyn said, or a church, or the public baths. My first glimpse of what had once been the power and glory that was Rome.

In what must have been the forum a man sat on the steps to a building that was not there any more, playing the reed-pipe to a small herd of goats. Lleyn asked for news of strangers, and he told us of a small party of horsemen who had ridden in the day before, asking where, if anywhere, they could get food and lodging for themselves and their horses. He had sent them up into the old fortress, where his master kept an inn at the sign of the Gladiator, a most noble inn, for passing travellers; and they were still there so far as he knew.

We thanked him and rode on, leaving him to his piping behind us.

The fortress on its higher ground was less in ruins than the lower city. Our horses' hooves rang on cobbles that the grass had not yet completely taken over, as we rode between the long straight barrack-rows. There were more people about; and many of the buildings had thatched roofs on them. Before one cluster of ragged buildings, a sign hung from a young ash tree, showing a fat pink cupid wearing an enormous gladiator's helmet and carrying a sword and shield. From somewhere within, a horse whinnied to ours as we drew rein before it; and a young shieldbearer with his mouth full and a crust in one hand appeared in a doorway and called behind him, 'They are here, my lord.'

And a few moments later, dismounted but with our arms still through our horses' bridles, for the most noble inn did not seem to have anyone to take them from us, nor even a hitching post outside, we were confronting three princes of the Cymru encamped with their shieldbearers among a rickety huddle of benches and tables at one end of a long barn-like hall, their horses being stabled at the other.

'I have brought him,' Lleyn was announcing.

Gorthyn, who had been delving into a fat-bellied pot on the table, looked up with a collop of meat on the end of his dagger. 'Prosper! God's Greeting to you!' he said, as though we had last met maybe a week ago. Then his gaze went over my shoulder, 'And this who follows you?'

'Conn, my body servant,' I said without thinking, and inwardly cursed myself the moment the words were out. This could have been Conn's chance to be simply a man among other men, at least for a while, and I had spoiled it. Yet there had to be some kind of reason for bringing him. I cast a hurried look of apology over my shoulder, and he received it with his slow quiet smile and the faintest shrug.

'It seemed that it was both or neither,' Lleyn explained to the world at large.

The thick-set formidable looking young man on Gorthyn's left snorted into the drinking bowl. 'Your second shieldbearer comes followed by a shieldbearer of his own. Hai Mai! Large ideas of themselves some people have!'

'I dare say he'll not be the only one – and like enough we shall need horseholders and the like,' Gorthyn said.

He sounded peaceable enough, but I saw the colour flare along the harsh line of his cheekbones; and the third man, older than the other two and maybe the leader because of that, cut in, smoothly as a well-burnished blade, 'And in any case it is not a matter to shake the earth on its foundations, on this night when the King's hosting begins, and there are other matters to be thinking of.'

'Such as food,' said the thick-set man reaching for another barley bannock from the basket on the table. People often thought that it was for his fighting powers that Gwenabwy had come to be likened to the wild pig. It was. But we who came to know him, knew also that there was another reason.

'Such as getting the horses fed and stabled,' said Gorthyn.

I looked doubtfully towards the other end of the barn; it seemed very full.

'There is more space through there,' Gorthyn flicked a finger towards a doorway that seemed to open into a courtyard of sorts. 'The forage store, too. When you have seen to the horses, follow your noses through to the cookhouse and demand food and another jug of this foul stuff they call wine.'

A short while later, the horses rubbed down and watered, with armfuls of hay spiced with beans from their own fodder bags spread before them, we returned to the long chamber, where a couple of torches had been lit in their iron sconces, and settled down with the other shieldbearers to fill our own empty bellies from the freshly brought pot of goat stew.

When the food was all gone we played dice, squatting on our heels in the pool of light from one of the torches, while our lords talked around the table, and Conn, a little apart from the rest of us, busied himself with mending a pack strap which so far as I knew was in no need of mending.

At first, the talk around the table seemed to be about nothing in particular, just a lazy blur of voices and the occasional laugh behind the rattle and roll of the dice. But after a while the voices cleared and hardened and I caught the words, 'war-trail' and began to listen. 'You think it *is* a war-trail, then?' Gorthyn said.

The older man, Tydfwlch the Tall, they called him, lightly thumbed an old scar on his jaw. 'I think so, yes. This call for younger sons, and each with two supporters, the old Arrowhead fighting unit . . . Yes, it has the smell of a hosting for the war-trail.'

We went on throwing the dice, but the pace of the game slowed, and all heads were tipped a little, eyes brightening. If we had been hounds our ears would have pricked. We were all very young, and to us a war-trail seemed a splendid thing.

'Why now?' Gorthyn said, thrusting back the hair from his forehead in the way that I had already come to know. 'Why not last year? Or next? Or the year after?'

Tydfwlch shrugged. 'Who shall tell what passes in the minds of kings? Maybe the Saxon threat draws nearer than we have heard among our own mountains.'

Gwenabwy laughed, flinging back his head and showing a cavern of open mouth. 'Who cares? A war-trail has always been good following for younger sons, and is not King Mynyddog called the Golden? There will be meat and mead and golden arm-rings for those who follow him!'

One of Tydfwlch's shieldbearers was shaking my shoulder, telling me that the dice box was with me and it was my turn to throw. I gathered my wits back to me, and rattled the box and threw, watching the three cubes spill out across the earthen floor. I had thrown triple six, highest cast of all, which men call Venus and everyone was shouting and laughing and beating me on the shoulders, taking it for a good omen for what was to come.

# – 6 –

# The Golden King and the Three Hundred

I shall never forget my first sight of Eidin Ridge as we came clattering up the final stretch of the old paved Legions' road from the south. We were a sizeable band by that time, having joined and been joined by other riders as we went along; men from Strathclyde and the old lost kingdom of Rheged, all answering the same summons. It was drawing on to sunset of a wild day, with shafts of harsh westering light lancing between the drifting cloud-masses of the broken skies.

One such lance of light struck suddenly along the whole length of the great ridge that rose ahead of us out of the low rolling country that washed it round. A moment before it had been dark and menacing, curiously alive with a life of its own like a crouching boar, and having nothing to do with the life of men. But in the acid-yellow light the huddled roofs and walls of living-places sprang out on its flanks and strung along its crest under a haze of evening cooking fires; and at the western end the ridge burst upward into a jagged shield-boss of rock, crowned with the sour white of lime-washed fortress walls.

'See,' someone said, pointing. 'Dyn Eidin!'

The shaft of light faded, and the sharp-edged ridge sank back into the storm-shadowed countryside, blotted out by a travelling squall of rain. Not long after, we came to the place where an unpaved track left the road. I had thought of the Legions' road leading us straight to the Dyn, but one of the Strathclyde men who had been that way before laughed and said, 'The Romans did not send their engineers to build their fine straight roads from chieftain's hall to chieftain's hall! This is the road to one of their frontier forts – over that way; Castellum they used to call it. The trackway here is the royal road of King Mynyddog.'

So following the royal road, we came on the edge of dusk to the place where the eastern end of the ridge sank into level ground almost at the foot of another great hill-mass thrusting towards the sky. 'That is the Giant's Seat,' said the Strathclyde man, showing his knowledge, as we passed beneath it. But we were weary with long riding and more interested just then in the huddle of buildings through which the track, swooping almost back on itself, seemed to lead up on to Eidin Ridge. A farm steading of some kind, though bigger than any of its kind that I had seen before, the first torches flaring ragged at the gateway, smoke rising through thatched roofs, and the general air of a place where food and shelter was to be found.

In the gateway we were checked to a trampling halt by a huge man who stepped out into the light between the torches and stood there, leaning on his spear. 'Who comes?'

Tydfwlch, still the senior of our little band, said, 'Younger sons in answer to the King's summons.'

'In a good hour are you come,' said the giant with the spear, and stood aside to let us pass.

In the open space amid the farm buildings we dropped from our saddles, and men came running to take the horses. I was doubtful for the moment about trusting my mare Shadow to a stranger's care, but the boy who was taking her bridle seemed to know what he was about, and surely in a king's stable the care would be good. I gave her a parting pat on her damp neck and went after the rest of our party. There were others who seemed to be of our kind there already – it was unlikely that we would be the first comers – but on the first evening their faces were a blur in the torchlight and the spitting rain that was setting in with the dusk. There were men there, women too, whose task seemed to be to give us welcome and tend to our needs; there was a long hostel-hall, new built – I mind the scent and colour of raw new wood and green thatch – and great tubs of heated washing water that smelled of herbs. And fingering its way in from some-where outside the fat reek of beef stew.

'Supper smells good,' I said hopefully to the old woman who was drying my back.

She cackled, 'So it should, for it is myself had the seasoning of it! But it is none of yours, for each night the newcomers of that day feast in the King's Mead Hall.'

So by and by, having pulled on the best we had by way of a change of clothing and huddled on our damp cloaks again over all, we made our way with the men of the King's household who had come to guide us, up the mile long road that led from the Royal Farm at one end of Eidin Ridge to the Dyn itself, the Royal Strong-hold at the other. People came to firelit doorways to watch us pass; some, girls mostly, called out a greeting. The chill of the spring rain was on the back of my neck, and suddenly sweet and unexpected, I caught the wafting scent of wet hawthorn where a bush leaned out from the black rocks of the defile as the last stretch of the road reared upwards to the gate of the King's Stronghold. And at the end, growing warm and torch-lit out of the wet night, another hall, new built and raw at the lower end like the long-house back at the Farm, old and long established at the upper; a hall that had been added to, that more men might feast in it.

What with weariness and the sense of being in a strange world, the whole of that first evening lies tangled in my memory with the confusion of a dream. Firelight and harp-song and candlelight – as many candles as I have seen in the great churches of the east, making the great hall so light that in places you could have seen to read a book in it. Coloured hangings and fine weapons along the walls; and gold everywhere, cups and arm-rings and the hilts of daggers. Even the King's favourite hounds crouched beneath the High Table had goldwork among the hunting studs on their collars. And crowding faces that shifted and came and went like the faces in a dream.

Only one thing in the dream stands out real and sharp-edged, and that was at the very beginning; the moment when the horns of feasting sounded and the dragon-worked hangings were drawn back from a doorway behind the High Seat, and the King came out to us. Mynyddog the Golden, Lord of the Gododdin. He came out between two of his household warriors, an arm on the shoulder of each. A man, the wreckage of a man, who must once have been a giant, but had shrunk and withered into himself until his mantle seemed to hang loose on bare bones, and the golden torque and armrings of kingship looked almost too heavy to be born. His face was yellow in the candlelight, with bruise-coloured eye-sockets pushed deep into his head. At first I thought that I was making some kind of stupid mistake, that this must be some aged kinsman of the King's; an uncle, or maybe the Queen's father, and in another moment the King himself would come through that inner door. But the men on either side of him brought him to the High Seat and eased him into it, and the only comers through the door after him were his Bard and his Champion and a tall woman with royal goldwork on her head, who took the seat beside him.

The warriors in the long hall rose to him with a shout as men greet the comings of their High Chief – Gorthyn and the rest of us maybe half a breath behind the others – and I knew that there was no mistake; the splendid wreck of a man at the High Table was the King. So was this not to be a war-trail after all? Or if it was, who was to lead us on it?

A little later, when the great food-chargers had been brought in, I went up to fetch Gorthyn's portion and bore it to him where he sat among the princes of Cymru, and looked questioningly into his face as I set it down, hoping that he had some idea of the answers. But he looked up and met my gaze, and shook his head very slightly. 'We shall know all things in due time,' he murmured, and reached for an oaten bannock from the red Samian bowl between himself and his neighbour.

And indeed, over the next few days, those of us who were strangers to Dyn Eidin did come in one way or another to know most of what was there for the knowing. For myself, I gained the answer to many questions and the making clear of much that seemed strange to me in a most unexpected way the very next morning.

I had gone into the stable court to make sure that all was well with my mare, Shadow, and there I came upon a merchant overseeing his men as they loaded up his pack ponies for the road. He was standing with his back to me, his shape lost in the muffling folds of his cloak, his head covered by a Phrygian cap of crimson leather; and it was not until he turned round that I knew him for Phanes of Syracuse.

If he had supped in the King's Hall last night we had missed each other; a thing not surprising, for I had been in no state to recognize faces on the guest bench, and it was clear that my face meant nothing to him at all. In the life of a travelling merchant there must be many faces that come and go and are forgotten, and I had been four years younger when we last met.

'God's greeting to you, young stranger,' he said, and would have turned away.

'God's greeting to you, Phanes of Syracuse,' I said. And he checked, looking at me more closely with those long dark eyes that had the look of distant places in them. 'In Gwynedd – Loban's smithy. He was mending a dagger for you,' I added, seeing him trying to remember. 'A silver hilt like an archangel, it had. That would be four years ago.'

He remembered then, and his face creased into a smile. 'Prosper, son of Gerontius! There was another boy with you, who – I think – was more interested in the blade.'

'Conn. He is with me still,' I said. 'Oh, but this is most wonderful to find you here!'

He laughed. 'Why, as to that, you should never be surprised to find one of my kind anywhere. But here is maybe the most likely place of all, for the King has a taste for the wares that I bring, and the wealth to pay for them; fine enamels, silk and sandalwood.' We had settled ourselves on the edge of the horse trough to talk more comfortably, and after a few moments he went on. 'Besides, there is old friendship between Mynyddog and me; I came here first when I was a boy, with my uncle, and Mynyddog was a boy also.' He put up a hand to push the crimson leather cap further back from his forehead, and I saw a thin silvery scar on the olive skin of his wrist; a very old scar left by the sort of nick that boys make when they swear the blood-brotherhood. He turned towards me. 'So – fair exchange in all things; what is it that you do here?'

'I follow the Prince Gorthyn, who comes from Gwynedd to answer the King's summons. We thought it was for a warhosting.'

'Something has made you change your mind?'

I was silent a little, tracing invisible lines with one finger in the water of the trough. I did not know quite how to put it. 'I saw the King in the Mead Hall last night.'

'Yes?' he said guardedly.

'He was very sick.'

'Yes,' he said again.

'What ails him?'

'An arrow between the ribs, from the cattle wars, three years past.'

I shook the chill bright water droplets from my fingers and asked the next thing. 'Then if the gathering is for war, will he mend in time to lead us?'

Phanes looked full back at me. 'Nobody mends from that kind of sickness. If he had been left to his own physicians he would have been dead long since; it was only the skills of the Queen that saved him, and even she cannot make him a whole man again.'

We were talking at half-breath, the life of the stable court flowing on around us. I would have liked to know more about the Queen's skills. Was she just herb-wise like Old Nurse, like most women who are the mistress of their household. Or was she more? Did she have the Wise-Craft? But that was only idle curiosity: for now, there were things that I needed more urgently to know. 'If it is a war-trail, and the King cannot lead us on it, then who?'

He spread his hands, 'Who shall say? If it were some matter of the Blues and Greens I would lay my gold on the Fosterling.'

That found a faint echo in my mind from last night. I groped after it. 'That would be the Captain of the Teulu, the King's bodyguard?'

'Aye, Ceredig, his foster-son.'

'Has he no son of his own, then?' I asked. 'None of his own blood to lead us?'

'Keep your voice down,' Phanes said, but with a hint of a smile in his tone. 'As to his own blood – the King is much changed by his sickness; but let you look in the Fosterling's face, and see if there is not even now a likeness. Above all, look at the eyes. The King has odd eyes, one green, one grey – it does not show from even a little distance – and the Fosterling has them too.'

That started me thinking of matters that I had not thought of before. 'That must be hard, to be a King and called the Golden, and not be able to buy a strong sword-arm, or a true-born son to follow him. What will he do when his time comes to go beyond the sunset?'

'For a son to take his place? Look to a daughter's husband, I suppose: after all, that has always been the way with the Pictish people beyond the Northern Wall. As to the strong sword-arm, at least his gold will buy him a band of younger sons with their shield-bearers behind them to unleash, when the time comes, against the Saxon hordes.'

'How large a band, I wonder?' I said. 'Would you be knowing? It seems that most things are known to you.'

'The word is for three hundred. Men such as your mountain princeling, others drawn from his own bodyguard.'

The rain had cleared in the night, but great clouds were coming up again from the south-east, spilling across the dark mass of the Giant's Seat like an advancing warhost. The Saxon threat seemed much closer here than among my own hills. 'Three hundred seems not over many,' I said at last.

There was a silence beside me and when I looked round Phanes also was watching those advancing clouds. 'With three hundred Companions Alexander won himself an empire,' he said. 'The Spartans held Thermopylae with three hundred. And with his three hundred your Arthur turned back the Saxon tide for fifty years, if the harpers' tales be true. There would seem to be a certain potency in the number.'

I said, trying to make it sound light, 'Then we should be three times potent, nine hundred, counting the shieldbearers – or will that seem greedy and spoil the magic?'

Phanes shook his head, 'I make no doubt that Arthur and the Spartans had their supporters and shield-bearers also. But it is only the three hundred, always only the three hundred, of whom the harpers sing.'

After a short while more, one of Phanes' men came to stand before him and report that the pack beasts were laden and ready for the road, and he got up, stretching under his cloak and I, getting up also, remembered that I had come into the stable court to see that all was well with Shadow.

At the last moment I remembered something else. 'The archangel dagger, have you taken it back to its master yet?'

'Not yet,' he said, turning to where his horse waited. 'I have had matters to keep me here in Britain this past few years. The Golden City must wait a while.'

When he had mounted and gone clattering and jingling out on to the track with his men and pack-train behind him, I wondered what the matters might be. Later, I came to know.

# 7

# The Gathering Feast

Phanes of Syracuse was right; by the end of the month, when the last comers had arrived, the King's war-band numbered three hundred.

And when the tally was complete, the King held a great Gathering Feast. There was not room for all the warriors, let alone their attendant shieldbearers, in the great Mead Hall with its smell of raw new wood; and so the long trestles were set up in the outer court, with fires and torches in between, so that it seemed Dyn Eidin was crowned with fire.

When we were all gathered, the feast horns sounded, and light moved and flared beyond the broad doorway of the King's Hall, and the King came out, leaning on the shoulders of his companions, to the High Seat, which had been carried out and set for him between the painted timber columns of the foreporch.

The horns sounded again, and the food was borne round from the kitchens and cooking pits behind the Hall; roast sucking pigs and huge joints of deer and cattle meat, swans with their feathers yet upon them and their wings half spread over the buckler-broad dishes on which they rested. We feasted then as I for one had never feasted before. Leastwise, the Three Hundred and the men of the Teulu feasted at the long tables, while we, their shieldbearers, served them according to custom; and when they could eat no more we had our turn, with plenty left for all, and the hounds chewing the bones under the benches, while the harpers told of past heroes, their battles and their loves. The torch smoke drifted across the darkened sky, and the strong yellow mead, sweet with its bitter after-taste, gave to all things a golden glow.

When the main part of the feasting was done, Mynyddog set his hands on the carved foreposts of his chair and thrust himself slowly to his feet. The horns sounded for a third time, and I saw him straighten himself, head up like an old war-horse at the smell of battle. Then, in the sudden silence, he began to speak to us.

'God's greeting to you all who come in answer to this summons; to you who come as strangers from all the kingdoms of the north and west; to you who come only across the fires from the ranks of the Teulu, my own household warriors, answering the same call. Let you listen to me this night, for I, Mynyddog of the Gododdin, must speak to you now at the outset of the thing that lies before us.' He must have had a great voice in his day; a voice for battle, like Prince Gorthyn's. But then he began to cough, and must needs let himself be eased back into his seat behind him; and one of those who had followed him from the Hall came quickly to his side and stooped close for a word with him, then turned to face the crowded court. By that time I knew him, a lean, dark-skinned man with yellow eyes and yellow teeth and a beak like a bird of prey under a grey-striped shag of rusty hair. Aneirin, the King's bard. Clearly he knew all that the King would say, and the thing had been prepared between them, that he might speak for Mynyddog if need be.

'The King speaks through my mouth,' he said. 'Hearken now to the words of Mynyddog the King.' He had a harper's voice, a trained storyteller's voice; no voice for a battlefield, but without seeming to raise it he could make it carry clear across the feasting court, and we listened to him with the silence that we would have given to the King. 'All of you who have ever listened to the harpers in your fathers' halls, you will know well enough of Arthur Pendragon and his Companions, of his twelve great battles, and how he thrust back the Saxon kind so that they came no more for the lifetime of a man. But all that is long ago, and now the Saxon flood comes thrusting in again.' He checked for an instant, I think for us to remember, though he did not speak of it, that he had been a captive of the Sea-wolves and suffered evil things at their hands. I had seen for myself the thickened white scar on his neck that marked the gall of a Saxon thrallring. 'Since Arthur's day Bernicia has been naught but an off-shoot of Deira, a few scattered settlements along our coast. But Bernicia has a king, Aethelfrith who men call the Flame-bringer; of him also, ye may have heard; and in the hollow of his swordhand Bernicia grows daily greater. Soon it will join with Deira into one great war-kingdom. And so now the time comes when, lacking the Pendragon – unless indeed he rise again to lead us –we must set in force the lessons that he taught to our forefathers in a desperate time. We must raise, as he did, three hundred light horsemen to unleash at any time and at whatever point the need is greatest, against the barbarians who would over-run our land. This, then, is the meaning of the summons that brings you here together. For as long as need be, you shall bide here, training in all matters of warfare, learning above all to become a brother-hood which thinks and feels and acts as one; and when the time comes indeed, I shall unleash you like hounds upon the quarry, knowing that as you have feasted at my table, so you will earn your mead.

'I am a sick man and my days for the war-trail are behind me, therefore I give you for your leader, when the time comes, Ceredig my son, who men call the Fosterling.'

I looked at the Captain of the Teulu standing by, and saw an odd look on his face – surprise, and a sort of bitter inward-turning laughter – and guessed that although the thing was indeed common knowl-edge, it was maybe the first time that the King had formally acknowledged his briar-bush son before all men.

But Aneirin was still speaking, and still in the King's words. 'One last thing I have to say. On a certain day, the hero Cuchulain' (he seemed obsessed by ancient legends and past heroes) 'learned from the Druid kind, that any boy who chose to take honour and gain his manhood on that day would come to be such a one as the harpers sing of round the fires for a thousand years but that he would not live to see the first white hair in his beard. Cuchulain chose to take honour on that day . . . If you take honour from my hands here and now, you also will each become such a one as the harpers sing of, but it may be that you also will not count your first white hairs. It is only right that you should know this, before you make your choice. This evening we have feasted all together, and with the feasting done, any who wish it, shall ride away. There shall be no shame; I shall choose out others to fill the empty places, that is all.

'But if you make the choice to become my men in this, then here and now you shall take the Great Oath to keep faith with me and with each other. And after that there can be no turning back with honour.'

Aneirin's voice fell silent, and he looked towards the King, and the King nodded and made a small gesture of finis with one gaunt hand.

No one moved. No one slipped away into the shadows. Only a dog snarled softly over a bone, and a knot in one of the pine torches spat sharply into the silence and far off along the Town Ridge a child began to cry.

We took the Oath then, sitting at the tables and around the fires. Warriors and shieldbearers alike, although I think that in truth it was meant only for the binding of the Three Hundred. The Great Oath which is the same through all the kingdoms, among all tribes and clans of Britain for it is older than clans and kingdoms.

'If we break faith with you, may the green earth gape and swallow us, may the grey seas roll in and overwhelm us, may the sky of stars fall upon us and crush us out of life for ever.'

'It is done, and it is well done. So do I count you all henceforth as sons of mine,' said Mynyddog, speaking for himself. His voice was dry and grinding in his chest, but the words came clear enough to all of us.

Then came the next thing.

He made a sign to the men of his household standing by, and the trestle boards of the High Table were drawn away, and great kists of carved and painted wood were brought from the Hall and set before him; and at his word they were opened and the swords which they contained were lifted out and freed of their wrappings of oiled linen. Great swords, some of them new from the smith's hands, some ancient and curiously wrought, hilts with goldwork, blades of fine blue-watered steel.

The giving of such weapons by a king to his followers in honour or reward or for the binding together of a brotherhood is a thing that all who have ever heard the harpers singing the high and ancient tales around the fires at night must know well enough, but I had never thought to see such a sword-giving in the world of my own day. It was like watching part of some half-lost hero tale, something that belonged to an older and darker and more shining world than mine.

There were no fine swords for the shieldbearers, of course, nor did we expect it. But I have not even now forgotten how the fierce splendour laid hold upon us all, in Mynyddog's flame-lit forecourt that night of early summer. And the faces of the young men crowding about the King for their gift-weapons, their eyes bright in the flare of the torches come easy to my mind.

I have but to close my eyes to see them passing, the men I came to know. The Prince of the Cymru, Madog, of little Elmet, Morien and Peredur, big fair Geraint from the far south, Tydfwlch The Tall; Gwenabwy who, so he claimed, had once killed a wolf with his naked hands; Cynan and Cynri and Cymran who were not strangers and in-comers like so many of us, but sons of Clydno who in his lifetime had been the King's judge, and who had crossed over from the ranks of the Teulu . . . As each came up Mynyddog laid a gaunt hand for an instant on the hilt of each sword, in token that it was his gift, before his captain and the grey-beards of his household bestowed it on its new master, until after a long while the kists were empty and none of the new Brotherhood lacked a sword.

I mind Gorthyn coming back to his place at one of the long side tables bearing an old sword with gold wires braided round the grip of age-blackened ivory, and a curling wave-break pattern engraved along the blade. It showed in the torch light when he half withdrew the scuffed wolfskin sheath, smiling at it gently and gravely, much as though it had been his first girl.

By the time the last sword had been given out it was late; way past the usual time to quench the torches and smoore the fires, and all things had taken on the golden glow that comes of much mead and the prospect of glory. But the King's Gathering Feast was not over. One thing remained.

And for this last thing, Ceredig the Fosterling became the King's voice. 'Mynyddog the King bids you, before you sleep this night, to drink together for the first time as a brotherhood.'

And while the words yet hung in the air among the smoke and the echoes of harpsong, light wavered again in the doorway of the High Hall, and the Queen and her daughters came through, bearing great mead bowls and followed by other women of the household with long-necked storage jars to keep them filled.

In Dyn Eidin they followed the old custom, and the women did not eat with the men on great occasions, but held their own feasting in the women's house. So though I had seen all of them from a distance more than once by then, I had not seen the King's women together; and they were worth the seeing. The Queen herself spear-tall, with a strong quiet face, and gold-work on her neck and arms, apples of gold hanging at the ends of her braided hair. Two of her daughters were out of the same mould, though with more of laughter in their faces; and the gowns of all of them not wool, but fine silks that must have come from the East in the pack-trains of merchants such as Phanes of Syracuse. The third daughter, walking last of the group in a gown of rose-hip red was the odd one out; smaller than the rest – which could have been because she was the youngest – with dove-gold hair and a narrow face that looked at first sight to be all eyes and no mouth.

The Queen held the golden mead bowl first for her lord the King, then for those who sat all across the foreporch where the High Table had been, while her daughters came down the lesser tables, holding their mead bowls for the warriors sprawled there. The youngest daughter, the Princess Niamh, was working her way down the long side table where Gorthyn sat, firmly concentrating on what she was doing, lest she spill a drop. And as she drew near, I saw that the reason her face looked to be all eyes was that despite her fairness, she had dark straight brows that should have been a boy's and overshadowed all the rest, and in her care of the bowl she carried she had sucked her mouth in until it all but disappeared. She looked much younger than her sisters, maybe younger even than Luned, but somehow, watching her come, I was not surprised if – as I had heard – the Queen her mother had chosen to pass on to her and not to either of the other two, her own physic skills.

She came to Cynan and his brothers sitting next to the men of Gwynedd. All three brothers looked like horses – the high cheekbones and flared nostrils and full dark eyes, the thick stallion crest of black hair – and none of them ever walked if they could ride, as though maybe there was a centaur somewhere in their bloodline. But as each rose to drink from the bowl she held, it was Cynan I noticed above the other two. It was always Cynan who I noticed, as though something in me knew already that somewhere in the future we had meaning for each other.

The bowl she held for him was of fine red Samian ware glowing in the flamelight almost the same colour as her gown. The colour made me look at it in the first place, and looking, I saw how his fingers crept on the sides of it to touch hers. I was not surprised; Cynan made laughing love to every girl who came his way, but this was different, a kind of teasing, and the look on their faces, glimpsed against the blue-shadowed and flame-fringed night was different, too, the look of old friends sharing a secret and maybe a jest. It was a very belonging look, and for that moment it made me think of Conn and Luned and me.

Then Cynan bent his head to drink from the tipped bowl. And after, the Lady Niamh passed on to Tydfwlch the Tall, to Gwenabwy, to Gorthyn who was still so busy dandling his sword that he scarcely realized she was there, until she stood close over him and his neighbour jabbed him in the ribs.

And in a short while after, came the end of the King's Gathering Feast.

# 8

# The Swordsmith

At the Royal Farm there were five more long-houses like the one that had received us on our first night below Eidin Ridge. All of them new-built and smelling of raw timber, and so roughly thatched that in times of storm the rain drove through and spat into our fires and soaked the bracken and skins of our sleeping places. (We did something about that ourselves as time went by, adding another layer of furze and broom to make the roofs within reason watertight.) And there we were lodged, fifty warriors to a long-house, and as many of their shieldbearers as could pack in with them, while the rest of us slept in the foreporch and lofts and wherever we could find space in the farm buildings round about.

From the very first, the Three Hundred were divided into troops of fifty and the Fosterling saw to it that each troop contained men from all the kingdoms, that there might be no danger of cross-loyalties to tribe or territory coming between troop and troop. And of course for us, their shieldbearers, it was the same.

We began our training almost without realizing that we did so, for in those early days much of it was the same as the training for manhood that we had known among our own hills: running and wrestling, the use of sword and spear, javelin and bow. (It was Morien, always the inventor in our midst, who brought out some story of Artos having used fire arrows in the taking of some Saxon stronghold, and set to work with linen rags soaked in pitch until he had achieved arrows of a like kind, one of which set fire to a store-shed roof, and gained him the name of Morien the Fiery which he bore from that time forth.) Cavalry training came later, but even that at first was a familiar kind. The Three Hundred trained sometimes by troop, sometimes all together as one war-band; and we, of course, did not train with them, not as yet. But we underwent all the same schooling on the same practice grounds at the foot of the Town Ridge, shouted at by the same war-scarred veterans of bygone battles; and at night, serving our warriors in Hall, we shared the same food and firelight and harpsong.

And by the end of the first few weeks we had begun to knit together into something whole and complete. The Three Hundred had begun to call themselves the Companions because that was the name by which men spoke of Artos' band of cavalry. We were never the Companions, but the bonding was for us also.

I have known much the same thing since, at another time and in another place, but that was the first time; and the first time for anything can only come once.

Some while past noon of a sweltering day – it was still early summer but thunder had been muttering among the hills all morning without being able to bring itself to the point of storm-break, and the sunlight was thick and heavy and the river levels quivering in the heat-haze – a knot of us were sprawling within the thin shade of the alder trees at the edge of the practice grounds, waiting for our lords and masters who were at their running and wrestling out on the open turf.

Nearest of all the wrestlers, Gorthyn and Cynan were heaving and straining at each other like a pair of antler-locked stags, and close beyond them Cymran, the youngest of the three brothers, had taken on Llif from beyond the old northern wall, a long lean Pict, sandy-haired and tattooed on breast and shoulders with the blue spiralling patterns of his people. I could see the blue spandrils leap and quiver with the movement of the straining muscles under the skin. I could hear the whistling breaths and the pad of bare feet on turf as men shifted their stance. But it had all been going on for a long time, each victorious wrestler moving up at the end of his bout to take on the winner of another pair, and we, waiting with our lords' clothes and rough linen towels to rub them down, were growing bored.

Looking back now, I do not know how it came about that we drew our knives and began to play Blade-bite. It is a boys' game that we should all have grown out of by that time, but we were bored, as I have said. We formed the circle and began, each pair of challenger and challenged in turn taking stance in the centre to try their blades against each other, the victor, as among the wrestlers, going on to meet the victor of the next pair. Only one strike allowed, and the victory to the blade that took the least damage. My knife was a veteran of more than one such contest, and had the notches to prove it, though since it was a good blade, and I had the knack, it had generally given more damage than it took; and when one of Cynan's shieldbearers, Dara by name, challenged me, I advanced to meet him in the middle of the circle with the confident air of a proved champion.

I remember the sharp clash and rasp as our blades met; and truly his suffered the deepest notch; I mind the shout going up, and the comparing of blades. But in the moment of impact I had felt something spring loose in the hilt, and when I looked to see what was amiss – being beaten about the shoulders in congratulations by my fellow shieldbearers the while – I found that one of the rivets holding the horn plates of the grip in place had sprung under the shock of blade meeting blade.

Conn was standing on the outskirts of the group, looking on. He seemed to spend a lot of his time looking on from the outskirts in those days, having no place of his own. He ran errands for everybody, tended horses, burnished harness and gear, fetched and carried, and was beginning to wear a sullen look, a down-tailed look like a masterless dog. I had noticed it for some while past, but had not known what to do about it.

I called him over and held out my knife. 'Conn, look you. This has sprung a rivet – there. Take it up to Fercos the weapon-smith, ask him to set it to rights, and wait you till it be done.'

He took the knife without a word, and turning, departed at his loping, faintly lopsided run, up the steep track that wound towards the Dyn. When I turned back to the wrestlers, Gorthyn had thrown his man. He straightened and stood back, shaking the sweat-darkened hair out of his eyes, then bent to pull Cynan laughing and breathless to his feet. They came back each with an arm across the other's shoulders, towards the shade of the trees, and Dara and I caught up the towels we had abandoned on the grass, and went to meet them.

A good while later, Conn had not returned. I had bidden him wait while the rivet was dealt with, and maybe Fercos was busy. The weapon-smiths of Eidin were mostly busy at that time, and Fercos, the King's armourer, must be in demand above all the rest. Meanwhile it was drawing on towards time for the evening meal. Eating with no tools but one's fingers is an awkward and messy business, and I should soon be in need of my knife – on this more than any other evening of the week for since there was no room for the whole Company in the King's Hall, each troop in turn supped with the King while the rest fed in their own hostels from the great cookhouses at the farm, and this evening it was the turn of our troop.

So, needing my knife, I headed for Fercos' smithy myself to find out what had become of it and of Conn.

It was while I was threading my way through the stone houses and workshops that clung about the outer wall of the Dyn that it came to me, out of nowhere, how seldom Conn had gone near the smithy at home. Only a few times, and then at my heels, in the years since Phanes had passed by with the archangel dagger. And with the thought came a somewhat confused understanding of the reason why.

When I came to the smoke-blackened smithy just within the gateway, it was unwantedly quiet; no ring of hammer on anvil or rasp of grinding-stone, no clatter and gasp of the goatskin bellows; only the tired roar of the flames sinking low on the forge hearth. Fercos the smith stood beside the anvil, a pair of tongues in one hand, looking intently down at the cooling blade which lay there. His striker stood behind him in the shadows, and on the usual bench before the door, my mended knife lying beside him, Conn sat forward, gazing in the same direction with the tranced air of someone listening to a harper's story that has captured his whole heart. He was not aware of my coming at all, and I checked in the doorway, not speaking. Fercos was tempering a sword blade and no one speaks to a smith or makes any sound to break his attention in that moment.

The blade cooling on the anvil had passed through the hot colours before I came, the white and yellow and red, and was glowing violet, changing to blue as we watched it, and the blue deepening to the colour of nightshade flowers. Another instant and it would be dulling on the edge of black. And in that instant Fercos grasped it with the tongs and with a swift movement plunged it into the trough of water that stood ready.

There was a hissing as of a disturbed snakepit and the smithy filled with throat-catching steam. And when the hissing had subsided and the steam begun to clear, Fercos took the blade from the water and laid it back on the anvil, dead and almost black, its rainbow fires all faded, and stood looking at it with his head on one side. In a few moments more he picked it up again, in his hands now, bending it into an arc, and letting it go with a *wang* like a released bow string.

'Reckon she'll do,' he said, and laid it down again.

All through the smithy the watchers let their breath go, and the tension fell slack. Conn looked up and saw me, and scrambled to his feet, catching up the mended knife.

'I lost count of time,' he said.

I took back the knife and thrust it into my belt. 'I thought that might be the way of it.'

He looked suddenly stiff and bitter. 'I am sorry – I forgot –'

'You forget too much,' I said, making my voice rough, anything to stop him saying what I thought he might be going to say – something about being my bondservant.

And he shut his mouth in a straight line.

The smith looked up from the blade on his anvil and said with quiet kindliness, 'Aye well, another day when maybe your lord can better spare you.' He smiled a little, consideringly, his head still on one side. 'Whether you have it in your hands or your head is another matter, but I am thinking you have it in your heart – the making of a swordsmith. We could be finding out.'

A short while later, having got him safely outside, I led the way across the crowded outer court to a certain place on the far side where the timber ramparts, ending on either side, left a gap between two black outcrops of rock, where the solid ground ended as abruptly as though sliced with an axe and fell sheer to the jagged mass of scree and rock and rough turf far below. There was some story about Epona, the Mother of Foals, having leapt her white mare from it, or maybe leapt from it herself in her mare form, in the years when the hills were new and she had raised the great rock for a fortress; and it had been kept unwalled and open ever since, in case she should pass that way again. Men tended to keep well clear of the place, though, for the occasional accident happened and when it did, it was still said, even in these days of the White Christ, that the Great Mother had called in her price for Dyn Eidin Rock.

So the midst of the gap, well away from either side, made a good place for private talk, a thing not easily come by in the crowded Dyn.

Conn followed me, dragging that tell-tale leg a little, and sat down at my side, both of us with our feet hanging into nothingness. But when I turned towards him he looked back at me with hot eyes and a mouth still shut into a straight line.

'Oh, don't be such a bird-wit!' I told him. 'I had to stop you blurting out – whatever it was.'

'Whatever it was?' he echoed.

I did not answer at once. The idea that had blown into my head on the way up from the practice ground had flowered during those moments in the smithy while the sword blade cooled from violet to blue. But it was still very new; so new that I needed a few moments more to get used to it and sort it out before I passed it on to Conn himself.

'I used to think,' I began at last. 'Well, I don't suppose I thought much about it really – that you had forgotten that idea about learning to be a smith. Well, you never went near Loban's forge at home, save when I dragged you. But you have not, have you?'

'I knew it was foolishness –'

'*You haven't, have you?*' I said. I had to be clear about that.

It was his turn to be silent, watching the long low tumble of hills in the westering light, half lost in the thunder haze. Behind us the outer court was growing yet more crowded as men gathered and began to drift towards the Mead Hall. The smell of hot meat wafted from the cookhouse. It would not be very long before I had to go. He pulled his gaze back from the distant hills.

'No, I haven't,' he said simply.

'Then listen. Did you tell Fercos – have you told anybody that you were my bondservant?'

'No. You told Gorthyn I was your body servant.'

'That is a different matter. There are free body servants. Not many but a few.'

He looked at me, frowning, puzzled as to what all this was about; and I pushed on, 'Don't you see? Conn, I cannot give you your freedom – I would if I could, but you are my father's, not mine. But if you want to be a swordsmith, then here is your chance to learn the skill, and when you have learned it – you're free.'

'You mean it?' he said.

'Of course I mean it!'

'Supposing always that Fercos will take me.'

'He'll take you; you heard what he said. There's not a smith in Dyn Eidin or along the Town Ridge who isn't in need of all the help he can get, since the King's hosting.'

Conn's gaze was very level. 'If it is forbidden for a bondman to learn the smith's craft, then it must be forbidden for a smith to teach him. If I ask him, I must tell him what I am.'

'No!' I told him. 'That's why I had to stop you spewing it out, back there in the smithy.'

He said stubbornly, 'To go to him and ask him to take and train me without telling him would be a thing without honour.'

I was so exasperated I could have taken him by the shoulders and shaken him until his back teeth fell out, if we had not been sitting on the edge of Epona's Leap; but the thing needed more careful handling than that. 'Listen,' I said. 'If you tell him and keep your precious honour bright and shining, he will do one of two things; either he will turn you away, and every smith of Eidin Ridge will do the like, or he will take you all the same, and may bring trouble on his head by doing it.'

'He may have heard it anyway, from someone else. Lleyn knows.'

'Neither Lleyn nor anyone else is likely to have been interested enough to tell him. If anyone does, he can always deny having heard it – so long as neither you nor I have told him. That way, if trouble comes, it will fall where it belongs, on my head.'

'On mine also.'

'No, for being a bondman you have no choice but to do as I bid you,' I told him ruthlessly.

Conn said, 'If I may not share the trouble, I will not share the lie.' And I saw that there would be no shifting him.

'So be it,' I said. 'If the trouble comes, I will throw you to the wolves to save my own hide. That makes you happy?'

The horns of feasting were sounding from the Hall and we scrambled to our feet and back from the edge.

'That makes me happy, O my brother and my lord,' he said with a sudden warmth like laughter in the back of his throat.

I spun him round and gave him a push between the shoulders. 'Then go you and ask him and God speed you in your asking.'

I watched him walk away, back towards Fercos' smithy, then turned and headed for the Hall.

I no longer had a body servant. I had never wanted one, come to think of it. I remembered my annoyance on the day my father had handed him over to me. I only had a friend. Much simpler than trying to combine the two; I have always liked things to be plain and uncomplicated.

# 9

# Ordeal by Wakefulness

Summer went by, and in the crop-lands below the Dyn the barley was tall and turning pale, and the birdsong beginning already to fall silent in deep-layered valley woods. Our first weeks of weapon training were over and we were beginning to work with the horses, learning the lessons of cavalry, to function together as wings and squadrons under our own troop leaders, though the leaders still changed from day to day until with time the natural leaders began to emerge. (Among the Companions no man held command because he was his father's son, but only because he was the best fitted for it, and the son of a one-valley chieftain might have the command over the sons of the great kingdoms such as Strathclyde. The Fosterling, as yet handling us in double harness with the King's bodyguard, saw to that.)

So, on the moors and the low heather hills around Eidin Ridge we were being tempered from the rough-riders we had mostly been among our own hills into ordered and disciplined cavalry such as Artos might not have disowned. With javelins and blunt-tipped lances we learned the opening moves of combat; we learned how to draw an enemy after us until it was too far from its own lines; how to deal with the spears of an enemy on foot; and, under the guidance of men old in the ways of horse-warfare before most of us were born, we taught to our horses the lessons that they also had to learn, training them to stand steady in the face of a hostile crowd and brandished weapons, to use their own forefeet as weapons (that comes easy to any stallion and even the geldings, but the mares had to be taught) to charge through banks of burning brushwood, listening to their rider more than their natural fear of fire ... And much of this training we took all together, Companions and shieldbearers alike, so that when the time came, no matter how the fighting went, we should each be able to bear whatever part was needful.

We learned and practised, together of course, the use of the three-man arrowhead, the warriors riding ahead as though into battle while the rest of us remained mounted and ready in the rear; the moves by which, if our warrior's horse was slain, one of us took up his own horse to replace it, returning on foot; if the warrior was slain, one went up to take his place, the other still remaining in reserve; and if the warrior was sore wounded, both of us went up, one to bring him off, the other to take his place. It sounds a simple enough matter, but it is less simple than it sounds. To come up always on the right side to have one's sword-arm free, to get a frightened and angry horse under control or a wounded man across one's saddle bow in the midst of a whirlpool of men and horses, takes a good deal of practice. (Gorthyn played the part whole-heartedly, I mind, and so did those, sometimes it was the Teulu, who played the enemy.) But we got into the way of it after a while.

I saw very little of Conn in those days. Fercos had taken him into his smithy, to work the goatskin bellows when need arose, but also to learn the craft, and the smith was a hard taskmaster. But at the odd times when we could snatch a few words together, Conn had the look of a man who has found his own path to follow. I tried to be glad of that and not to miss his quiet company.

Ah, well, I was forming other bonds, as I have said. And I had other things to think about. Towards the time of the Lammas fires, Ceredig the Fosterling devised a new kind of ordeal for us; and from then on, far into the autumn, groups of the Companions would draw lots from an age-eaten Roman helmet, three white pebbles and the rest black, and each time, those who drew the white pebbles were issued with three days hard ration of oat or barley cake, and sent out from the Ridge with orders to go where they would, hold together and keep themselves and each other from sleeping for three days and three nights. Again, it seemed a simple matter, but those of us who had ever trained a hawk and been through the three nights and days of keeping it awake which is the final point of the training had some idea of what was entailed.

It was into early autumn by the time it came to the turn of our troop; and night after night the draw was made, until Gorthyn and Cynan and Llif the Pict drew the white pebbles. They divided up their shieldbearers according to their own whim, as had become the custom. I had hoped to be with Lleyn, who had become a friend by that time, but our Lords thought otherwise, and I found myself cast with Dara and with one of Llif's shieldbearers, Huil by name, who I scarcely knew.

The lots were drawn overnight, and afterwards we ate all that our bellies would hold, and slept like hogs; and at dawn we scattered in threes into the wilderness.

Dara and Huil and I joined the old paved road that headed north-westward towards the long-forsaken Legionary fort on the shores of the Firth. Castellum, I had heard it called. The place had an unchancy reputation, for it was said that it had been garrisoned, not by Red Crests, but by men who called themselves Frontier Wolves and had some sort of kinship with the four-footed kind, and whose ghosts still came back in wolf shape to run through the ruins at full moon. That would have seemed a good enough reason for keeping well clear of the place, especially as the moon was near to full. So why we chose to spend our three nights vigil there, I am not sure. Maybe it gave the whole exercise a heightened smell of adventure. Maybe we thought it would be something that we could crow about afterwards to less valiant souls. Also I think we played quite deliberately with the idea that the whiff of fear might help us to keep awake.

From the place where the Eidin Ridge track turned off from it, the road was almost lost, for few people travelled it any more, and the tide of heather and bramble and rough grass had come flowing in. Sometimes, for a short distance, our feet sensed the hardness of stone under the grass, but at other times it was as though no one had ever passed that way before. The little thin wind blowing up from the Firth began to have the smell of salt in it, and the crying and calling of shorebirds was the voice of a great loneliness as we came down the last stretch to the old lost frontier fort. It was not the first time that we had come that way; by that time there were few places within half a day of Dyn Eidin that were not known to us; but I had not been so aware of the loneliness, the emptiness of the place before. There were birch and rowan in the ditch, and the past summer's willowherb turned to grey seed-silk massing in the gap where the gateway must have been; and midway between the fallen stone stumps of the gatehouse towers, a path had been trampled through the willowherb. Not so empty of human life, after all.

The sight pulled us up in our tracks. And Huil said, 'We are not the first-comers, by the look of it.'

'Like enough it is an animal – fox or wolf,' I said.

But Dara thought otherwise. 'Never saw anything but wild pig leave a trampled track like that – wild pig or man – not ghost-wolf, anyway.' And he giggled. Dara was a stout good natured callant with pale eyelashes and a giggle that came out of him like water out of a bottle. But having made his jest he glanced about him uneasily. It was not quite the place to be jesting about ghost-wolves.

Huil, who like all his kind had a nose like a hunting dog, dropped to his knees and crouched forward, sniffing at the trampled stems.

'It is man.'

He got up, and the three of us stood for a moment looking at each other, wondering whether we should go elsewhere. But it seemed a poor spirited sort of thing to do, to turn away as though someone else had a better right than we had. I said, 'The place is big enough for two lots of us.' And we prowled in, swaggering a little for the benefit of any eye that might be watching.

We had taken our time on the way, and it was a while past noon: and it seemed to us, especially with others beside ourselves loose in the old fort, that the first thing to do was to find our quarters for the days and nights to come: somewhere that would give shelter from possible wild weather and which could be defended in case of need. We scattered to the search, but not widely, keeping within call or sight-signal of each other all the while, and cast around among the turf hummocks of fallen briar-grown walls like hounds on a thin scent. In the gate gap between breast-high banks, that gave out into what seemed to be some kind of outer part of the camp where it ran into the grey waters of the Firth, Huil picked up the scent of the first-comers again, and after a careful testing of the grass and bushes (he was a tracker to equal the Little Dark People, was Huil) told us, squatting on his haunches, 'They have not come back. Not this way, anyway.'

'So. Then we bide clear of beyond the gate,' Dara said. 'That gives us the high ground at all events.' And we turned back into the ruins of the main fort.

We found our shelter after a while; a kind of undercroft, a storage place perhaps. The front half of whatever had been above it had fallen in, half blocking the ragged entrance gap, but further in it seemed sound enough, the earth above it held up by arched stonework and the roots of trees. Shelter from night and weather and wolf.

We built a hearth of fallen stones close to the mouth of the cave – more like a cave than a building it seemed – and gathered dead wood for a fire when night came, but no bracken or the like, as we would normally have done, to pile over the root-broken stones of the floor – the more we made ourselves comfortable, the harder we would find it to keep from sleep. We went down to the burn that ran through its steep gorge below the western rampart and drank and filled the leather bottle we had brought with us, for the evening's stirabout, where the water ran clear and deep above the remains of a paved ford. There was an upright stone, I mind, marking the place where an old track from the fort must have entered the water, heading westward; a black stone, dappled with grey and golden lichen. I set my hand on its rounded poll, and got the odd uncanny feel that it was used to the touch of men's hands in passing. But that must have been long and long ago . . .

We came back to the cave, and built and lit our fire, with Dara's strike-a-light to kindle the spark. The sparks fell on to the dry fir fronds and the dead twigs caught, and Huil stooped and blew between his hands on to the licking tongues of flame; and as we fed it with longer and longer sticks and branches, the fire on our hearth caught and flared up, casting its light a little way into the cave as the daylight outside faded, picking out stones and dragon-coiled tree roots, and the faces of the three of us gathered about it. We undid the oatmeal bag and took out the dinted iron pot, tipped in a third of the meal and the water we had brought up from the ford and set about making the evening stira-bout.

With neither salt nor a knob of honeycomb it was dull eating, but it stayed our hunger. We finished up every crumb and smear from the inside of the pot, and put the bag safely aside for tomorrow night and the night after; then sat and looked at each other, listening to the wind that had begun to rise outside.

That first night went easily enough. All of us were well used to missing a night's sleep now and then for one reason or another – hunting or a mead drink or a turn of wolf-guard over the lambing pens. We told stories that first night, feeding our small fire sparingly to make the wood store last, each of us bringing out tales from among our own hills.

I told of Branwen who was wedded to a King of Eriu and carried back to his kingdom across the western waters and misused and abandoned, and how at last she won back to her own land, and of her vengeance that followed after. I told of Gwyn ap Nudd and the Wild Hunt, tales with which Old Nurse had used to frighten Luned and me on windy autumn nights when we lay in our beds listening to the hound-babble of the grey geese flying over.

Dara told of a Queen of Strathclyde, Languareth by name; how she gave a ring that the King had given her to her warrior lover. The King saw the ring on his hand (he cannot have had much sense between his ears that warrior lover!) and with drugged wine caused him to fall into a deep sleep, and while he slept took the ring from his finger and threw it in the river. Then he asked the Queen why she no longer wore it; and when she made an excuse, saying that it was too big for her hand and she feared to lose it, flew into a passion, accused her of having given it to another man (which after all was the truth) and threatened her with death if she did not instantly bring it to him. Making some desperate excuse, she managed to gain a breathing space until next morning, and as soon as the King had left her, she ran to the holy man who lived nearby and begged him to help her. The holy man took pity on her – or maybe he was thinking that a queen would make a useful friend – and bade her send a fisherman down to the river, with orders to bring her the first fish that took his line. The fisherman went down to the river and cast his line, and a fish came up and took the bait. He carried the fish to the Queen and when she and her maidens opened it, there inside, gleaming in the first light of morning, was the King's golden ring.

It was a good story and Dara, who enjoyed anything that savoured of gossip, put much rich and colourful detail into it. But myself, I liked better the strange unchancy tales that Huil told that night. They were not easy to follow, for being of the Pictish people his native tongue was not ours, and though he spoke our tongue none so ill, he pronounced some of the words strangely; and beside that the stories themselves were as many-stranded and interwoven as the tendrils of the white bindweed or the patterns tattooed on his own breast and shoulders. Stories from a world that still counted wealth in cattle and bondwomen; an older world than mine or Dara's, a shadow world in which even the ghosts and water-horses and battling heroes seemed stranger than our own.

It was after one of Huil's stories that I needed to go outside and make water. I did not much care for the idea, for he had peopled the dark beyond the fireglow with too many strange and hair-lifting things, and I would have gone only just beyond the cave entrance. But not wishing to admit myself scared by a bairn's ghost story, I made myself go further, half across the old fort. It was so, through the thin spitting rain, that I glimpsed a blink of firelight away beyond the northern gate. So I knew where the other three had made their lair, and I wondered, on the way back, whether they had seen the blink of our fire also, in the damp and windy dark. I wondered also who they were, those other three. Maybe Lleyn and his two fellows, maybe our own three warriors, but there had been more than one set of white pebbles drawn last night. It might be something to pass the time with later, to find out . . .

At first light, we went down to the burn again; and drank and doused our heads to wash the night fuzziness out of them in the cold swift-running water. Then we returned to the cave and the question of what we should do with the daylight hours until we could eat again.

We could have spent some of the time in setting makeshift traps in the hope of catching something to sweeten the evening bannock, but there was a sense of ritual on us; the oat and barley meal that had been issued to us was proper food for the vigil. Also I think we wanted to use the time to do something, make something, that would leave the mark of our having been there.

'We could rebuild a wall,' I said, standing in the cave mouth and looking about the traces of old footings breaking like outcrops through the grass. The rain had stopped and the early light was waking starling colours in the fallen stone.

'Which one?' Huil asked. 'I am thinking there are enough and more than enough to choose from.'

'Any one,' I said. 'It makes no odds.'

Dara let out his bubbling laugh. 'We could build a cairn and stick the bannock-cloth on top of it for a banner.'

'Too showy,' I said.

And thankfully, Huil agreed with me. 'A wall would be more use.'

'Use for what, in the name of light?' Dara grinned at us. 'To keep the ghosts out?'

'To keep us from going to sleep,' I said. 'Either will serve for that – let's toss for it and let the Gods of Castellum choose,' and I fished in my pouch for the only coin I had on me.

So we tossed for it, and the Gods of Castellum chose a wall.

Close before our cave were the remains of a very small enclosure, a store-shed maybe. At the near corner the wall stood pretty near elbow high; at the lower end it was almost lost under rank grass. In one place a rowan tree had seeded in the rubble filling and sent its roots down into the footings, heaving the stones aside. We hacked back the docks and brambles until the whole oblong lay clear, and began building. There were plenty of loose stones lying about, and we heaved them up and stacked them one upon another, fitting them together in the manner of dry-stone walling. None of us were expert builders of walls, but we brought great care to the task. If we were going to build a wall, it should at least be a wall that we could be proud of. Also the more care we took, the more we thought about what we were doing, the less we had to think about the emptiness of our bellies, the less likely we were to fall asleep. It became very important to us, that wall. We held a deeply earnest council, I mind, as to what we should do about the rowan tree: build round it, or leave a gap. In the end we left a gap, carefully squared up. Huil, with his feelings for curves, would have had us build round it, but we were two to one against.

That was towards the end of the day, and all things were becoming just a little unreal, to me at least, but I was pleased to find that I was not at all sleepy. That was when, heaving up yet another stone, I saw something scratched on the under side of it, and rubbing off the staining lichen with the heel of my hand, saw that it was a running wolf, not properly carved but crudely scratched as though with the point of a dagger, yet with something of life in it all the same. I squatted down with it across my knee, to look at it more closely. I was still aware of the world around me, the others still busy on the wall, the crying of the gulls whirling overhead, but the wolf was blurring a little on my sight, fading and yet at the same time growing towards life. Wolf running – running among trees . . .

And then Huil had me by the shoulder, shaking me back to wakefulness. That night, our second without sleep, is hazy in my mind. Looking back, I have wondered more than once, why we did not come to an agreement and take turns, one to keep watch while the other two slept. None of us could have betrayed the other two without also betraying ourselves. But we did not, nor do I believe that any of the rest of us did so. We kept faith with the orders we had been given, and got through the slow dragging hours somehow, as best we could. With the fire re-kindled and the evening ration eaten, we returned at first to our storytelling. But in truth we had all lost our taste for it, and the effort to concentrate on telling a story or even on listening to it seemed suddenly more than it was worth. And as the stories began to tail away, we turned more and more to talk, to word games and riddles, getting up to stretch and stamp about every now and

then when the flame light began to blur. We played
dice for pebbles, we tried to play Flash the Fingers, but
that must be played at lightning speed if it is to be a
game worth playing at all, and our reactions were so
slow that we abandoned the attempt. We talked –
mostly about our elders and betters.

The first night had been Huil's, with his chill,
uncanny stories from beyond the edge of the
world; but that second night was Dara's, he being
born and bred on Eidin Ridge, and having, moreover,
a nose for other people's affairs that would have done
credit to some old hen-wife. From him, that night, I
came to know things about the royal household and
the King's Teulu aye, and the Companions, that I had
not known, or known only vaguely and piecemeal
before.

I learned what lay behind the white mark of the
thrall ring on the neck of Aneirin the Poet; how he had
been taken captive by the Saxons when on an embas-
sage to their King, taken under the Green Branch of
peacetalk, which is against all the rules even of war,
and held for ransom; and how, when his fellows returned with the word, Mynyddog, ashamed to haggle
for the life and freedom of a friend (and was he not,
after all, called the Wealthy?), had had the demanded
gold brought from his treasury, and bidden Cenau of
his Hearth Companions to take it south. Dara, who
was feeding dry sprigs of last summer's heather to the
fire as he talked, looked up with an eyebrow cocked in
half question; we knew the man? Huil and I nodded.
We knew the man: Cenau, son of Llwyarch Hen, the
grim little fighting man who most us believed would
take the Fosterling's place as Captain of the bodyguard

when he left it to lead the Companions on the war-trail.

'Go on,' Huil said, leaning closer with his arms gripped round his knees.

And Dara went on. 'This is a ransom that should be paid with spears,' Cenau said. But he had his orders, and he took the ransom-gold south, with a band of warriors for an escort, and one of the merchant kind who knew something of the Saxon tongue, to act as interpreter. (I did not even wonder if the merchant was Phanes of Syracuse; I simply assumed without question that it was.) They came to the court of the Saxon king and he received them well enough in his Great Hall, but when the gold was on the High Table, he swore that the captive had escaped, and claimed that the gold was due to him all the same, for calling off the hunt and leaving him free to live or die as the Fates decreed. Then Cenau cried out, 'Did I not say? This is a ransom that must be paid with spears!' And he and his men snatched fire brands from the hearth and flung them up into the thatch and the roof timbers and in the tumult and confusion they fought their way out, leaving the gold and three of their own men dead behind them, and while the Saxons strove to save their king's Hall, they set off, questing like hounds through the surrounding buildings. And Aneirin, who all this while had been chained by the neck close by in a store-shed half underground, heard the uproar, guessing the meaning of it, or maybe knowing by the inner sight of his kind, lifted up his voice and began to sing. And Cenau and his men heard the voice and the song that were Aneirin's and made towards them. They battered their way into his prison-place and hacked his neck-chain free of the beam to which it was made fast, and bore him off to where the horses waited, and so back to Dyn Eidin.

It seemed that that was the end of the story, but we waited, hoping for more, and in a short while Dara looked up from his fire-feeding again, and went on, 'I saw them ride in. I was but seven summers old, but I mind yet, what Aneirin looked like.'

'Bad?' I prodded.

'As though he had had the Wild Hunt on his tail.'

'Had the Saxons tortured him?' Huil ran the tip of his tongue which was narrow and pointed over his lips.

'I would not be knowing. I have heard it said that he was very sick for a long while, and that the King would have had him taken into the house of the Holy Brothers and tended there by the Infirmarer who is also one of his own physicians. But the Father Abbot would not accept him unless he received the faith of the White Christ, and sick or not, Aneirin had other thoughts as to that. It must have been a scene worth the watching!' Dara let out his bubbling giggle. 'In the end, the Queen and her women tended him. I dare say he was better off that way.'

I nodded. 'I have heard it said that the Queen has the gift of herb healing, she and the Princess Niamh also.'

'As to that, surely every woman passes her skills on to the chosen one among her daughters.'

'I wonder if the Queen chose that one because she lacks the beauty that the other two have, and could do with a skill to make up for it,' Huil said thoughtfully, then shook his head. 'More likely because she had the skill born in her and it only needed to be trained and nurtured.'

Dara said quickly, 'In any case, she does not lack beauty for those with eyes to see.'

'Such as yourself? It seems you have a special interest in the Princess Niamh,' I began, mocking a little, but it seemed that it was no mocking matter.

'Because I am Cynan's shieldbearer, and take proper interest in his affairs,' Dara said stiffly. 'And she would come running if Cynan whistled.'

I laughed. 'As to that, every girl along Eidin Ridge would come running if Cynan whistled.'

'This is different. An old story. She used to run at his heels like a puppy whenever she could escape from her nurse. Once he got tired of it and set her on the high branch of an apple tree and went away and left her there. It is different now, of course, but –'

He broke off. Huil had tensed like a hunting dog. Nose up and a faint quiver running through him. He got up and moved soundlessly, crouching a little, towards the entrance. Dara and I waited, straining our ears, ready to spring after him; and I'll not deny that the thought of the ghost-wolves was chill for the moment in the back of my neck, though it was far more likely a spy from the party beyond the north gate. Then Huil was back, and squatting down again in his place beside the fire.

'What was it?' we asked him.

He shook his head. 'Something – man – it has gone now.'

And after a while of listening for it to come back, we broke silence and began to talk again, but of different things – things which mattered little and are gone from me.

But when the darkness thinned and we went out into the first light of morning, a bright knot of rowan berries lay exactly in the midst of our newly-walled enclosure.

'It seems that we have had visitors in the night,' I said. 'Maybe tonight we should return the visit.'

# – 10 –
# The Night of the Running Wolves

We spent the third day on our wall. But I remember little about it save that towards the day's end one corner of it fell down, because we – one or all of us – had misjudged something in the building of it. And after a sudden flaring quarrel as to whose fault it was, as though it mattered, we set to work to repair the damage, as though that mattered either.

And when darkness came down, we kindled our fire for the last time, a very meagre fire, for dry wood was growing scarce in our part of the fort, and squatting around it we ate the last of our barley bannock, which by then was as dry as sawdust and prone to crumble.

Our throats were like lime kilns, not only from the bannock but from the endless talking for the sake of talking. We had told all the stories we knew, and in any case our weary minds flinched from the bare idea of trying to sort out the tangled skein of even the simplest tale. I mind looking at the other two and seeing that their faces looked dull and blotchy in the light of the fire, and their eyes red-rimmed. For myself, I felt as though my eyes were full of hot dust, and I seemed to see everything through a slight haze. My whole body ached to lie down and let go and slip below the dark sucking wavelets of sleep, and I began to have the feeling that I was not really there at all. And after I had more than once roused from this state to find Huil or Dara shaking me, and had myself caught Dara in the last instant before he rolled quietly forward into the fire, I knew that we were going to have to take some kind of desperate action if we were to get through that last night without sleeping.

'Sweet Mother of Foals, will it never be morning?' Dara groaned, rocking on his haunches.

Huil let out a long whistling breath and sat back, stretching and shaking his head as though he had a bee in his ear.

And into the foggy darkness behind my eyes came the remembered sight of the bright knot of rowan berries lying so exactly in the midst of our walled enclosure. Huil had thrown it out, and we had not spoken of it again, nor the idea that we should return the visit of those who had left it there . . .

I heard my own voice, thick with sleep, saying, 'It is the last night, let us make it a night to crown the other two.'

Huil rubbed the back of his hand across his face and squinted round at me. 'What then shall we do? Pull up the Giant's Seat by the roots?'

'Not such a great matter as that would be. There remains the matter of last night's visit still to be repaid.'

'A raid, you mean?' Dara said with quickening interest.

'They began it, setting foot unbidden in our enclosure. It will serve to pass the time, and like enough they'll be glad of that as we shall.' We looked at each other round the fire, the three of us, while the aching

need for sleep drew back into the shadows. Then with
no other word spoken, we got to our feet.

'Silent hunting,' I said. 'It will be no sport if we do
not take them by surprise.'

Huil looked up through the jagged entrance hole,
smiling like a lover. 'We have a raider's moon for it,
anyway.'

We smoored the fire with turfs and set out. The sea
mist that had rolled up from the Firth and hung about
most of the day had cleared, and certainly we had a
raider's moon; a harsh white moon that seemed too
near for comfort, and the light and shadow of it among
the ruined walls and bramble brakes made striped
wild-cat patterns black and white in my head. We fell
into the familiar single-file of the hunting trail, moving
with as much care for silence as though the thing had
been deadly earnest, not the mere whim of the moment, a half savage jest meant to pass the time and
hold sleep at bay. We skirted the open space that might
have been the parade ground, making use of every
bush and hummock and patch of shadow, and gained
the maze of half-lost ruins beyond. Once something
rustled in a patch of broom; once a white owl swept
across our path on wings padded with silence, and a
few moments later, away to our left, something small
and shrill cried out in its death agony.

Then we were crouching together in the breast-high
ruins of a gatetower laced together by the roots of
thorn trees, looking out over the remains of the old
outer fort where it thrust northward into the paleness
of the Firth, over traces of fallen buildings and jetties
where I suppose the supply ships had come in when
Castellum had been a place of living men who needed

gear and feeding. And in the midst of the desolation and the grey tide of moonlight, I saw again the dim red blink of a watchfire sunk to embers; lower than we had ever let *our* watchfire sink in the two nights gone by.

We went forward on our bellies, that last bit of the way, expecting every instant a shout to tell us that we had been discovered. But no shout or movement came. The other three had made their lair in a place not so very different from our own, among the wreckage of what might have been the fort's bath house. The faint fire-glow and the cold whiteness of the moon showed the still standing pillars of the hypocaust, and the dark mouth of the stoke-chamber. The fire had been made in the mouth of the stoke-hole, and the three who should have been wakeful round it were sleeping peacefully.

Clearly sleep had come upon them unawares and probably only a short time before. At any moment they would rouse; but for now, one lay face down with his feet almost in the fire, one had slumped back against the pile of stones and fallen floor-tiles behind him, one still sat, with his head on his knees. We checked, looking at each other. Then with no word spoken, we rose and hurled ourselves upon them, running low and howling like wolves.

Afterwards I realized what a stupid dangerous thing we did, but at the time we knew only the jest of it. They woke and rose to meet us, and within a racing heartbeat of time the battle was locked and reeling to and fro, scattering the red gleeds of the fire underfoot. In the utter confusion one of them went for the knife in his belt. I dived on him and we went down together with him underneath. He caught his head sideways on a stone, I heard the crack of it, and knocked himself witless for the moment, and I managed to twist the knife out of his grasp before his wits came back to him. 'Don't be a fool!' I was shouting. 'It's only us!' But he did not seem to hear me. The others were trampling to and fro, close-grappled and striking out at each other in a rough and tumble that was already half in earnest; but with him it was something else, a kind of panic, I suppose. He had begun squealing, a horrible sound like something in a trap; writhing and squealing; and lacking his dagger which I had flung a good way off, he ducked his head and tried to bite my wrist. I was lying on top of him by that time, and I mind getting my other hand under his chin and forcing his head back. My hand slipped and shot up the side of his face and into the thick hair that was almost silver in the moonlight, and clenched on a handful of it. In the same instant it was as though a wasp had stung me on the palm; and in the same instant also his squealing changed from fear to pain, and he let out a shrill yelp and arched himself sideways, heaving to fling me off yet still struggling to get his teeth into my arm.

Then the other four were upon us, tearing us apart, hauling us to our feet. The battle was over, and the stillness of the moonlight came flooding back. I found myself looking at Faelinn, shieldbearer to Peredur of Caer Luil, who was among the few to answer Mynydogg's summons from the half-lost kingdom of Rheged. They were all touchy, the Rheged men, all shadowed by the death of their own king, though it happened in their fathers' time, not in theirs, all a little unsure, even those whose fathers had been loyal, of whether other men might be finding them guilty; all of them a little prone to pick a quarrel or nurse a grudge in consequence.

And Faelinn stood and stared back at me, with blood trickling out of his hair and down his neck. He put his left hand to the side of his head and held it there; and glancing down at my own, I saw that I was holding a long tassel of barley-pale hair, and tangled with it, the blue glass earring which he always wore. There was blood on my hand too. Some of it mine from a cut palm, some of it his, from where I had torn the ring out of his ear.

Then one of his fellows demanded thickly, dabbing at a bloody nose, 'In the name of thunder, what game do you think you are playing?'

'Nay, we did but seek a little harmless practice for the kind of game that we shall be playing in good earnest by and by,' Dara told him. 'Also we came in all courtesy to return the visit that you paid to us last night. It was no fault of ours that we found you all sleeping.'

And that was something that would have been better left unsaid.

We stood and stared at each other in silence round the scattered gleeds of the fire. They were too proud to protest that they had not been asleep, to ask our promise of silence on the matter, and at least we had enough sense left not to insult them by promising unasked. But the thing hung like a naked blade in the air between us, none the less. And for Faelinn it was worse than for the rest, because he had squealed like a stuck pig, because he had panicked and gone for his knife, and had a torn ear that would keep him from ever forgetting it. And I made matters worse by holding out the earring to him, saying, I suppose rather scornfully, 'Here you are; hang it in your other ear and take better care of it next time.'

He looked at me with hot eyes, while I waited, holding the bauble between finger and thumb. He wanted to turn away, leaving it where it was, I could tell that; but even more he wanted his earring back again. So we stood, the other four looking on. In the end he took it from me with his free hand and tossed it up, a spark of blue in the moonlight, and caught it again, as though to make light of the whole thing, but turned away with hunched shoulders which somewhat spoiled his effect.

Someone laughed, and the thing was over, or it seemed so.

Down on the mud flats of low tide, a curlew began calling, though as yet there was no light save that of the moon.

In the first green light of dawn, with the shorebirds crying and calling, we stamped out the last embers of our fire, the three days and nights being over. We went down to the burn to drink for the last time. The tall stone beside the ford caught the first light on its lichened flank, but I did not touch her again, feeling that I had not the right. The men who had made for themselves the right to touch her were all gone.

The last thing we did before leaving the ruined fort was to make our marks on the wall that we had rebuilt. We made them on the stone under the running wolf. Being best able to write, I went first, scratching my name with the point of my knife – I should have to take it to Conn for re-sharpening, before I could use it

again – and after me, Dara managed his own name
with the letters very small and jigging up and down.
Huil could not write, but he scratched a careful pattern
of interlacing lines with a strange bird's head at the top
of it which did just as well, since we were not doing it
that the world might know that we had been there and
re-built a wall, but for some other purpose altogether.

Then, the other three having gone ahead of us, we set
out for Dyn Eidin. I do not know whether it is possible
to sleep while walking, but certainly I found myself
turning in among the outbuildings of the Royal Farm
without any clear memory of how I got there.

# The Champion's Portion

That autumn we began to go out on mounted patrols, half a troop, usually, three or four days at a time, riding the ragged fringes of Gododdin territory that were fretted by Saxon raiders. Not war patrols, just 'showing the sword arm', though once or twice there was a brush with the Saxon kind along the coast, and once or twice the patrols came back with a dead or wounded man lying across his saddle in their midst, the loss to be made good from among the shield-bearers. Most nights we found lodgings in some farm settlement among the birch woods and the low heather hills around the hall of some one-valley chieftain; but when that failed we slept in the open with our horses wherever we could find any kind of shelter from wind and rain. One night we camped on the lee side of Traprain Law, where only the hummocks in the ground and the traces of a trackway snaking up and round the hill showed where the old capital had been, before the Saxon menace drew too close, and the King – Mynyddog's father, it would be – had burned it to the ground and moved his Royal Hall to the old war capital of Dyn Eidin.

It seemed an unchancy place to camp, but Cymran who was that day's leader demanded to know were we old women or Saxons to be scared of bogles; and certainly, though the horses were fidgety all night, we heard and saw nothing worse than the wild geese flighting down from the north, black wavering arrow-heads high overhead against a scarlet sunset sky, and all night long the soughing of a wet wind through the long grass and the bramble domes.

Winter came down upon us suddenly, closing the ways with snow that turned to slush and froze again beneath fresh falls. The patrols ceased for the while and so did the coming and going of envoys between Mynyddog and his fellow kings which had been going on all summer and autumn long; and so too did any news of the outside world. Indeed it was as though the outside world had ceased to exist, and the great ridge itself was the only thing to stand clear in a nothingness of cold and wind and drifting snow and driving rain. But in Dyn Eidin and along the Town Ridge, life went forward with such crowding purpose that the very air seemed to pulse like a softly tapped drum. All day the charcoal smoke rose from the smithies and armourers' shops and the ring of hammer on anvil told where ancient weapons were being mended and new ones forged. Our training went on by day as usual under the watchful eye of the Fosterling and the most seasoned of the household warriors, and at night we shared feasting and harpsong in the King's Hall and in our own hostels. The leggy two-year-olds were brought in to the horseyards for breaking. We took a hand in that, most of us being well used to the same work among our own hills; and when the snow let up enough, we went hunting; wolves for the sake of the lambing pens later on, boar and deer for fresh meat. The music of the hounds made me think of Gelert and my father's pack and the day when we rode with Prince Gorthyn after the white hart.

At midwinter Mynyddog called a great three-day feast, and decreed that on each night, two of the six troops of the Companions in turn should feast with him in the High Hall. But on the first day the whole Company went up from the Royal Farm to the great Gift-making in the outer court which was for all of them together, though only the two chosen troops for that evening would remain after the horns of feasting sounded. Only a few of the shieldbearers went up to attend upon their lords at supper. The rest of us watched them away, and then turned back to our own affairs and the warmth of the fires in the long houses.

At dusk, with the smell of our own feasting beginning to waft in from the baking pits, they returned to us, the four troops who did not feast with the King that night. They came with a flare of torches that made a golden mill-race of the driving sleet, with one of the King's harpers to lead them striking clashing flights of notes from his harp and declaring Cuchulain's battle in the Pass of the North – though indeed you could scarcely hear him, for they had drunk mead and were singing as they came.

> I'll sing you seven-ho! Green grow the rushes-ho.
> What are your seven-ho?
> Seven for the seven stars in the sky
> Six for the six proud walkers
> Five for the symbols at your door . . .

The singing broke up; they divided and came thrusting into their own hostels, the sleet melting dark on their hair and shoulders, tossing down the King's gifts on their sleeping places or beside the fires. Shirts of fine ringmail that had been captured in forgotten wars, or for the younger and lesser men leather tunics with plates of horn stitched on to them in the places that would be most vulnerable to sword cut or spear thrust; shields and well-balanced lances, fine saddles and horsegear, gold torques for the necks of warriors, heavy arm-rings of gold and silver and enamelled bronze.

Not for nothing was Mynyddog called The Wealthy.

Many of the gifts were, of course, war gear that would have been issued to the Companions in any case when the time came; but given so, among firelight and mead-drinking and the thunder of Cuchulain's chariot wheels, they had a potency and a power of binding loyalty that might have been less strong if they had been issued in the cold light of morning.

The tables had been set up and the bondservants brought in the piled dishes and the feasting went forward. I mind that Gorthyn ate one-handed for the most part, keeping the other free for reaching under the table to touch the mail shirt and the bull's-hide buckler with its bird-shaped mountings of gilded bronze which lay there at his feet. And he was not the only one.

And when the eating, though not the drinking, was over, they must all try their new toys, struggling into war shirts on top of their festival tunics, trying the weight and the balance of weapons, challenging each other to mock combat with much laughter and shouting, while we who had barely started on our own feeding, toiled to and fro and in and out after them with our mouths full of hastily snatched up food, keeping their mead cups full and hauling them in and out of their war gear (a good ringmail shirt is almost too heavy and awkward for a man to get into unaided).

They sobered somewhat after a while and fell to talking and dicing around the fires, plaguing the harpers for this story and that story; and we were left free to finish the filling of our own bellies at last.

At the upper fire, close to where I sat with a lump of blood pudding for company, Gorthyn and Cynan and a handful more had begun to hark forward to the time when they would be taking up their gift weapons in earnest, riding out on whatever war-trail the King might order. Questioning when the day would come, questioning where the trail would lead.

'Before another turn of the year, anyway,' someone said, thumbing the new slim spearhead that lay across his knee.

'Down into Bernicia or Deira, for sure,' said someone else.

'Bernicia and Deira are not the only stretches where the Sea-wolves gather on British coasts.'

'No, but their threat is the nearest,' Gorthyn said. 'They say that Aethelfrith and Aelle are drawing closer into alliance with every moon that passes; and if they join spears indeed, they will be as strong as all the warhosts of the kingdoms joined together.'

Cynan smiled gently into the fire, 'Yet men on horses count always for more than men on foot, as Arthur Pendragon showed in his day. If the King's embassies to Strathclyde and the Pict lands bear fruit, there could be a fine hosting come the spring, and we may ride south in brave company as soon as the grass stands high enough to feed the horses.'

Llif, the Pict, said suddenly and loudly (he was somewhat drunk – they were all somewhat drunk by that time, and it was loosening their thinking and their tongues), 'How if they bear no fruit after all, these embassies? How if there is no warhosting in the spring?'

The others fell upon him, banging his head on the floor to bring the sense back into it, and I mind Cynan, who had sprung to his feet, standing over the scrimmage, laughing with his arms flung out, 'Then we shall ride south alone. The odds will be no worse than thirty or forty to one. Ten to one if you count the shield-bearers!'

The other thing I remember about that night is that later, when the fires were smoored and the sleeping rugs spread, and Lleyn and I were hauling Gorthyn out of his mailshirt, he said, staggering a little as we heaved it over his head and shoulders, 'The King should not be alone in giftmaking at the turn of the year.' And he sat down on the sleeping bench and pulled up the sleeve of his tunic; and by the light of the candle in the horn-paned lantern that hung nearby, I saw the thick silver arm-ring, the King's gift, which he had come back wearing from the High Hall, and below it and on his other arm the matched pair of enamelled bronze that he had worn there ever since I had first known him. 'I feel myself somewhat too splendid in all this finery. So –' He pulled off one of the gleaming things. 'Hold out your arm,' he bade Lleyn, and sprang it into place. Then he turned to me, 'That for the first of my shieldbearers, and this for the second.'

It was not the first gift I had had from him since we came to Dyn Eidin; a new cloak at the start of winter, a better dirk than I had brought from home, but those had been the things that any warrior must provide for his followers. This was different. I felt the bronze warm with his own warmth as he sprang it on to my arm, saw the quiver of his hands forcing the ends together. I felt the proud weight of it as I should feel the lightness and the lack if now, after all these years, I were to take it off.

The next day quite a number of the shieldbearers, though not all, were wearing or carrying something passed on to them by their Lords, an arm-ring, an enamelled brooch, a dagger with a hilt of narwhal ivory. I felt sorry as from a great height for the have-nots. I felt sorry for Faelinn when I passed him with the sleeve of my tunic well thrust up so that everyone could see what lay beneath. Generally, since that night in the old fort, we had taken care not to meet each other's eye – his ear had healed but the split lobe remained, and he did indeed now wear the blue glass drop in his other ear – but that morning in the clear snow-light, his glance caught the glint of polished bronze and flickered up to my face before he could stop it. He saw, I think, that I was sorry, and flushed crimson and looked as though he could have knifed me for the price of a broken shoe-string.

That night, the second of the midwinter feast, was the night when Cynan and his wild brothers, having received fine saddles among the King's gifts, rode their horses into the Royal Hall, announcing themselves as the Three Battle Horsemen of Dyn Eidin of the Many Goldsmiths; up one side of the roaring and rocking hall between the long fires and the feasting warriors to the foot of the High Table itself, and down the other

side of it and out again, without so much as a spilled
mead jar behind them, which said something for their
horse skill, for sure.

Nay, I did not see the thing with my own eyes; it was
not yet the turn of our troop to feast with the King and
we had no place in the High Hall of Dyn Eidin. Nor, of
course, had our Three Battle Horsemen; we missed
them early from our own feasting, and knew no more
than that, but later the story ran like forest fire from
end to end of Eidin Ridge.

It was the third and last night of the great feast, *our*
night for the High Hall, that we all but burned Dyn
Eidin round our ears.

The day had been filled like the other two with
hunting and sport. Down on the practice ground, softened a little by an overnight thaw, there had been a
splendidly bloody game of 'Cattle Raiding', the pick of
our horsemen against the pick of the household
warriors while the rest of us yelled ourselves hoarse on
the side-lines. And we had won, getting the calf's head
back through our own garlanded gateposts nine times
ahead of the Teulu, and came to that night's feasting
already a little drunk with our own victory. Mynyddog
himself was not in his Hall that night, but had gone,
wrapped in furs and carried in a litter, to celebrate the
birth of the White Kristani with the Holy Brothers
according to his custom, summoning the Fosterling,
the Captain of his bodyguard, to go with him; and the
bard Aneirin was shut in his own quarters with the
kind of fever that comes with a cough and a streaming
nose. And but for our own sense of victory and for
those three empty places, I think that maybe the thing
would not have happened . . .

It began when the great bowls of meat stew and dried salmon-char had been emptied and the first keen edge was gone from our hunger, and the sizzling carcasses of roasted boar – the fruits of yesterday's hunting – were borne in on huge chargers, each carried by four men, decked and garlanded with holly and fir and juniper, to be the crowning splendour of the midwinter feast. The horns of feasting sounded again at their coming, and a roar of greeting went up from the warrior benches, men tossing up their mead cups as they were borne up the Hall.

One after another the charges were set down, the full length of the High Table before the King's empty seat, and the King's carvers stepped forward with their long knives to break up the still sizzling carcasses. The tumult quietened somewhat, every head turning towards the High Table as the good work began. And in the quiet, Amalgoid, one of the Teulu, rose in his place and demanded the Champion's Portion, the first slice from the left shoulder of the kill – in this case when there were more beasts than one, that must mean the first of them to be carved. I had heard of the claim being made in ancient times, as in the song of Bricrue's Feast, but I had thought of it as belonging to the world before the Romans came. Certainly I had never known it in my father's Hall. Maybe old customs lingered on more strongly north of the Romans' Wall, I thought. But there seemed to be something of surprise in the moment's stillness that greeted his claim.

From where I was standing far down the Hall I could not see much of what was happening, but I heard clearly enough – the old dry voice of Bleddfach the

King's steward making formal reply, 'By what right, Amalgoid, do you make claim to the Champion's Portion?'

'By this right,' Amalgoid replied, 'that my spear was first at the kill of yesterday's king boar. There is no hunter like to me under the King's roof this night. So do I claim the Champion's Portion!'

And the old tired voice said, 'The Champion's Portion is yours.'

A murmur ran down along the crowded benches, and at our end of the Hall the Companions looked at each other. Then Tydfwlch the Tall, who always found delight in a battle of any kind, sprang to his feet and shouted up towards the High Table, 'Not so fast! I also claim the Champion's Portion, I Tydfwlch from the eagle haunts of Yr Widdfa!'

But we knew that he made the claim as it were for all of us, out of the rivalry that was between Companions and Teulu. At the High Table by the Royal Fire, the old steward, trying to keep the thing from taking hold, protested, 'Your claim comes too late –'

'How so? It was not told me that the claim was to be made, therefore I did not make it earlier.'

Bleddfach the steward was silent a moment, while the murmuring along the warrior benches rose and fell. Then craning, I saw him spread his hands in a gesture that was like a defeat. He said, clinging to his dignity, 'By what right, Tydfwlch, do you make claim to the Champion's Portion?'

Tydfwlch was already striding up the Hall. 'By the right that in today's game of Cattle Raid I bore the calf's head back for the ninth time through our gate-posts, leading the Companions to victory.'

It was as good a reason as any to put forward on the spur of the moment.

Amalgoid began shouting a furious protest about green untried warriors laying claim to honours that were for better men. Tydfwlch countered that so far as he was aware there were no better men in the High Hall of Dyn Eidin that night, chanting his victories against boarder raiders and the Water Horse of Pwl Ddu to prove it.

The thing was half in jest at that stage, but no more than half and the jest beginning to wear thin. Quite cheerfully, but with purpose, the Companions rose from their benches and began to move forward up the Hall towards the Royal Fire and the High Table and the shouting match that was going on there. And in the upper Hall, the men of the Teulu, backing Amalgoid, rose also and stood ready to receive them. We, the shieldbearers, pressed at the heels of our own warriors, and through the broad doorways opening on to the snowy night, others of us who had been hanging around the cookhouses and baking pits came thrusting in to join the rest as sound of what was afoot spilled out and spread abroad.

Lleyn and I pushed our way up behind Prince Gorthyn, shoulder against shoulder amid the surge of others all around us. Somewhere up ahead the shouting of personal insults had given way to the sound of fighting, and then the full joyful roar of battle as Teulu and Companions came together; and the voice of the old steward desperately trying to keep order, which we had heard distantly without paying the least heed to it, was lost in the general uproar.

The memory comes to me now through a haze that was only partly of mead, for we were drunk also with the knowledge that we were the Companions and their shieldbearers, the Shining Company who would be unleashed presently against the Saxon kind, and the Teulu were goaded with the sour knowledge that though they had the glory of being the King's bodyguard they would remain leashed at home when we came to the shining hour. At the moment we had quite forgotten, as I think they had too, that many of the Three Hundred, Cynan and his brothers among them, had been of the Teulu before the Companions came into being.

The roar of battle burst upwards to the rafters and surged to and fro between the walls of the Mead Hall; but in that enclosed space we were too close-packed for serious and enjoyable fighting, and only the foremost from each side could come at each other, while the rest shouted and thrust at their own kind to get through, pushing up tighter and tighter from behind. I mind thrusting head-down in Gorthyn's wake, and being carried sideways by a sudden cross-surge of the mob, and finding myself trampling among the outer embers of the central fire. I mind something of myself that seemed to be outside the rest of me, thinking that if the thing went on much longer, someone was going to get killed; for in that mob one would only have to go down to be trampled underfoot.

Yet the battle smell was in the back of my nose, and the joy of the fight within me kept me yelling and thrusting with the rest. But the sideways surge that had carried me through the fringes of the fire continued and whether others had the same thought as myself and enough sense left to act on it, or whether it was just a blind instinct to burst out and gain more elbow room for the fighting, I suddenly found myself being swept out through one of the side doorways into the winter night.

Through side doors and great main doors and even through the high windows, bursting the shutters open as they came, the battle was spilling out into the forecourt. Some had thought to bring the wall torches with them, and the sleet that was falling again fell spitting and hissing into the flames that gave us a ragged fighting-light. I had lost Gorthyn and Lleyn, but it did not matter; out in the broad court there was room for all of us to find our enemy. I found mine almost at once, one of the Teulu's calf's-head team earlier that day, and bloodied his nose for him even while I spat out blood of my own and a broken tooth.

Then I heard Prince Gorthyn's shout: that splendid trumpet shout of his carrying clear across the turmoil, 'Lleyn! Prosper! To me!' and I drove in a final blow that sent my opponent reeling, and got my head down and butted through in the direction from which it came. Dodging random blows, and narrowly escaping falling over the hounds who had spilled out with the rest of us and started a dozen dog-fights of their own among the legs of the battle, I came up alongside my lord only a few moments after Lleyn got there. Gorthyn was locked in a wrestling grip with one of the Teulu, and almost in the same instant, twisted and threw him on his hip; a juddering tooth-shattering fall, and turned to us, panting a little, his smile wide and happy. 'This is a night for keeping close together!'

The size of our warhost was swelling as others of the Companions and their shieldbearers, getting wind in one way or another of what was happening, came roaring up from the hostels along the royal road to join us. Soon the Teulu would be outnumbered. Meanwhile a knot of them came at us with heads down and flaying fists. Lleyn thrust out a leg and tripped the foremost of them and I went down after him and got him by the ears and banged his head a few times on the half-thawed half-frozen ground to cool his hero-light. But Gorthyn's hand was twisted in the neckband of my tunic, hauling me to my feet, and suddenly the press about us seemed to be slackening, the surf-roar of battle beginning to sink. I snatched a glance at his face and saw that he was looking across the heads of the mob towards something on the far side of the court; and craning the same way, I saw on the edge of the torchlight and by the white radiance of the moon which swam clear of the snowclouds at that moment, the shapes of four women in the gateway from the inner courtyard, and the women's house. They were cloaked against the cold, but their hoods lay back on their shoulders and their faces were clear in the mingled light that struck sparks from the goldwork in their hair.

The Queen and her daughters had come to put an end to our rioting before blood was spilled or Dyn Eidin went up in flames. They made no movement, only stood there, letting themselves be seen, and little by little the quiet began and spread, as more and more of us became aware of them.

But in the middle of the court around the weapon-stone where the fighting had been hottest, men had not yet seen them, and were too busy about their own affairs to hear someone's upraised voice shouting 'Break off! The Queen is here!' And to the battling dogs, of course, their coming meant nothing at all.

Then a frenzied yapping broke out above the deeper tumult that was still going on. One of the little creamy lapdogs which the royal women kept for playthings and which were seldom allowed in the outer court must have slipped out after them, and seeing and hearing and smelling the nearest hound-fight, had hurled itself joyfully to join in. And next instant the Princess Niamh came swooping after it, calling its name on a high seabird note.

'Cannaid! Cannaid!'

I saw her for a splinter of time poised by the weapon-stone in the reeling heart of things, and then, and then – I do not know what happened, I could not see, a knot of warriors maybe somewhat drunker than the rest of us, and close-locked still in conflict, came spilling in from the side, and the battle closed once more around her.

'Lleyn! Prosper! With me!' Gorthyn shouted, and we were with him, butting and thrusting our way through and shouting as we went. She had caught up the little dog and was clutching it high against her, her back against the weapon-stone when she came in sight again, and we had almost reached her when a couple of fighting hounds crashed into her, and she lost her footing on the icy slush and went down. We got to her in only a few moments more. It was all so quick, the whole thing had been so quick since we first saw the royal women standing in the gateway that a score of heartbeats could have covered it from first to last. But we were not the first, for Cynan was already there, standing over her as I have seen him since then standing over a wounded comrade, and thrusting back the tangle of men and hounds.

She was up again at once, and tried to take a step and almost fell with a sharp cry, 'Ah, my foot!'

The little dog had run shivering and yelping against my feet, and I scooped it into safety. Cynan had caught up the Princess high against his shoulder, and turned with her towards the gateway where her sisters had started forward to meet them. We closed round them, his brothers also and a few more of the Companions as they realized what had happened, and shielded them from any buffeting as he carried her back to the waiting Queen.

Behind us the tumult was sinking as we went, and men were beginning to haul apart the still snapping and snarling hounds.

The women closed round her, supporting her as Cynan set her down, but she looked back, calling still, 'Cannaid? Please, Cannaid?' I set the shivering little thing in her arms, though one of her sisters took it from her so that they could help her away. The noise had sunk so low that her voice was clear as she tried to thank us all over her shoulder at the same time. And into the quiet came the sudden clash of hooves as the Fosterling, with his cloak flying, clattered in through the open gate from the royal road and pulled his horse up all standing on the edge of the crowd. I suppose the steward must have sent word to him in the house of the Holy Brothers, and clearly he knew what the battle had been about and had no need to ask the meaning of that night's work.

The last of the tumult had died away; only the snarling of a stray dog-fight still fretted at the stillness. And Teulu and Companions alike, battered and somewhat bloody, we turned to face the Fosterling's chilly gaze that raked us through and through.

'So, it seems that I come somewhat late upon the scene,' he said, and there was a flicker of amusement in his voice. 'I am a truthful man, and therefore I cannot claim that the devil's uproar you have been raising here reached me before the altar and interrupted my devotions; but certainly, returning in answer to Bleddfach's summons, it met me half way!'

We scuffed our feet in the frozen slush and mumbled like boys caught stealing apples; suddenly aware of the bitter cold. And the Fosterling's mouth twitched. 'Since it seems that the royal ladies have quelled this riot for me, it is my mind that now you should return to the Hall that we may continue our interrupted supper.' He swung down from the saddle, somebody coming quickly to take his horse, and his eye lit on the knot of hounds still battling over something – a ragged lump of baked meat I suddenly saw it was. 'What remains of supper, at all events. I imagine that the question of the Champion's Portion is now well and truly settled.' And laughter took us like a gale.

But next morning in the grey chill of the thaw, we were all stone-cold sober, still battered, but sober, when we gathered again to the King's forecourt, in answer to the summons that had called us there, Teulu and Companions alike with the shieldbearers hanging on the outskirts.

The King half sat, half lay in his great chair that had been brought out into the foreporch of the Hall, swathed in soft skin robes to his bearded chin, with the Fosterling standing at his side and the closest of his household warriors ranged about him.

The Fosterling stood with his thumbs in his sword belt and looked us over at leisure with those strange two-coloured eyes of his, while we waited, looking back. 'God's greeting to you, my heroes,' he said, pleasantly, when he had looked enough. 'Now let you tell me, why this sudden hunger for the Champion's Portion, which no warrior has claimed in Dyn Eidin in the lifetime of a man?'

Amalgoid said, 'It was for a jest as much as anything. Also it was for the honour of the Teulu.'

'So. A jest that had a sharp edge to it.' The Fosterling flicked his gaze to Tydfwlch the Tall. 'And you? This claim is still the custom among your own hills?'

Tydfwlch shook his head. 'Not in the lifetimes of three men.'

'Then why now?'

'Because Amalgoid of the Teulu made it first; and the Companions also have an honour to maintain.'

I mind the silence that followed; and in the silence, the sense of oneness that had been growing within us almost unknown for a long while, enclosing us like a rampart.

Then the Fosterling hitched at his sword belt in the way that he had, and turned to the King, but pitching his voice for all of us to hear. 'My Lord the King, it is true, as our forefathers told, that no man may for long handle two teams at the same time. It is in my mind that now the time has come, as we knew that it must, for you to choose a new captain for the Teulu, for the Companions have become their own thing and must have their own captain.'

'And you are that captain?'

'So it was agreed between us.'

'Sa, sa, sa . . . Meaning that you want them all to yourself,' said Mynydogg rather surprisingly; and the shadow of a smile on his gaunt face, echoing the smile on the Fosterling's own, made it clearer than ever that they were father and son.

'I do not think that anyone else can handle them,' said our new captain. 'But yes, I want them all to myself.'

The roar that we sent up might have lifted the roof off the King's Hall if we had been within it.

Only the Teulu, losing their old captain, were silent.

# – 12 –
# Epona's Leap

The winter months wore on; bitter months that brought the wolves in out of the wildwood to hunt close about the living places of men, so that men must mount guard over the sheep folds by day as well as through the long nights. Day after day the wind drove snow or freezing rain across the great whale-backed mass of Eidin Ridge; and when the snowclouds cleared for a while and the iron frosts set in, there were nights when the whole sky northward was flickering with strange lights. I had seen such lights faintly from the high hills above my home valley, but never such a show as this, that sent rippling tongues and ribbons of cold fire far up the sky. I knew now why men called them 'The Crown of the North' and also why it was said that they foretold great happenings for good or ill, victory or pestilence, the birth of heroes or the death of kings.

But a day came when the wind went round to the south and had a new smell to it, promising a world still there after all, beyond the lowland hills, promising afar off the return of spring.

As soon as the mirey ways were in any sort fit for travelling, while the burns ran green with thaw-water from the melting snows, before even the salmon began to come up from the sea, Mynyddog's embassies were going to and fro once more between himself and his fellow kings of the north. On an evening of squalls and sunbursts, with the cloud shadows flying like a charge

144

of cavalry across the moors, an embassy from Aidan of Dalriada rode into Dyn Eidin: three tall men cloaked in magnificent skins; the leader, who looked to be long past his own warrior days, the tallest of them all, with a small fierce eye and a mouth like a wolf trap.

On the day after they rode in, they were shut away in the King's private lodging with Mynyddog himself, the Fosterling, and Cenau who was now Captain of the Teulu in his place, and Aneirin who as chief bard to the King must always be present at such meetings.

For the rest of us life went on as usual. A good part of the day was passed in practising for the great display with which we were to dazzle and impress the Lords of Dalriada on the morrow.

Towards evening Gorthyn's big sorrel cast a shoe; and when I took him over to the shoe-smith at the far side of the Royal Farm, I heard a great bell-clashing of hammer on anvil and thought that some other horse was being shod. But when I hitched Bryth to the ring beside the doorpost and looked inside, there was no horse there, and the men sweating in the red firelight were making horseshoes to add to an orderly stack of them against the wall. That did not surprise me, for as the swordsmiths and armourers had been busy all that winter mending old weapons and war gear and making new, so the blacksmiths, in between their usual work, had been beating out horseshoes against the time that the Company would be needing them.

'Can you spare one of those?' I asked, flicking a thumb at the stack. 'My lord's horse has cast a shoe at the practice.'

One of the smiths looked up from a half formed shoe on the nearest of the three anvils, and I saw – in the red gloom of the smithy and the smoke and the flying sparks I had not known him until I saw his face – that it was Conn. And that did surprise me.

'Conn! What brings you here? I thought it was a swordsmith you were.'

He rubbed the back of his hand across his sweating forehead, leaving a black smear. 'Fercos' ruling is that a smith should learn every branch of his craft on the way up, and that even a high king's swordsmith should be able to shoe a horse or forge a ploughshare. Just now the need is for horseshoes.'

'Then let you re-shoe Bryth, and make sure that his other shoes are secure for this fool's frolic the King has decreed tomorrow for the impressing of Dalriada.'

He glanced towards the Master Smith who nodded without looking up from his own work, and a short while later when the shoe before him was finished, he replaced the cast shoe and tested the rest, picking up each round hoof in turn while Bryth slobbered at his shoulder. And afterwards, Conn standing with one shoulder propped against the doorpost, I with an arm over the sorrel's neck, we lingered for a short while. It was some while since we had had the chance of a few words together.

'Is it well?' I asked. I always asked that, I still felt oddly responsible for Conn.

And he looked at me with that slow grave smile of his. 'Why would it not be?'

'It doesn't irk you to be spending your time and skill down here?' I knew how much I should hate it, if I were on the way to being a swordsmith, no matter what Fercos' ruling might be.

'Did I not say? No need of ploughshares, maybe, but any smith who goes with the field-forge must be able to shoe a horse as well as sharpen a sword or beat the dint out of a war-cap.'

Goes with the field forge . . . I had known, I suppose, that there must be a field-forge. No cavalry force, once away from home, could function without one, but I had not thought to wonder who its smiths would be.

'You?' I said. 'Conn, that makes good hearing!'

He shook his head quickly. 'I'd not be knowing. But Fercos is too old for such rough work, and he must send one at least of his family.'

'And the one might be you!'

'I shall try for it!' he said; then turning the subject almost as Luned used to do, 'Will you be needing Shadow's shoes checked for tomorrow?'

'No. It is a thing only for the Companions, praise be to Epona.'

'Not champing at the bit to show off your own skills?'

'I don't see much point in it,' I said. 'Not for those men.'

'They *are* Dalriada,' Conn said.

I knew what he meant. The King's purpose was clear, to show off to this embassy his fine new warbands drawn from all the northern kingdoms, hoping that they would go back and persuade Aidan their king that men of different tribes could stand together, and that in the face of a strong enemy it is better so than to stand alone. The old story of the sticks which, singly, may be snapped between the fingers of one hand, but which bound into a faggot, are beyond the breaking of the strongest man.

'Prosper, son of Gerontius, does not believe it will work?' Conn said after a few moments, his thoughts clearly having followed the same path as my own.

I shrugged. 'You know what they say of Aidan of the Dalriada. He's a warlord more than a king; and his wars are glorified cattle-raids, whether he goes against the Saxon kind or his neighbours.'

'Still, I suppose he – Mynyddog – has to try,' Conn said thoughtfully.

'Oh yes, he has to try.'

Someone was shouting for Conn from within the smithy, and he turned back through the firelit door-way, while I went on my way, taking Bryth down to the horse-lines.

Next day we made a great showing for the Lords of Dalriada who stood looking on, mantled in their magnificent furs in the squally rain. All together, for a good part of the shieldbearers had been drawn in after all to play the enemy, we showed off our horse-skills, wrestled and raced and fought mock battles. And all the while our Captain, standing among the strangers with something of the look of a man who has bitten on a sloe, clearly relished it as little as we did.

Towards day's end we were all gathered once more in the King's outer court thinking that the show was over. But it seemed that it was not. Not quite yet . . .

Mynyddog himself had come out to join us, walking unaided to his great chair that had been set for him in the fore porch of his Hall, though God knows what the effort must have cost him. And Aneirin had settled on the bard stool at his feet. He looked at us and we looked back at him with the knowledge that we had done him credit. The day was fading, and ahead of us lay fire's warmth and deer-meat stew and mead and harpsong that we felt was well earned.

Then Mynyddog looked up at the envoy standing beside him and said something. I could not catch the words, but it had the sound of courtesy. Something about hoping that the day's display had pleased them, I suppose, for the tall man, his voice pitched to carry, made reply, 'Today's display has indeed been well worth the watching, so far as it goes. Indeed I have seldom seen it greatly bettered, save by the Teulu of my Lord Aidan.'

We bristled like a hound when it smells wolf.

The King began, 'You find something lacking –' his face was flushing but the red was tinged with grey, and his dry brittle cough cut him short.

The Fosterling stepped forward, saying quickly, 'My Lord the King, let me. It was I who trained them and their honour is mine.' And to the envoy, he said with cold courtesy, 'You find something lacking in our childish games?'

'Nothing in the world,' said the Dalriada. 'Yet what does it all prove – save training, and one may train a hound. There must be more –'

'Let you tell me what more,' the Fosterling said in a voice like wild honey.

'So, I will tell. If my Lord Aidan were to call out any man from his Teulu and bid him leap from the Rock of Black Annis, he would do it without thought. Can you say the same for these men of yours?'

The Fosterling said, 'I do not doubt it. But I will not be squandering the life of a man by putting it to the test. And if I were to do so, what would it prove beyond obedience? The blind unthinking berserk frenzy of the Saxon kind. Other things than that are needed for the forging of a fighting brotherhood.'

The two stood facing each other with their gaze locked together while a man might count to ten. Then the Fosterling said, 'Here among the Companions there are warriors of every tribe of the north and west, some even who are ancient enemies. Yet if I were to call out three at random, one to run blindfold towards Epona's Leap where the rock falls sheer a score of spears' lengths to other rocks beneath, trusting to the other two to catch him back from dashing out his brains, and all three were to do without question the thing that I asked of them – that, I am thinking, might prove something worth the proving.'

'Such as?' said the envoy, with mockery deep in his throat.

'Such as – that it is possible for men of different tribes to find or forge new loyalties among themselves.'

'So, then let you put *that* to the test,' said the Dalriada, and as the Fosterling stiffened as though to meet a spear under his own ribs, he added musingly, 'Yet how shall I know that you are not choosing men of the same tribe, even close kin?'

'Choose them for yourself,' our Captain said between shut teeth.

The thing was of no great matter, and without even much danger to it. But it was a thing that we had not been trained to, and at the end of a hard day, when we were tired and hungry . . .

The envoy picked out his men at random, the runner and one of the catchers from among the shieldbearers. None of them were closely known to me, and so the choice did not set my heart jumping. We all pressed back, leaving an empty space straight across the outer court, a road ending in the nothingness of Epona's Leap; and the chosen three walked out into it. There was a pause while something was found to bind the runner's eyes. In the end Geraint of Dumnonia pulled off the striped silken scarf which he always wore knotted round his waist under his sword belt, and passed it through the crowd, shouting after it, 'Have a care now. A girl gave me that, and I don't want it fouled with blood and brains!'

It was a grim jest, but it was something to laugh at, and we laughed accordingly.

Against the weapon-stone the runner stood to be blindfolded with the vivid silk. When its knot was tied, he put his hands up to each side of his head as though to settle the folds and test how firmly they were in position, and took up the stance that runners take at the start of a race, bearing forward on to the ball of his left foot. The other two moved onto the lip of emptiness which was Epona's Leap; I could see them speaking with their heads together a moment, then they crouched down facing each other, with only the sky and the distance of lowland hills behind them. For the first time it dawned on me that what danger there was was for them almost as much as for the runner. Then somebody gave the starting shout, and the runner sprang forward on a line for the Leap and the tensed catchers. It was the merest sprint, not enough for a runner to find his stride; but I suppose it had slipped all our minds that a man running blind tends to pull to the right. He began to veer almost from the first step, and at the last instant the other two flinging themselves sideways, just caught him from going headlong into the right-hand fang of rock.

They disentangled themselves and he pulled off the blindfold and looked about him, slightly bemused by the clamour rising on all sides, then flushed crimson as he realized what had happened.

The envoy flung up his head and laughed on a mocking note. And the runner looked from him to the Fosterling and asked levelly, 'Would you have me try again? If the catchers call, it will give me the direction.'

The envoy nodded, 'Again, yes, but with another three, I think.' A happy thought seemed to strike him. 'And one more after that; three casts of the dice for luck!'

'I suppose we shall get supper sometime,' Dara muttered in my ear.

The runner handed the silken scarf back to its owner who had come thrusting through to reclaim it, and dropped back into the crowd, his catchers also, rubbing their knees and laughing. And the envoy picked another three. The runner was Cynri, the brother of Cynan.

He stepped out to have his eyes bound with the reborrowed scarf, and took his forward-leaning stance for the run.

This time the catchers called to him, 'Cum, cum! Sweff! Sweff!' as men call to their hounds, and he headed straight towards their calling. And they braced themselves, arms out for the catch. For a heartbeat of time, I thought they must all three go over, but when the shock and chaos of arms and legs sorted itself out, all of them were still there. Cynri pulled off the scarf, and bowed with a flourish to the envoy, to the King, to the Captain of the Companions, and strolled off in the direction of the gate and the road that led to supper.

'Sa, sa, that was better,' said the envoy. 'This is a sport that I have not witnessed before. Now the third cast of the dice.'

He hitched his great furred mantle about him, and with a glance of shared amusement with his two fellows, came strolling out yet again into our midst, looking about him like a man at a horse fair where nothing really takes his fancy. Almost, I expected to see him slap someone aside as a man may slap aside the woolly rump of a colt that is across his way.

He passed closely by where I stood, and as he did so, the wind gusting up from the south, whipped my hair into my eyes. I put up my hand to thrust it back, and the sudden movement must have caught at his awareness, he glanced round in passing, then checked and looked full at me, down from his height. 'You will serve well enough for the runner,' he said. 'Out with you,' and moved on.

For the moment I did not quite believe it, almost I glanced back, thinking that he was speaking to someone behind me, but friendly hands were on my shoulders, pushing me forward into the cleared space, and I walked out to the weapon-stone, and stood there, my heart beginning to thump in the base of my throat. The man holding the scarf came up beside me, standing ready, and I did not see who the envoy had chosen for my catchers until they came to join me.

One was Ywain of the Companions, a thick set, steady looking man who often led his troop. He gave me a quick reassuring grin. I grinned back and looked at the other, and my heart fell over itself and began to

race. The second of my catchers was Faelinn. Faelinn
with the blue glass drop in his right ear catching the
light of the sodden sunset. It was the first time we had
looked at each other directly since the night in the
ruins of Castellum, and the moment was not a comfortable one. His pale eyes, his whole face, had a kind
of careful blankness, as though he were taking pains
that I should not be able to see what lay beyond the
skin, but it did not quite hide a shimmer of triumph,
perhaps he did not mean it to; and I was cold scared.
Oh, I did not think he really meant to let me go over
Epona's Leap, but it would be very easily done, very
easy to fumble his half of the catch and make it look
like an accident.

Someone was binding the scarf over my eyes, shut-
ting out the dazzle of the sunset barring the west with
gold, and I was alone in the darkness, with fear. All too
clearly in the darkness I saw the edge of Epona's Leap
and the emptiness beyond, and the black rocks below
. . . I crouched forward on the ball of my left foot, the
starting shout was in my ears, and I was off, heading
for the guiding calls of my catchers, 'Cum, cum! Sweff,
sweff!' My memory of that run is partly that it went on
for a great while, partly that it was over in the time it
takes to blink. 'Cum, cum, cum! Sweff, sweff!' The
shouts ran out into a sort of grunt and I was tackled
and brought down and heaved over backwards between stride and stride, with most of the wind knocked
out of my body.

Somebody pulled off the blindfold and I scrambled
to my feet, and the brightness of the wet and windy
sunset was dazzling into my eyes again. It seemed odd
that I had not been in the dark long enough for the

world to change at all, that even the raven which had been planing up against the gusts when the blindfold went on was not yet out of sight beyond the roof ridge of the King's Hall. 'Come away back a bit, I don't like it here on the edge if you do,' someone said, and, blinking against the brightness, I saw that it was Faelinn. And we looked at each other, face to face a second time, with the unease between us all gone. Suddenly we laughed, sharing the laughter, and I knew that Faelinn had never had the remotest idea of letting me go over the edge. He had known that in the moment of seeing him there as one of my catchers, I had been afraid. And that moment had been all he needed to even the score. Ywain joined in the laughter, not knowing what it was all about. And laughing still, though somewhat breathlessly, the three of us pulled back from Epona's Leap.

But whether it all made a feather-weight of difference to the King's hopes of a confederate warhost from the kingdoms of the north was more than anyone could guess.

# – 13 –
# The Rider from the South

The promise of spring had turned into spring itself; a harsh spring of squally rain and a wind that seemed stuck in the east, but in the cleared crop-lands plough-ing had begun, and the Long Moss was alive with the crying and calling of marsh birds above their nesting places. There was a day when I found a clump of wash-faced primroses among the roots of an alder tree, and foolishly, wished that I could share them with Luned. And so the homing-hunger came upon me, as it did from time to time; as it still does even now . . .

That evening a group of us on our way back from the horse-runs and with nothing much to do until the horns sounded for supper, were sprawling at ease in the faint sun-warmth on the turf slopes below the Dyn. Tydfwlch the Tall, Cynan and his brothers together as usual, little dark Morien, Prince Gorthyn and a few more, with the usual fringe of shieldbearers, and the hounds who always tagged along with us.

Someone came through the greening broom bushes into our midst, and I sat up – I had been lying on my back and watching the first swallows hawking among the midges overhead – and saw the short strong shape and strange yellow eyes of the King's bard. The rest of us were rolling over, sitting up, the hounds thumping their tails in welcome.

He was carrying his harp in his hand, out of its bag

and readied for playing; the little black bog-oak crot
that we knew had been his since he was a boy, and that
no man but he might lay hands on.

'Oh flower of all harpers, have you come to sing to
us?' Cynan asked.

And 'Sing for us – sit here and sing for us!' others
joined in, while a couple of the hounds yawned,
stretched themselves to their feet, and came to thrust
their muzzles into the hollow of his hand.

Harpers of Aneirin's rank, bards and praise-singers
to Kings, keepers of their people's history, seldom
wake their own harps in Hall save on the most high
and splendid occasions; they make the great hero-
songs, but it is lesser men who sing them. But from
time to time Aneirin would bring forth his harp and set
himself down with it among a knot of us taking our
ease as we were doing now.

He sat himself down, his harp on his knee, and we all
drew a little closer. 'Oh my children, what then shall I
sing?'

'Sing something easy,' said Cynan, chewing on a
stalk of winter-lean grass; and there was a murmur of
contented agreement from the rest. The trouble with
Aneirin's songs was that often they made one think;
and after a long day's schooling in the horse-runs,
none of us wanted to have to think.

A smile flickered at the long corners of Aneirin's
bearded lips, and settling the harp into the hollow of
his shoulder, he set free a small shining flight of notes
and began to sing, very quietly, a song that most of us
knew by heart, for whatever tribe we came from, we
heard it from our mothers or our nurses in the beginning of time.

Dinogad's coat is of many colours, many colours,
I made it of the skins of martins. Phew! Phew! A
  Whistling!
Let us sing to him, the eight slaves sing to him,
When your father would go hunting
With his spear shaft on his shoulder and his club in
  his hand.
He called to the swift hounds
'Giff, giff. Seize, seize. Fetch, fetch –'

I found myself thinking again of the primrose clump
among the alder roots, and Luned, and Gelert's muzzle
in my hand, and the smell of water mint in the pool
above the ford at home; and I think that I was not the
only one.

When the song of Dinogad was over, we called for
another, and Aneirin sang again.

The fort opposite the oak wood,
Once it was Bruidge's, it was Cathal's,
It was Aed's, it was Arbell's.
It was Conairy's, it was Cushling's,
It was Madduin's –
The fort remains after each in turn.
And the kings sleep in the ground.

And the homing-hunger that the first song had
woken in us deepened to sadness of another kind. And
I mind Aneirin looked about him with raised brows,
and said, 'Hai Mai, what sorry faces!' And sang again
– a fool's song about seven men riding on a pig that
had us all dissolved in laughter.

'Harper most dear, you are playing with us,' Gorthyn
said.

'Does it seem so indeed? Nay, but upon you, maybe.

Every harper plays upon his hearers as he does upon
the strings of his harp. It is so that the music comes,
between the harp and the hearts of men . . . If you
would have me sing again, choose you what I shall
sing.'

And for a while he played to our call like some
strolling horse-fair minstrel, snatches of every song
and every tale we called for. There is a glow to that
hour in my memory even now.

In a while one of the brown-robed brothers from the
monastery came by, heading up through the broom
bushes towards the Dyn. Brother Felim the fat little
Infirmarer, I saw it was, as he drew nearer. He would
not go out of his way to avoid the harp notes, but he
pulled his hood forward and walked a little faster, his
head turned away, his hand, to judge by its position,
holding the crucifix about his neck. And there was
something about the very whisk of his skirts above his
sandalled feet that told us his feelings.

Aneirin sent a mocking flight of notes like a dance of
butterflies after him.

'I do not think that he loves you greatly, nor us because
we sit here listening to you,' said Tydfwlch the Tall.

Aneirin shook his head. 'Few of his kind have
much love to spare for mine. Also he does not like it
that I, who have only the slight healing knowledge of
most of my kind and maybe a little more learned from
the Queen, shall ride with you when the time comes.
He thinks that it is his right to go with the bandage
linen.'

'But does he *want* to ride with us?' Morien said. 'He
is not the right shape.'

'Hardly. But he feels that he and his God are both

slighted. He thinks that your immortal souls would be safer in his keeping than in mine, and forgets certain skills and advantages which I possess and he does not.'

'Such as?' Morien asked, to keep him talking. Aneirin talking could be as good listening as Aneirin in song.

And the King's bard listed his advantages gravely, sticking out a finger of his free hand for each one: 'For the first, I have been a fighting man in my youth and am even now in better shape than he for long hard riding. For the second, it is said of us, of the Druid kind, that with a fire of rowan wood we can raise a magic mist to conceal a whole army. That is a thing that I have not tried for myself, though I have heard of one that covered all Roscommon. For the third – I can make songs.'

'And so you will ride long and hard with us, and raise us a magic mist to cover us from the Saxons' eyes, and make us songs to keep our hearts high within us,' said my Lord Gorthyn.

'All these things; but the songs will be chiefly for the time when the fighting is over,' Aneirin said, beginning to make his harp ready for its bag as though it were a thing living and beloved. 'Am I not the King's bard, the keeper of the long story of his people the Gododdin? I am the one to be there, seeing over the fighting when it joins, that I may make of it afterward the Great Song that others will sing for a thousand years.'

And Tydfwlch said, 'That will be a triumph-song worth the singing!' fondling the little dagger in his belt.

There was a pause, teased with the flitter of small birds in the broom bushes. And then Llif from the Pict lands beyond Bannog, rolled over on to his belly, his chin propped between his fists, and demanded, 'Let you sing of us all by name, that we may live as long as the song.'

'All three hundred of you?' Aneirin said, with his eyebrows quirking. 'By name aye and by reputation.'

'Sing of me how I have slain a wolf with my bare hands,' said Gwenabwy, spreading his hands out with the fingers hooked like claws. 'I will tell you the way of it, that you may get it right when the time comes –' There was a general laugh, for we had all heard that story, and more than once.

'That tale I will tell,' Aneirin promised, drawing up the silken cord of his harp bag. 'As I will tell of you, Morien, why your brethren call you the Fiery. And of you, Gorthyn, how you hunted a white hart, but guessing that he was a faery beast called your hounds off and let him go.' (I felt Lleyn wriggle slightly beside me, and knew where *that* story had come from.) 'And of you, Llif, of the Painted People –'

The list would have gone on, but in that moment the faint and fitful wind brought the sound of a horse ridden at speed on the road from the south.

'Someone comes in haste,' Aneirin said.

And I – there's no knowing why, for horses came and went often enough along that track – I was back in the curve of the turf rampart above my father's house, and Conn and Luned with me and Gelert's rough head under my hand, on the evening that Gorthyn's summons came; and the same smell of change was in the wind.

Before night the news had run from end to end of Eidin Ridge, that Aelle, King of Deira was dead – a mischance on the hunting trail – and the wood being gathered for his funeral fire; and the sounds of Dyn Eidin making ready for the war-trail had taken on a new urgency.

In the first light of next morning men rode out, mounted on the best horses in the King's stables and heading for Dalriada and Strathclyde and the Pict lands and my own Gwynedd, all the kingdoms of the north and west.

A little later that morning, having spoken with our Captain, Gorthyn called Lleyn and me to attend him, and bade us burnish his sword (it did not need burnishing) and help him on with his mail shirt and his cloak of grey wolfskins such as had lately been issued to all the Companions, and follow behind him up to the Inner Court and the place before the royal house where the King sat daily to give audience and pass judgements and listen to his people.

A state visit from a king's son to a king.

Mynyddog half lay in his great chair spread with creamy ram skins, and with fine fur robes muffled about him for the chill of spring was in the air, and even when the sun shone it seemed that he was scarcely ever warm. His leather-clad Champion stood behind him, and his bard and men of his bodyguard on either side.

I mind his eyes met and followed us, seeming to draw back with us as we came, the life that was so low in the rest of him banked there like a smoored fire.

Aneirin spoke for him at first, asking with all proper formality what thing it was that brought the Prince Gorthyn seeking speech with the King.

Gorthyn knelt before the muffled feet. 'My Lord the King, last night came word that Aelle of Deira is gone beyond the sunset.'

'That I was aware of,' said Mynyddog.

'And this morning your messengers to the kings have ridden away.'

'That also.'

'My lord, give me leave to go back to my father's court. It may be that I can do better than a mere messenger, because I am his son – make him listen and send the war-bands we need –'

I had a sense of cold shock. Gorthyn was but speaking openly the thing that was in the minds of all men. The thing was true, but it was not such a truth as young warriors speak to kings. I think that for the moment we all expected the skies to fall. I certainly feared for that moment to see a signal from the King's hand, and Gorthyn cut down by the great two-edged sword of the King's Champion. Maybe Gorthyn had the same fear.

Then, 'The thought is a good one,' said the King's tired voice. 'But if I were to send you, and the rest of your kind – remember you are not the only king's son among the Companions – it would be too many to spare out of the Three Hundred.'

Gorthyn's head went further up, and I saw the muscles tense and thicken at the back of his neck. 'Does My Lord the King doubt that we should return?'

There was a smile like a shadow on Mynyddog's sunken face. 'Na, na, never think that I cast doubt upon your honour.'

'Then I may go?'

The King shook his head, and the smile seemed more than ever like a shadow. 'Aelle is dead and the thing is upon us, and if I read the signs aright, the Company must be on the march south before the swiftest horses could bring you back to it. War-bands can maybe follow on behind, but for you and your kind, *there is not the time.*'

The King spoke truth. There was no time. Five days later Phanes of Syracuse rode in to Dyn Eidin alone and on a foundered horse, bringing with him in place of his usual baled silks and fine weapons, the news that Aethelfrith of Bernicia, coming down in state to attend King Aelle's death-feast, had set himself in the King's Seat at Catraeth, claiming the rule of Deira in double yoke with his own kingdom, since the dead king's sons were too young for the task. He was still there, and his housecarls with him, and many of the dead king's men also, a war-band of something over three hundred in all.

There was more. Something about the whole war-strength of both kingdoms taking down the weapons from their walls, but all that came later in the day. The merchant had got no further than the first part of his tidings, when he keeled over and dropped like a poled ox – so said those that saw it – and they found smashed ribs and an axe gash that had bled him almost white under his cloak.

That was at noon, and they had carried him off to the monastery for tending, and the Infirmarer had brought him back to himself. When he had told the rest, a black goat was brought in from the flock, and its throat cut, and hazel rods charred at one end were dipped in its blood, and given to swift riders. And before evening they were away, carrying the Cran-Tara through the Gododdin lands; the call to raise the

warhost; the hosting place Habitancum on the road
south, the day five days hence, allowing time for the
men from the further hills to arrive. And for the
other kingdoms, riders also, carrying on the news from
Catraeth, though without the Cran-Tara that had of
course no power beyond the frontiers of the Gododdin.

We knew, seeing them go, that we should not see any
coming-in of war-bands in answer, for we should be
gone on our own road south with the second day's
dawning. The time for unleashing the Companions
had come.

There seemed surprisingly little to be done on that
final day, for the ready-making for the march had been
going on ever since word of Aelle's death had reached
us. Horses had been shod, and all weapons and gear
that had not been given out during the past year issued
to us. There was not much, for most of it we had had
long since, so that both us and our horses should have
time to grow used to the weight and balance of it; but
I mind that my tunic of boiled leather with the horn
plates on breast and shoulders seemed to take on a
new significance. The Companions were given, as a
final gift to each one, a thing such as I had not seen
before – a coif of fine linkmail hanging straight and
close to their head with a mask of the same fine mesh
that could be hooked across the face covering all but
the eyes. When Gorthyn and his fellows put them on
to try the feel of them, they no longer looked like the
Companions, but remote and beautiful and terrifying
as if they might be warriors come from the faint stain
of brightness in the night sky that men call the Milky
Way.

Iron rations were issued for both men and horses, though we were to live as far as might be off the country; each horse had four shoes in a bag tied to the saddle, against mischances on the road; the tools and gear for the field-forge lay piled with the pack saddles beside the farm smithy ready for loading; and Conn, with the old dirk bestowed on him by Fercos, had slept beside the stack for three nights, with Credne, one of the shoe-smiths, and the boy whose task was to fetch and carry and work the goatskin bellows. It was a lightness in my heart that Conn was riding with us.

In the King's Hall, a while before the evening meal, the Captain spoke with his six troop leaders; and later, in their own long-houses, the leaders passed on each to their own troop all that he had said, while most of the rest of us, crowding lofts and doorways and high windows, listened on. Lleyn and I were absent at the time on some errand for Prince Gorthyn. But when we returned and the evening meal was over, he gathered us into a corner among the great kists and storage creels stacked at the gable end, and while we squatted there, burnishing our weapons for the march, he told us in our turn, all that there was to tell.

Rain had come on with the dusk, and I mind the whisper of it across the rough thatch and the spit and hiss as it came down through the smoke hole and into the fire. I mind the trestle tables being pulled away and the usual coming and going of hounds and men, laughter and a snatch of song and the quick flare of a quarrel, quickly quenched, all making a background to the thing he told.

'Aelle is dead, and Aethelfrith has seized the double kingship and sits in Catraeth, the Royal Village, with his household warriors about him,' Gorthyn said.

That much we knew already, but he must be left to tell the thing from the beginning in his own way. Only Lleyn glanced up from the spear blade on his knee, 'Around three hundred, that would be?'

'As Phanes tells it. The usual number for a chief's bodyguard. But there is word of all Deira and Bernicia sharpening their weapons for a warhosting.'

'Deira could not be sharpening their weapons *against* Aethelfrith?' I said.

Gorthyn shook his head. 'It seems that with their own king dead and his sons too young to carry his sword after him, Deira will make the best of an ill job, and follow Bernicia's king for the sake of his strength to lead them. And his leading, now that he has both warhosts in his hand, will be northward and westward into our heartlands.'

'And we are just to ride down and toss these warhosts back into the sea?' I asked, half-laughing, half incredulous as the idea opened up before me.

'That might be beyond even our powers, and must be for the warhosts of the north that by God's grace will take the trail after us. It is for us to get down to Catraeth before the Saxons can gather there in strength, and give battle to Aethelfrith and his house-carls while they stand alone.' He leaned forward and brushed the strewing rushes from the floor in front of him, and pulling out his dagger, began to scratch something on the bare earth.

Lleyn and I leaned forward to watch, and saw that it was a map – a picture of a countryside as an eagle hanging in the eye of the sun might see it, looking down.

'See, here is the Grand Road linking north and south, and here comes in another from across the Penuin Hills. Then five miles or so south of the joining-place, the road crosses a river, and beyond is Catraeth – Catteractonium, the Romans called it, from the rapids and broken water thereabouts. Here is what remains of the town, and here, maybe a mile on, the Saxon Royal Village. We all know that the Sea-wolves are afraid of stone-built cities and the ghosts that the Legions left behind them, and so unless we can take them by surprise and fire their own thatch over their heads, they are most like to meet us somewhere on the open ground south of the river. But be all that as it may, our task is to take the town – the Fosterling was there once; he said there's the remains of a fort in the north-east corner – and hold out there, cutting the road, and making things as difficult as may be for the Saxon battle-lords in their coming together, until our own main warhosts can come up with us.' He brushed his hand across the floor, rubbing out the scratched lines. 'If the summons gets to them through their marshes and forests, the men of Elmet could reach us within the first days; they're the nearest.'

'And if they do not?' Lleyn's face had a sober look that I had seldom seen on it.

'Then still we hold on, waiting for the Gododdin – and Dalriada and Gwynedd and Pictland and Strath-clyde. . . . We are the buyers of time for the rest.'

'Us, and the Spartans at Thermopylae,' I said. And then wished I had not said it.

'And we know what happened to them. A classical education is a fine encouraging thing.' Lleyn's face cracked into its familiar grin.

One of the hounds whimpered in his sleep, and I heard again the hiss and spit of rain falling into the fire.

# – 14 –
# The Road to Catraeth

We stood beside our horses with the re-mounts and the slim baggage train in the open ground below the Royal Farm, we, the shieldbearers, waiting for our Lords. The Companions had taken their own horses up to the Dyn the night before at the King's bidding, that they might make a fitting ride-out through the town in the morning, a ride-out for men and women and bairns to remember afterward.

I mind the fidgeting of the horses. Shadow stamped and shook her head, made restless by the smell of coming events, and I soothed her with a hand on her neck. 'That mare of yours is as full of fads and fancies as a fine maiden,' Lleyn said, over his shoulder. The dogs who always run with a warhost were already leashed. I mind the feel of my leather tunic and the faint creak of it as I moved. My leather war-cap with the iron rim hung from my saddlebow, my oxhide buckler beside it. All of us were craning towards the place where the royal road that led as straight as a spearshaft the length of the town ridge curved out from among the crowded buildings to join the trackway looping south.

The storms of the past few days had cleared, and it was a morning of changeful wind and sunshine, cloud shadows drifting across the hills, and a thin shining rain. And as we watched, suddenly from away in the mile distant Dyn, where the King himself would be watching, the hunting horns were sounding, thin and shining like the rain, and we heard the voices of the people begin to rise like a far off sea.

'Here they come,' Lleyn said.

We were too far to one side to see them coming; we heard them though, or rather, we heard all Eidin giving tongue as they rode by, and then the distant shingle-surge of horse hooves over cobbles, and the hounds pricked their ears to listen. A great tide of sound sweeping nearer and nearer. And a great wing of sunshine sweeping with it along the ridge before the west wind.

The waiting was over, and we swung into our saddles and gathered the horses under us. The drumming of hooves and the sea-roar of voices broke over us. And the first of the riders swung out into the open, and behind them all the rest. The Fosterling was in the lead, and beside him Aneirin in his favourite cloak that wear and weather had changed from crimson to the colour of old spilled wine; and next behind them Geraint from the far south, with the Red Dragon standard that the Queen and her women had stitched for us through the winter, lifting and rippling on the spring wind. Every rider wore his mail coif, but with the mask left open so that his face was bare. Grey wolfskin cloaks hung loose over a glint of colour or a flash of gold beneath. Some had a few primroses or a knot of blackthorn blossom stuck into a shoulder brooch, a token tossed to them by some girl in passing. Cynan had three. Two and two they rode, a shining company, and the sun and rain clashing together as they came. And for that one moment the thought came to me – an odd unchancy thought to be pushed away hurriedly –

that it is not good for mortal men to wear that particular bloom of light.

So they passed, and when they were gone by, the long skein of them, stringing out along the foot of the ridge, we spilled forward after them, with the baggage beasts in our midst and the field-forge with its team of weapon-smiths and farriers. So we made for the old half-lost road that struck south-westward through the Long Moss. Men and women and children followed us for a while in flying column along our flank, and then fell back.

To take the direct way by three peaked Eildon and on down the great upland road through the heart of Gododdin territory would have seemed most likely, but once past the hosting place at Habitancum it would bring us overnear to the empty land – empty for the good reason that in the past years it had suffered too many raids from Bernicia – and our left flank would be dangerously exposed. It would be no good thing to come in contact too soon with the Saxons, and waste time and lives, and like enough have word of our coming carried ahead of us. So we followed the western road, three days longer than the other, but well clear of the Saxons' reach almost all the way; and for most of the way through a still-living land, a thing to be considered when a war-band has to live for the most part on the country it passes through.

At noon, over beyond the Long Moss, we halted to rest the horses, and when we went on again, by the Captain's orders we took up the proper order of march. Now, each pair of shieldbearers rode with their warrior, to guard his back and each other; not that there would be need of that until many miles further on our way, but it was well to get into the way of it. It was good to find ourselves back in the familiar arrowhead again. The advance guard, one troop, rode ahead in small scouting groups, making a long line abreast that was maybe a mile from wing-tip to wing-tip; and the rest followed after, troop by troop, widely spaced, with the Captain and his standard bearer in the third. Our troop, that day, was the last of all, rearguard behind the baggage horses; and we rode seeing the standard far ahead, a lick of crimson in the changeful light.

Each day the troop changed places, but always the Fosterling our Captain rode with the third of the line, and always that blink of crimson told us where he was, and always Aneirin who was to sing our Triumph Song rode beside him, hooded and muffled in his weather-stained cloak.

The first night we were still in Gododdin territory, and the people of the local chieftain came out to us with what grain and cattle they could spare from their lean end of winter store. No, more than they could spare, for the Cran-Tara had passed that way, and they were getting together weapons and journey food on their own account.

That day, and the one that followed, we did not hunt, nor send out foraging parties. But before evening of the second day we were into the old lost territory of Rheged; a land almost empty of men, where the farms as well as the forts were hearth-cold and forsaken. And from then on we kept to the proper order of march in grim earnest, and lay up in the old forts at night with a strong guard on the picketed horses. From there also we began to hunt and forage as we went.

Three days brought us to the Wall, and we made a loop eastward, crossing by way of the bramble-grown wreckage of the nearest wall-fort to avoid passing through Caer Luil that the Romans called Luguvallium; for a living town full of merchants and travelling folk might have links with the Saxon kind, and nine hundred horsemen would not pass through unnoticed. The fort where we made our crossing was empty as though it had never known the footprints of men. Wolves, maybe – there was an animal smell among the roofless barrack rows, but wolves would not carry word of our passing to their two-legged kin.

We pushed on south, and next morning rejoined our road. The land was still Rheged – or what had been Rheged – lowland country at first, though with hills rising afar off on either side; and must have been rich cattle country in its day, though there was little enough cattle-grazing now; gently wooded country, too, with the hazel and alder thickets already hazed with green. But before the day's end we were heading up into the high valley of the Eddain, and the oaks of the low country behind us were giving place to rowan and birch and wind-shaped hawthorn following the course of the brown streams off the moors. Curlew country now, and the great blunt hills of Penuin beginning to rise on either hand. And the rush of falling water was never out of our ears save when for a little while the road ran clear of engulfing grass and heather and the stream sounds were lost in the clatter of hooves on the old paved way.

Towards evening of the second day from Caer Luil we came to another forsaken fort with heather washing to its walls, and the road running straight through, in at one gate-gap and out the other. We had been five days on the march, and made good time, and the Fosterling deemed that we should lie up there for one day to rest the horses before the last two days' push that should bring us down upon Catraeth.

Rest for the horses, but not for us, for he set us to fighting practice among the roofless buildings and the narrow ways between, as though he feared that our battle-readiness might grow dull and our hands forget their killer cunning if we sat quiet for a few hours and watched the grass grow. All save the hunting parties, that is, and Conn and his fellows who set up the fieldforge where the remains of what seemed to have been the cookhouse gave them a hearth to work on, and saw to loose horseshoes and the honing of weapons already sharp enough to draw blood from the wind; and Aneirin who spent the time perched in the stump that remained of the signal tower, looking south-eastward with a fold of his cloak pulled over his head.

But towards evening, with the meat brought in by the hunters beginning to scent the cooking smoke with sweetness, with the horses that had been grazing under guard watered and oat-fed and tethered for the night, and the light beginning to fade over the high moors, at last there was time to draw breath.

Conn and I drifted down through the horse-lines in search of a short spell of peace and quiet, and came upon an upright stone standing man-high beside the way. Not a milestone, we were used to those, but something else, that made me think of the stone beside the ford at Castellum. It was dappled with moon-coloured lichen and all about it there clung the odd magic that belongs to boundaries and threshold places.

'Boundary stone?' said Conn, only half questioning. I nodded. 'Like enough; Rheged on this side of it, Deira on the other.'

We found a hawthorn-fringed hollow below the road on the Rheged side where there was a pocket of shelter from the small thin wind, and squatted down into it side by side, looking back towards the sunset.

It was a while and a while since we had had the chance to be quiet in each other's company, but that evening it seemed to have come about of its own accord, and in the little space of time that was like a gift, we turned from newer friendships, newer bonds, back to the old one that belonged to our old world; knowing, both of us, that we might never have the chance to be quiet in each other's company again.

Neither of us said anything as to that, of course; one does not speak such things even to one's nearest friend. Especially to one's nearest friend.

The sunset brightened moment by moment, the bars of faint brightness under the grey cloud-roof strengthening to saffron and silver; and the evening was full of the spiralling springtime call of the curlews that had come in from the coast to nest on the high moors; and in the silences between the hushing of the wind through the hill grass we could hear faintly the voice of the young river below in the valley. We could hear too, behind us, the shifting of the tethered horses, men's voices from the fort, and a snatch of song and the sudden baying of a hound. But none of that seemed for the moment to be any affair of ours.

We did not talk much. There was not much that needed to be said, and we had never been given to talking for the sake of talking. But after a while, the quiet and the distant calling of the river that I had had no time to hear all day returned into my mind the memory of the dream that I had woken with that morning and forgotten almost before my eyes were fully open.

'I had a dream last night. I dreamed that I was walking up the valley, past Loban's smithy. You and Luned and Gelert were there too – somewhere – but I could not see you.'

'And?' Conn said, after waiting for me to go on.

'That's all. Silly sort of dream – not worth having, really.'

'Maybe there was more that you do not remember,' Conn said, his arms across his updrawn knees, eyes narrowed into the fading brightness of the sunset.

And indeed there was something more, taking shape in my mind as I went back over the dream memory. 'Phanes was sitting on the door-bench; and someone with him – I didn't see properly – shining and silver, with wings . . .' I shook my head, wishing I had not remembered that bit, 'Probably just the light through the alder leaves.'

'More likely the silver hilt of that dagger of his, grown to proper archangel size. It had magic for you, that dagger hilt, didn't it?'

And I saw with relief that that was what the figure was. I did not want Phanes of Syracuse to be dead; certainly not the Holy Brothers' kind of dead, with shining angels. He had been still alive in the care of the monastery's Infirmarer when we left Dyn Eidin; and I wanted him to be alive when we got back – if we ever got back.

'As the blade did for you,' I said.

'But I did not dream of it,' said Conn, and then after a while, 'I wish I had had that dream too.'

But I do not think it was the archangel dagger so much as the track up the valley that he was thinking of.

And only the next moment, a voice just behind us demanded, 'How if I had been a Saxon?'

And we wrenched around and scrambled to our feet to find Cynan standing among the hawthorn bushes within arm's reach of us.

With my heart hammering in the base of my throat, I said, 'Then, my Lord Cynan, I am thinking you might very well have been a dead Saxon. There are two of us to the one of you.'

'Save that if I had been a Saxon indeed, I would not have given you warning by speaking before I used my seax,' he retorted. 'Keep a better look-out behind you when you sit out beyond the camp fires in strange territory. How long were you thinking to take your ease out here by the enemy mark-stone with the dusk coming down, if I had not come out to take a look at the horse-lines and chanced to see you?'

'Not long – with the smell of supper in the air,' I told him. We were not short on respect for our betters in and around the Company, but speech was free among us, even between a shieldbearer and his troop leader.

'And I have been too long from my forge, I am thinking,' Conn said, scrambling up from the little hollow with a hand on a hawthorn root for aid, and shook himself and started back towards the fort.

Cynan looked after him. 'Your friend is saddle-sore?'

'No. It is an old hurt to his knee,' I said. 'He drags that leg when he is tired or when –' I broke off. To go on would have been a kind of betrayal.

But Cynan seemed to understand something of what I had left unsaid. 'I am sorry I broke in. There is little enough chance for a few quiet words with a friend on this kind of trail.' He shook his shoulders as though to rid himself of something. 'I am thinking that we had best be getting back, or they will have eaten all the meat and there will be only bannock left for us.'

We turned back towards the horse-lines together, and I mind – such a boy I still was – that there was a bright hard knot of pride in me because I was walking with Cynan Mac Clydno.

The wind had died into a long trough of quiet, but as we walked, suddenly there was a faint stirring in the heart of the tangle of thorn and bracken maybe less than a spear-throw ahead. It might have been only an eddy of the wind, but all around was completely still.

I glanced aside at Cynan and saw him looking the same way. He made a quick sign to me for silence, and slipped his dagger from its sheath. I followed at his heels as he moved forward, crouching a little. The wind had come back, and the stirring in the hawthorn tangle was lost among the rest; but in the fading light we could see where it had been, and see also when, at the last moment something – a man clad in rough sheepskins – broke cover and ran for the denser scrub of the valley floor.

He should not have left it so late. But I suppose he had hoped that if he froze, we might pass him by. Only that one unwary movement had betrayed him.

I heard a flurry of shouting as the men on horseguard woke to what was happening; but Cynan and I were upon our quarry and, even winged by fear, he was not the runner that we were after our months of training, and in a couple of bowshots we brought him down. I twisted the long knife out of his hand and sent it spinning, while Cynan slammed his own dagger home into its sheath to have both hands free for man-handling.

The man fought like a wolf, and cried out sobbingly, something in a strange tongue, as we twisted his arms behind him and hauled him round towards the fort. 'Here's your Saxon!' Cynan said, and it was true, from the look of him and his tongue and his smell – the Saxons have a different smell from us, some say because they eat wheat instead of the oats and barley that are proper for a man. We began to haul him back the way we had come, into the midst of the men who had come running from the picket lines.

'What have you there?' someone asked.

'Wolf hiding in a thorn-brake,' Cynan told him. 'Some of you go and see if there are any more – you'll find his knife out there somewhere.'

We brought him before the Captain where he sat beside the High Fire with Aneirin and the other troop leaders about him, eating singed deer meat and slab-thick stirabout.

'We found this,' Cynan said.

The Fosterling looked up at the man through a blue waft of smoke. 'What was he doing?'

'Hiding in a hawthorn thicket.'

'Armed?'

'He drew a knife on us. It is back there in the bracken somewhere. The usual kind.'

'A Saxon?'

'Aye.'

The Captain turned to speak to the man directly. 'What purpose had you? To spy upon us?'

The Saxon, who had stood panting but with no word, broke into a stream of guttural speech. It had in it the sound of desperate protest, but we could not understand a word of his barbarous tongue, as clearly he could not understand a word of ours. I could feel the twitching tension of his whole body, but from where I stood, holding his left arm twisted behind his back, I could not see his face, and I was glad of that, having a fairly clear idea of how the thing must end.

Aneirin licked the fat from his fingers and looked up. 'Maybe I can be of help in this.'

The Fosterling nodded. 'Ask him what he was doing here. Did he come to spy on us?'

Aneirin put the question into the Saxon tongue and turned the answering string of protests back into ours. 'He said he is no spy but only a man seeking for a lost sheep.'

'In the midst of a war-camp?' the Captain asked, and again Aneirin turned the thing to and fro between tongues.

'He says he did not know that the Red Crests' palace, which is a place of trolls and evil spirits, had become a war-camp. Sheep may stray far, and he has found them before now, harbouring in this place.'

'And why the hiding and the running?'

'He says when he found horses and armed men here, he was afraid, and thought to wait till dark to get away unseen.' And then after another stumbling flood of words, 'He says he means no harm. He begs you to let him live and go back to his sheep.'

'Sheep? In this high moorland country?' the Captain said. And then, 'I dare not.'

There was a small sharp silence, and then someone cried, 'How if it is true?'

And someone else, his mouth full of deer meat, said, 'He is still a Saxon.'

'And if he is a scout for his own people, he will have means of sending on word, a man on a fast horse could reach Catraeth many hours ahead of us; and there are other means – pre-arranged smoke signals. Explain to him, Aneirin; tell him the sorrow is upon us, I dare not risk it.'

Aneirin told the man his words, and I felt the muscles of his arm and back shudder and strain. He began to cry out and plead and rave. It was horrible. And then, seeing no giving in the faces around him, he gathered himself together and spat across the fire on the Captain's feet. The spittle fell short and in the silence I heard it hiss on the hot stones. And the Saxon, as though in acceptance of what was coming, stood suddenly still.

The Captain made a small signal to Cynan, and I sensed, for I could not see, the quick movement as he slipped the dagger from his belt, and almost in the same instant, the shock of the blow driven home.

The Saxon gave a convulsing jerk in my hold, and with a kind of grunt, sagged to the ground.

'I never had to do quite that thing before,' Ceredig the Fosterling said levelly. 'I hope I never have to do it again.'

The man had rolled over in falling, and lay face up in the light of the fire, and for the first time I saw his face. Not a face of the blue-eyed savages we thought of the Saxons as being; blue-eyed, certainly, but just a man's face, weather-beaten, square cut, neither young nor old, the kind of face one might have thought of as dependable.

So, that was my first experience of war. Despite the last year's patrol skirmishes, despite all that was to come so soon after. And it has remained, as my first experience of war, in my memory ever since.

There was a cold sickness in my belly, and for a moment I was horribly afraid that I was going to throw up there and then before the Captain and the troop leaders.

Then Cynan's hand was on my shoulder, spinning me round. 'Behave!' said his voice in my ear. 'Go to Prince Gorthyn, he will be wondering what has become of his shieldbearer – and send my two to me here. You and I have done our part in this, they can haul him away.'

# – 15 –
# Night Attack

The next day's march was a long one, over the high crest of Penuin, watershed country where the rivers of east and west have their beginnings, a great emptiness with no sound but the wind and running water and curlews crying, save for the sound of our own passing. Another night passed in another half-lost fort so like the last that we began to feel as though we were travelling in a circle, save that there was no frontier stone and no dead Saxon lying beside the hearth. But by evening of the next day the highest of the great hills were behind us and we were coming down the head-valley of the Tees. We saw below us forests still bare and dappled like a thrush's breast rolling away and away into the blue distance, with afar off, on the edge of everything, a grey streak that might be the sea.

And so, with the forest reaching up towards us, we came to the remains of yet one more fort in that land of lost forts, and made our last night's camp. It was not much of a fort, maybe only a permanent marching camp in its time, and being on the edge of forest country the wild had taken it back more completely than those of the high moors. The cleared space that must once have surrounded it was submerged in scrub, hazel and alder and crack-willow, even a few oaks creeping back from the dark tide of the forest, and little remained of the buildings but turf hummocks and bramble domes.

That night, when the evening bannock had been eaten and the horses fed and watered, and there had been a few hours of rest for men and beasts, Ceredig Fosterling sent out the three best scouts among us, on spare horses that had not been ridden that day, to see what was to be seen, and bring back word. The rest of us slept in watches with our blades loose in the sheath, and kept a strong guard on the picket lines, for now we were deep into enemy territory, and no knowing how close there might be Saxon settlements in the forest. And when we rode on next day in the clean green dawn, the Captain had tightened the pattern of march, so we rode in close formation, two troops centred on the road and a light scouting screen ahead, the rest in wings into the country on either side.

Just as we were making the noon halt, last night's scouts rode in with their horses in a lather. And almost before their report had been given to the Captain, it was running through the troops. Aethelfrith the Lord of Bernicia and Deira was still holed up in Catraeth, and the first-come of his gathering warbands with him, all crowded into and around the Royal Village, leaving the old town and its fort empty, according to their usual custom.

'Can we make any guess at their numbers, now?' Gorthyn asked of the world in general, with his mouth full of oat cake.

And one of the others, newly come to the shareout, murmured over his shoulder, 'The scouts reckon, counting the shieldbearers, much the same as our own.'

I thought it was good news, that we were not as yet outnumbered, but Tydfwlch who was older and more experienced than most of the Companions said soberly,

'Not so good. The Legions reckoned, at least according to my grandsire, that an attacking force needed at least twice the strength of the defenders, to over-run a defended position.'

'Hark to our own croaking raven,' Morien said.

And Cynan called across from where he stood with his horse's upturned hoof in his hand while he got a stone out of its frog. 'That's if the quality of attackers and defenders are equal. The war-bands of Aethelfrith are no more than farmers with weapons in their hands and the blood-lust behind their noses. They are not the Companions, nor have they spent a year in the Mead Hall and the training grounds of Mynyddog the Golden.'

And then it was time to be on the march again.

In the midtime between noon and twilight we came out on to the great Legions' road leading north and south, and on the edge of dusk, we were lying up along the woodshore, with Catraeth town across its loop of river not much more than a mile to the south.

Ahead of us the land was roughly cleared, though overgrown with hazel and alder scrub between broad intake fields that showed faintly green here and there with promises of a threadbare crop. Always the Saxons clear the forest and plant their wheat where the land is not good enough for crops, though it might support black cattle. But the forest would have been better left for timber and hunting. The forsaken town looked from that distance like little more than a kind of grey shingle ridge; save where on the highest ground the remains of the fort crouched like an old hound in the last thickening light of sunset. Of the Royal Village another mile beyond it, there was no sign at all.

A wind had begun to rise, blowing from the south-
west, which was good, for it would help to cover the
sound of our coming. And I mind as we waited, dismounted along the edges of the forest, the fading
petals of blackthorn coming down before the gusts,
freckling the darkness of Shadow's mane with white.

The scouts had been sent forward again, and while
we waited for their return and for the dark to cover us,
we watered the horses at the nearby stream, and fed
them what was left of their bean ration, and ate our
own evening bannock and the ration of dried meat
saved for our last meal before battle. And all the while
the wind rose until it sounded like a charge of cavalry
in the woods behind us.

Some while after dark there came a sudden stir further along the line that we knew must mean the return
of the scouts. The fourth troop, dismounted to act as
archers, were going ahead on foot, their horses left
with the remounts and baggage train in care of the
horse-holders; but we knew little of that at the time.
Our own troop was still cavalry as we followed Cynan
forward into the near-dark, with a red night's work
ahead of us.

The Legions' road led straight between the usual
gravestones and a huddle of fallen buildings that might
have been warehouses or the like, to the gates of
Catraeth town; but the road was not for us, even if the
bridge that carried it across the river had still been
standing. We swung westward and forded the river
further up beyond the cleared land, where it ran shallow over shelving stones, tearing down the bank for a
spear-throw on either side by our passing. Troop by
troop, we crossed, the foot somewhere on ahead of us,

and skeined away into the dark like wild geese at the autumn flighting. And the wind covered the noise that we made with its soft turmoil among the bushes, as we headed for the Royal Village. Presently we had the place ringed round. There was no moon in the sky of hurrying cloud, but beyond the stockades there were lights, not the alerted hurrying of torches, but cooking fires and the glow from doorways, and as we waited the wind brought us fitfully the sound of voices roaring out in song. Aethelfrith's housecarls were feasting as we had feasted in Mynyddog's Hall. It seemed that they kept no watch; and the advantage of surprise was with us still.

The first flight of arrows went over our heads from the archers in the scrub behind us. Not man-killers but the fire arrows of Morien's conjuring, trailing fiery tails of spirit-soaked rag dragon-wise behind them as they flew, to lodge in the stockade timbers and the thorn-work of the gateways; a few, the furthest travellers, to pitch down into the thatch of the huddled roofs within. Dogs began a frenzied barking, but our own warhounds, trained to silence, made no reply. A man shouted, and his warning yell was taken up by others. The singing in Aethelfrith's hall came to a ragged halt. Shadow fidgeted uneasily under me as I swung the shield on to my shoulder and shifted the balance of my spear, and I soothed her in a whisper, 'Soft now! Softly, *cariad*, all's well.'

From the far side of the steading, clear across the uproar that was beginning to rise between, sounded the clear high note of the hunting horn, telling us that all was in readiness, and our own took up the call, like two cocks crowing against each other in the sunrise. I drove my heel into Shadow's flank as we broke forward from a stand into a canter, heading for the now blazing gateway. I remembered the fire-rides in the practice ground below Dyn Eidin, which had seemed to have little purpose at the time but had purpose enough now. The canter quickened to full gallop, and above the rolling thunder of hooves we were yelling like fiends out of hell as we came.

The first troop, the Captain's own troop, was through and over the blazing thorn-work of the gateway, beating the fire under their hooves and scattering a bright spindrift of flame, and into the midst of the men who came running with snatched up weapons to meet them. And after them we plunged, choked and half blinded, across the glowing way that they had left behind. Vaguely, I was aware to left and right of riders crashing through the burning stockades – through and over in a score of places. I was aware of yelling faces and flamelight on the swinging blades of axes and the long straight Saxon knives, and the narrow heads of our own spears. I think I killed, and more than once, but of that I am not sure; none of it seemed to matter as much as that single killing of three nights ago. Our hunting horns were sounding again, and from the heart of the steading before the long barn-like building that must be Aethelfrith's Hall – Aelle's Hall – there rose the sudden hollow booming of the Saxon war-horn. We thrust on towards it. The fire arrows had set the high thatched roof alight, and against the wavering sheet of flame, high on the gable end, a spreading pair of antlers marked the place for what it was, the Mead Hall of a king; and below, the upreared horse-tail standards marked the battle-stand of Aethelfrith himself.

We went for it, charging and charging again behind the Red Dragon of Britain, ploughing through the fanged masses of the Saxon kind, with our own dismounted men, their arrows spent, running beside us to guard the horses' bellies, and the hunting horns from the far side of the steading sounding nearer and nearer yet.

The Saxons were taken all unawares, many of them were drunk from the Mead Hall; but they fought like wolves, and the King's housecarls forming the shield-ring, stood rock steady, swinging their mighty axes, and died like heroes when the time came for dying. Again and again the horsetail standard lurched and all but went down; but each time was caught and heaved aloft once more as another man stepped into the place of the fallen standard bearer.

Much of this comes into my mind like memory, but truth to tell, I think that is because I heard it told so often afterward, and because I knew that that must have been the way of it. And at the time all that I knew of that fight in the Saxon royal steading was a clotted mass of snarling faces in the light of burning thatch, a sense of chaos, and the smell of blood and sweat and dung. I remember small isolated things: a hound leaping at a Saxon's throat, a wisp of burning thatch that I struck away from Shadow's neck before it could singe her mane. I remember seeing Dara drop beside me with his head split open by an axe, and not believing it until later . . .

In the end the shield-ring crumbled and went down. In the end the hand-to-hand fighting that reached from end to end of the steading broke up also. Companions and shieldbearers were plunging in and out of blazing

buildings dealing with any who they found within; and
the remaining defenders broke and ran, streaming away
over the blackened wreckage of the stockades, heading
for the refuge of the forest and the marsh country. We
did not go after them; they were few enough.

When the last fighting was done, a spent stillness
came over the Royal Village. Only the soft gusting of
the wind, only the ugly sounds of wounded men and
horses, and the lowing of frightened cattle in the corral. Men were slaking the flames of burning roofs as
best they could. Presently we would fire the whole
place, but not yet, not till we had stripped it of all that
we could make use of, weapons and grain and cattle. I
had slipped from the saddle and was standing with my
arm over Shadow's neck, leaning my weary weight
against her while she turned her head and lipped at my
shoulder. I fondled her, and as my head cleared somewhat, began to look around for Gorthyn, my lord. He
was standing with Llif and a few more, close-gathered
about the Captain, looking down at the bodies of the
housecarls sprawled about the horse-tail standard.
Urging Shadow forward I went to join them, not really
thinking why, just following the pattern whereby unless he has reason to be elsewhere, a shieldbearer's
place is with his warrior. Lleyn was there, too; and the
arrowhead was complete.

Men were turning over the dead, looking at their
faces by the light of a firebrand. Looking for someone,
it seemed. One of the searchers lifted aside the fallen
standard, its flowing white horsetail stained and
clotted crimson, and under it lay a very tall man, his
face hidden by the great wolf-mask helmet that he
wore. I had glimpsed that helmet earlier, rearing half a

head taller even than his housecarls at the centre of the shield-ring.

'Aethelfrith,' someone said.

Ceredig Fosterling himself stooped and seized it by the crest and dragged it off. There was a faint smile as though of amused triumph on the dead face, but the hair – Aethelfrith's hair was molten red – was brindled grey, and the face belonged to a man much older than the Saxon king.

There was a leaden silence. The thing was too bad for any outcry, any cursing, to make it better.

The Captain straightened up, still holding the great helmet, and looked at those about him. 'Make search,' he ordered. 'There is always the chance that he is hiding somewhere, or among the dead elsewhere.' And men scattered to do his bidding, but we knew, as he knew, that the housecarls had made their shield-ring, and stood up to die, the tallest among them wearing the King's helmet, to cover the escape of their king himself.

'They were brave men. Pity it is that their chief was not worthy of them,' Llif said.

And Gorthyn agreed, in the tone of one making an interesting discovery, 'I did not think that he would show us white feathers in his tail.'

The Captain swung round on him wearily. 'Use what wits you have, man. Aethelfrith is no coward, only hard-headed. He knew that had he remained to die here with his men, we should have gained the victory that we came for. While he lives his hosting war-bands still have him to lead them, and we have no true victory after all.'

'So, what do we do now?' someone asked, nursing a sword-arm that dripped red.

'See to our own dead and wounded, take all that may be of use to us and make for the fort,' the Fosterling said. 'All that follows after must wait until these things be done.'

Men were going through the Saxon dead, stripping them of weapons and useful gear. They lay everywhere. There were women and bairns, mercifully not many, for those belonging to the steading in Aelle's time must for the most part have gone in one way or another when Aethelfrith came upon them, and the newcomers would not yet have brought in their own women. We handled them more gently than the men, but where there was a gold ring or an enamelled belt clasp for the taking we took from all alike, according to the custom of war. We gathered our own dead together for burial, digging out for them hastily a long grave-ditch where the ground was soft outside the stockade. We had not lost heavily, not yet, more horses than men, and those we left lying where they had fallen, finishing off the wounded beasts for kindness' sake.

Lleyn and I carried Dara to the grave trench, and laid him in it with his cloak across his ruined face. He was really Cynan's affair, but Cynan and Cymran had a grave-laying of their own to tend to, for they had found Cynri lying where the bodies were clotted thick in the mouth of the Mead Hall.

We stripped the royal steading of all that could be of use to us – weapons, beer, corn, even cattle-fodder – and loaded it on to the farm sleds. We gathered the few cattle from the corral in a small lowing herd; and so with horsemen flanking them in case of surprise, we drove and hauled the spoils back to what remained of the Roman town, through the windy darkness that yet remained of the night. And when the last load was away, we set torches to the thatch again, wherever the fires had been quenched, and left the place to burn over its dead.

# Waiting for Elmet

Catraeth, Catteractonium as the Romans had called it, was a double cohort fort, and so there was room enough for all of us within the crumbling defences, but not for the horses, so we picketed them outside the fort but within the turf walls of the town, keeping a strong guard on them. Mercifully the river, running quiet after the white water further upstream, looped close under the town walls, making it easy to water them, at least for the present. There were wells and springs in both the town and the fort, but most of them had fallen in.

That first day is a jumble of crowded and shifting memories in my mind. We found a barrack-row with part of its roof still on, to make a shelter for our wounded, and started up cooking fires – there was plenty of dead wood about the place. We slaughtered some of the cattle. The rest would be kept for later need, but men fresh from battle need hot food with blood in it. Conn and his mates, coming in with the rest of the horses and their holders from the place beyond the river where they had been left before the attack, set up their field-forge in what had once been the armourer's shop. I mind that they brought in with them a little dark man with a thrall-ring round his neck. Some of the steading's thralls had been caught up and killed in the fighting, others, seizing their chance, had run while the running was good. This one had

come back, being minded to kill a few Saxons in his
turn, and being a local man became one of our scouts.
Conn's first task was to cut off his thrall-ring.

I mind coming up from the horse-lines and seeing
Aneirin sitting beside one of the fires, looking with
interest at a Saxon harp that must have come from
Aethelfrith's Hall. There was blood on him; he had
been working all day among our wounded, but it
might have been his own, for he had been with the
archers last night. I paused beside him and demanded,
as though I were the greybeard and he some young
hothead, 'And what would we have done for a praise-
singer if the Great Ones had not had a care of you last
night?' (My excuse? That it was not a day since I had
helped to lay Dara in his grave, and I was face to face
with the fact, which had not quite broken through to
me before, that in battle my friends and those most
near and dear to me might actually die.)

He looked up at me with an air of great serenity
about him, and said only, 'Nay now, if I am to sing the
Great Song of the Gododdin at Catraeth, God and all
the Great Ones will hold me safe for the sake of the
singing that is in me. If I am not, then what value is my
life above the lives of other men?'

There was still hope in us at that time – we waited
for the war-bands of Elmet to come in. Elmet that was
so much the nearest of the northern kingdoms and
must therefore reach us ahead of all the rest. And in
those few open days before the warhosts of Deira and
Bernicia closed in, we sent off scouts to keep watch to
the north and west for the men of the kingdoms and
bring us word of their coming. (We are better scouts
than the Saxons, because we are hunters and they are

not.) Also Ceredig the Captain called out Madog, he being an Elmet man, and ordered him away into his own hills to tell his tribe that we were in Catraeth and waited for their coming . . .

After their going, we set ourselves to get the grain sacks and the great jars of Saxon beer stacked under cover. Beer has a cold bitter taste, not like the fire-hearted yellow mead that we were used to, but the cold of it warmed in the belly and dimmed one's sorrows and weariness, though it did not give the same shine to life. We got the few black cattle fenced in and hunted out anything that would serve as pails and water troughs for them and the horses, against the time when we might not be able to get to the river.

Next day two of the scouts came in, and almost at once after their coming word was running through the fort that a big war-band was on the road from the south, and that the tall red haired man at their head – so said the scout who had once been his thrall – was Aethelfrith.

Of the Elmet men there was still no sign.

From the rampart and the stump of the signal tower we could see afar off the bright blur of the Saxon fires strung along the woodshore to the south, where they had made camp that first night. The next night there were more of them, from the north across the river, as well. The first night the Fosterling held us like hounds in leash, but the second night he called out Cynan and Tydfwlch and said, 'Are your troops ready?' We had been ready all day, and we told him so. And he said, 'Go then, and good hunting to you.'

The brushwood barricades across the main gateway were pulled aside and we went.

After that, for a while there were no more fires in the dark, for the Saxons had learned the un-wisdom of showing their whereabouts in smoke by day or flame by night; but it made little difference, for the scouts brought us word of where the camps were pitched.

But the camps grew more and bigger as the days went by.

In some ways those raids of ours were like the cattle raids that many of us had known among our own hills, and called for the same skills and the same reckless speed. In others they were more like hunting, but a deadly hunting in which the quarry was men. Sometimes we took them on the march, coming on them out of the woods at twilight or out of the westering sun, with the thunderbolt crack of cavalry upon a rabble of men on foot. Sometimes we skirmished about the camps, beyond the firelight. All the while we cost them men and more men, of Deira and Bernicia which I have heard they call Northumberland now. But all the while, despite all that we could do, the numbers against us grew; and they cost us dearly also, in men but even more in horses, until, except when the purpose of things demanded cavalry, we took to holding the horses back and making our raids on foot.

That called for a different kind of fighting, ringmail left behind because of the faint chime that it makes in movement; a closing in, silent as shadows, until the last moment came . . . That eased the drain on the horses, but it cost us yet more heavily in men.

And still the men of Elmet did not come, nor the combined warhost of the north and west, nor even the warrior bands of the Gododdin, though the Cran-Tara must have reached many of them before we crossed the border on our road south.

In a while – I do not know the exact tally of nights and days – the whole of the two-fold Saxon war-horde was gathered to the mustering place, and we were encircled in their midst. The Saxons built stockades across the roads to the north and south and wherever the ground was possible for a breakout. To attack the stockades would only be to lose men to no purpose, especially as escape was not among our orders; and the barricades would rise again.

Even to get the horses watered now cost men. The time of the wild-riding sorties was over, as the siege tightened about us, and there were daily skirmishes as they sought to drive us in from the crumbling town defences. Soon we should be penned fast within the fort itself, and that would mean losing most of the horses and the best of the still surviving wells. It was on the last mounted sally, the last riding out to guard the horses at their watering, covered by our archers from the town walls, that Gorthyn's horse was killed under him. I mind the slipping shambles as man and beast came down together, and the bright arc of an axe blade up-swung. It took him between neck and shoulder, slicing through the ringmail into flesh and bone. Lleyn's dirk was in the Saxon's throat almost before Gorthyn hit the ground, and an arrow from the walls took him under the arm. But that was too late for Gorthyn.

We slung him across my saddle bow and got him back into the fort, Lleyn covering our rear. And all the while his blood spurted over my bridle arm. Once back in the fort, we got him down, and lashed his own neck-cloth and mine round his shoulder to check the bleeding, and carried him up to the barrack-row that sheltered the wounded, and laid him on the bare ground – there was no more straw nor fern for bedding – and Aneirin came and did what could be done for him. It was not much. Nearly all the salves and medicines that the Queen had sent with us, even the bandage linen, were gone by then. And in any case, he had lost more blood than a man can well lose and yet live.

The wound sickened and turned foul almost at once. That was the way with most of our wounded, as it generally is when wounded men must lie too close together and there is not enough of anything, even water. It took him three days to die, but I think that he was out of his body for most of that time, even before the fever took him.

Lleyn and I nursed him between us when we were free from other matters.

We were both with him on the last morning. Earlier, he had been bright-eyed and raving, but as the light grew he had slipped into a kind of sleep that was not like true sleep. There was quiet, save for his quick, shallow breathing, in the corner of the barrack-row which we had curtained off with dead men's cloaks strung on spear-shafts to give him a private dying-space. Such quiet that faintly, from the woods down river, I heard the cuckoo calling; the first cuckoo of the year.

Then, almost at once after the alarm call of the hunting horn and the light flurry of sound, swelling and growing ragged, that meant the out-break of fresh fighting; another attack on the town gate. And then the hurrying of feet, and voice calling to voice as men snatched up their weapons and hurried down to join

the gate's guard. But that was all from the world
outside. In the corner of the barrack-row there was
still no sound but Gorthyn's shallow breathing, growing more shallow as the moments passed.

Lleyn's head went up, and I drew my legs under me
to be away in answer to the call. But Gorthyn's hand,
the one that still had life in it, was fast about my wrist.
He had been holding it so before he fell asleep, and in
his sleep had kept his hold unbroken. I checked in the
movement I had begun, and looked across to meet
Lleyn's gaze; and the decision making went wordlessly
to and fro between us.

'Bide here,' he said, and, 'Your turn next time.' And
he got up, slipping his dirk from its sheath, and went
out. I heard him calling back to the cuckoo: 'Cuckoo,
cuckoo!' as he went down to join the fight.

The flurry of sound had swelled into the full-
throated roar and weapon-clash of men locked in close
combat, but still it all seemed small and far off, and the
only sound that really concerned me was that faint
stressful rasp of Gorthyn's breathing. It changed, and
looking down through the shadows I saw his eyelids
begin to twitch. They opened, and he lay looking up at
me. His face had always been bony and now it looked
like a skull, a young skull if there could be such a
thing, with only the eyes alive in it. But his eyes were
clear and awake, with the crazy-brightness of the
wound-fever gone from them. And for one moment I
thought that he was better, that against all the odds he
was going to mend. Then I understood that the change
was not that; not that at all . . .

'Prosper,' he said, drawing breath for the word as
though it were a cart rattling over stones.

'I am here,' I said.

And his gaze drifted away from mine and went searching into the shadows, then returned to me again. 'Lleyn?'

'Down in the gate. The Saxons are attacking again.'

'Lleyn – of my own hearth-kin,' he said. 'Kin follows kin. But you – if I had not – come hunting the white hart in – your father's runs, you would not be – here today.'

'I would not be anywhere else,' I said, and for the moment it was true.

His voice was getting weaker, the painful breath rattling in his chest, but there was a trace of a smile at the corners of his parched mouth. 'There's glad I am – that we did not kill the white hart.'

'I also.'

His breath caught and strangled. A trickled of blood came out of his mouth and nose, and his head rolled sideways. There was no sound at all in the cloaked off corners of the barrack-row.

I freed my wrist from his hold as gently as I knew how, and put his hand that had been alive only the moment before, with the hand that had been two days dead, together on his breast. Then I got up, freeing my own dirk, and went out and down towards the gate.

The sound of fighting was dying down, and the struggling mass of men about the gateway thinning out, the wave of the Saxon attack streaming away towards the river, sped by a last flight of arrows from the gatehouse.

Men were falling back, carrying wounded among them, while already others were struggling to renew the thornwork barricade. And in the gateway our newest dead lay sprawled.

Close under the gate tower Cynan crouched over someone, something that ran red like a broached wine jar. I went to see if there was help to be given, and saw that it was Cymran. He was almost broken apart midway, by a blow from another of the great Saxon war-axes, part still and part writhing like a snake crushed under a cartwheel. It was horrible. As I reached them he cried out shrilly, 'Oh, for God's sake, finish it!' And Cynan slipped his dagger from his belt left handed – his right arm was under his brother's head – and finished it as calmly and competently as he might have slit the throat of a kid for the cooking pot.

I did not look at his face. I did not dare. I turned blunderingly away: and in so doing all but fell over another body with the barb of a Saxon arrow that had passed clear through, sticking out between the shoulder blades. I turned it over, but there was no need; one does not need to see a friend's face to know him from other men; it was Lleyn. He could not even have got into the fight; his dirk was still in his hand, but it was clean.

I do not think that I felt anything, just then. We had grown used to the faces of dead friends, anyway. The thing I mind most sharply of that moment is that somewhere down-river the cuckoo was still calling.

After dark, we buried the day's dead in the lower town as usual, in what must have been the gardens of temples and rich men's houses, while others of us stood guard on the crumbling walls. They had been overgrown with trees and the in-flowing of the wild when first we made our tattered stronghold in Catraeth; we had hacked down most of it now, for firewood or shelter or barricades, or simply to clear the ground outside the fortress walls. But a little remained. An ancient maytree growing beside a fallen marble bench was just breaking into flower, and a young moon cast the shadows of its branches over the long grass and gave us light to work by.

We would have buried them in their war-gear with their weapons beside them had we been able, but our own need was too sore. We left them their adorments, though; to each man the brooch or arm-ring or twisted golden torque that was his own. We could not spare the time nor the space for separate graves; we dug out a broad trench, deep enough to keep the wolves out, but no more, and laid them side by side, Companions and shieldbearers together. Gorthyn and Lleyn together. We laid the earth back over all.

It was not until the thing was done and over, and I was on my way back to the fort with the rest of the burying party that what had happened struck home to me. That morning I had been one of three; and tonight I was alone.

With the cold ache of desolation in my belly, I checked in the gateway and looked back. From the slightly higher ground of the fort, I could still see the topmost branches of the maytree in the moonlight. I could see also the Saxon watchfires. We were encircled and penned fast, and the Saxons knew that they had no need now to keep themselves dark.

Someone was beside me; a shoulder brushed against mine in turning, and I looked round quickly, somehow for that one instant expecting it to be Lleyn, and it was Faelinn. The moon made a tiny blue spark in the glass bead he still wore in his right ear, and showed his face with the same look on it that I suppose was on my own.

I knew that his fellow shieldbearer had gone down days ago, but I had been so deep taken with my own two beside the maytree that I had no awareness that Peredur also was among that day's dead.

I do not think anything was said between us. We went back into the fort together like a pair of masterless hounds. We sat down side by side at the first fire we came to, and when the lean evening ration was shared out – the last of the cattle were dead and we had not eaten meat for days – we shared one sour wheat cake between us.

Between moonset and dawn they attacked the picket lines, the first time that they had brought themselves to face the trolls and devils within the town walls after dark. It was only a small skirmishing band of them that time, and the horseguard killed several of them before they could cut the ropes and stampede the horses, and the rest melted back into the darkness before we got down to help. It was over and done with so quickly that it seemed of little moment, not much more than a kind of wild sport. Much like our own cattle raiding. But when the troop leader passed on the Captain's orders that the horses were to be brought up into the fort, we began to understand its real purpose: the loss of the river and then of the remaining town springs. With the horses packed within the fort walls, how long before the water ran out? Some of us muttered that it would have been better to leave the beasts out to take their chance than have to kill them ourselves if relief did not reach us within the next few days.

But at dusk on the same day Madog got back to us through the Saxon screen. One of the look-outs brought him in, looking like a famished and storm-driven ghost in the light of our watch-fire. And those of us who saw him come knew the word that he brought before ever he told it to the Fosterling.

'So the Elmet men will not be coming,' Faelinn said.

And the bitterness rose in me like gall. 'I suppose they think that their forests and marshes will keep them safe enough.'

'There are other kingdoms, still.'

I doubted it. 'If Elmet does not come, how is it different for the others?' I said. 'We all told ourselves that Mynyddog was Artos the Bear over again, but he's not. The kingdoms of the north will not combine warhosts again at the call of a High Chief from beyond their frontiers.'

That still left our own war-bands, the Gododdin within the summons of their own king's Cran-Tara. But neither of us spoke of them. We had looked for their coming too long. And even if they came now, what could they do, the fighting strength of our tribe against the double warhost of all Deira and Bernicia, except share with us in the dying?

# – 17 –
# The Last Day

Later that morning Ceredig the Captain called us all together in what I think must have been the mess hall of the fort. (Our numbers were small enough for that now: less than a hundred of the original Company, less than two hundred of the shieldbearers.) All of us save for the handful left on watch. Even Conn and his mates from the field-forge, and Aneirin, who had spent most of his time when he was not with the wounded sitting alone by himself in what remained of the signal tower with the fold of his old wine-coloured cloak over his head.

Now he sat on the fallen stone that served him as a song-stool, in the bard's proper place at the Captain's feet, and gazed into the fire as though he were reading pictures in it. And Madog crouched at the Captain's other side, holding on his knee the oat cake that clearly he was beyond eating, and staring into the fire also with red-rimmed eyes in a face that was so furious and shamed that it hurt to look at it.

And there, standing between them, Ceredig the Fosterling spoke with us as a man speaks with his friends. I saw him in the flamelight across the crowding shoulders of other men, tall and raw-boned, with that mane of rough tawny hair and those strange eyes of his, one grey and the other green, shining jewel-wise in his famished face. (Indeed we all had the famine look on us by that time.) He was silent for the first moment after he stood up, his gaze raking to and fro into the furthest shadows so that when he began to speak, we all knew that he spoke to *us*, not only the Companions who were crowded closest to the fire.

Na, na, I do not remember word for word, after so many years, but the gist of it, that I remember well enough.

'My brothers, there is that which I have to say to you, and the time has come for saying it. The orders of Mynyddog the King, on which we rode south, you already know: to attack and over-run Aethelfrith and his war-bands, to take this fort of our Roman forefathers and hold it, working all the damage that we can upon the Saxon warhost as it gathers, until our own warhost comes to our relief, or until we are over-run. To those orders we have been true. Not Cuchulain himself in the Pass of the North could have wrought more greatly than we. But sorrow upon me, Aethelfrith himself escaped our first attack and left us with an empty victory. Even so, there are many and many of the Saxon kind who will not take blade and burning forward into our valleys, because we have laid them down here to sleep a red sleep. We have held them back by this – that they dare not move forward leaving us alive behind them. So – we have held them, playing for time; time for the tribes to join war-spears behind us and come down to the fight.

'But now it seems that there is no more time to play for, no such joining of war-spears behind us. Madog has returned to us from his own people –'

There was a low muttering round the fire, Madog's hand clenched on the bannock so that it burst and crumbled between his fingers, and a hand came round from behind him and scooped up the larger bits. We were too hungry to waste good oaten crumbs. 'They are no people of mine any more,' he said through set teeth.

'From the Lords of Elmet,' the Fosterling said after a moment. 'Bringing us their word that they dare not send us their war-bands, for they have hearths and women and cattle of their own to guard.'

Someone put in, still clinging to a ragged hope, 'The other kingdoms maybe are of a different mind from Elmet!'

And Ceredig turned to look at him kindly, man to man. 'If Elmet does not come, why should any other? Our own men should have been here long ere this, answering the Cran-Tara, and they have not come.'

The words fell clear and heavy into our silence. And in the silence Cynan spoke up, I think for all of us. Almost the first word that we had heard him speak since Cymran's dying. 'The King has failed in this thing that he sought to bring about. But he has not failed in all things; he has not failed in the making of the Company. And the Company will not fail him, now that it is time to earn the mead we drank under his roof and the golden torques and blue-bladed swords we have had of him. We are his men – so, let you tell us the thing that we do now!'

All round the fire men were giving tongue, a hoarse and ragged outcry that the Captain quieted with an upraised arm. 'My brothers, I will tell you what it is that we do now. It is for that that I have called you together. We have waited for a warhost that has not come, and truly I believe that it will not come now. We could hold on, waiting a few more days

– not many, for even if we begin to eat the horses, the wells are running dry. Our numbers are sinking fast. We are too few, and the Saxon circle drawn too tight about us for any more raiding. The Saxons know this, and they also will wait, until we are too weak to lift sword against them; and at the end of those few days we shall die like a badger in its holt when they send in the ground-dogs. That is no end for this shining company.

'Therefore, not tonight but tomorrow night when we have had time to prepare all things fittingly, let us make an end of our own choosing. Let us make one last charge against the Saxons, where their spear-wall is thickest, and where to judge by their horsetail standard, Aethelfrith himself should have his battlestand. We shall not break through; it is not for that we make our charge. We shall go down. But we shall take down with us such a harvest of the Saxon kind that it shall be long and long before their war hordes can gather full strength again.'

He broke off, and stared round at us in the spitting firelight. But we kept the silence, knowing that there was something more to come.

'Yet this is a last ride that should be made only with willing hearts,' he said at last, his voice suddenly hoarse. 'Tomorrow night after moonrise, I shall make it. I shall rejoice if you ride with me. I am a man who likes to choose with care the company he dies in, and I should be full fain to die in yours. Nevertheless, the choice is for you to make, each one for himself. And if I ride alone, I shall not therefore forget that I have loved you, and had, I think, your love in return.'

For a moment longer the silence held us, then we rose to him as one man, shouting round the fire that we were his, that we would ride with him, all of us, all – all.

'Not quite all,' the Fosterling said when we were quiet once more. 'One must go back to Dyn Eidin, and others for his escort.'

And we waited, in a new silence that made the stamp and whinny of a restless horse in the picket lines sound very loud.

'For the escort riders, Conn and Credne and Flamn of the field-forge, who can best be spared, because our need of them will be over. To guide them Garym who knows these hills and has scouted for us all this while. And for the one –' he looked down at Aneirin. 'Prince of Bards, this you will do for us.'

Aneirin lifted his gaze slowly from the heart of the fire. 'How if I refuse?'

'One must go, to carry word of our end back to the King. And who but the one who, living, can sing our passing so that men may remember us for a thousand years?'

Aneirin said, 'This is a hard thing that you ask of me. I was a fighting man in my youth, and for these bright and bitter days I have had something of my youth again.'

And Cynan leaned forward beside the fire. 'Harper dear, it is a hard thing we ask of you, but you must leave your youth with us, and live on without it, for if you die, we shall die unsung and unhonoured. Remember the Great Song you promised us, on the day the orders came.'

I mind thinking that the song he had promised that day had been a triumph song, not a lament. But I suppose that also is not without triumph in its way. We all added our voices to Cynan's and Ceredig the Fosterling had the final word.

'To be a bard is a greater thing than to be a warrior. If you win back living to my father's Hall, count yourself ransomed by your power of poetry, and make us our Great Song for men to remember us by. No man likes to die unsung, and we shall have earned a shining song, Harp-Lord.'

Aneirin was silent a moment, his eyes half-closed, gazing once more into the fire, then he opened them wide and turned his hawk-yellow stare upon us, 'You shall not die unsung, if I win back to Dyn Eidin,' he said.

So the thing was settled and made sure, and when the little food that there was had been eaten, he tuned his harp and sang to us, the first time that he had done that thing since we rode south; not the old songs that we knew, but another that he must have begun to make in the ruined signal tower during the past days; rough-edged as yet, not honed and tempered as it would be in later days.

'The men went to Catraeth, fierce in their laughter,
    Pale mead was their feast drink, a year in Eidin's Hall,
    Their spears bright as the wings of dawning . . .'

He sang snatches of half-formed song as they came to him, for this man and that. He sang of Gwenabwy and his wolf, of Llif still living and Gorthyn dead. He sang deep into the night, of the three hundred men wearing golden torques and bearing swords that were the King's gift. Not of us, the shieldbearers, of course; we did not expect it. I do not suppose the men of other states who stood with the Spartans at Thermopylae expected it, either.

That night I slept well in the few hours we were allowed, lightly and quietly, and woke to the first ashen light of the dawn that would be the last we saw.

It was an odd day; nothing felt quite real, and yet all things had slightly clearer edges and more luminous colours than was usual. Friends tended to drift into twos and threes and little groups, holding together as we went about the ready-making for the last fight that would come after moonrise.

All the details of that day remain with me yet. But the order in which things happened was hazy to me even at the time, so that the day remains a tumble of clear-cut scenes and images that can be taken out and looked at separately, and dropped back again wherever they chance to fall.

Faelinn and I were still together, not friends, but held together by our lost-dog state. Together we gathered up the armour and weapons that had belonged to our lords, and together we found an unclaimed corner and settled down to burnish it and make all ready for the night. I mind rubbing up Gorthyn's sword and looking to the rivets that secured the hilt; I mind grooming his grey wolfskin cloak as one grooms a living hound, burnishing the rust spots from his battle-shirt and the fine linkmail coif with its strangely beautiful mask. His war-cap had gone when his horse came down, and without the mail would not be much protection against a sword cut. But I think it was not so much for the protection, that I made it ready, as for the sake of the man who had worn it last. I had washed the blood from the shirt on the day that the axe gash was made, and now I mended it as best I could with a leather thong, for the same reason.

I mind coming upon Llif in a patch of sunlight, stripped naked and with a little pot of woad in one hand and a stick with the end chewed soft in the other, tracing warrior patterns wherever there was space among the tattooing on his breast and shoulders and thighs.

I checked beside him for a few moments, watching, then asked, 'Why the beauty work?'

'It is the custom of my people to wear such patterns when we go into battle,' he said.

'That I understand, when you go into battle naked. But in leather and ringmail, who will know?'

'I shall know,' Llif said, squinting at the blue spiral growing below his shoulder.

Most of us combed our hair at some time in that day, before we armed up. We groomed the horses too, as best we could in such close-picketing. It was all part of the same ritual, I suppose, the making of all things worthy . . . the horses were in a sorry state by that time, famine-drained as ourselves and with all condition lost; gaunt ghosts of the proud high-crested animals we had ridden out from Dyn Eidin a few short weeks ago. Shadow turned her head and nuzzled at my breast with delicately working lops, still hoping for the honey-crusts I had been used to give her, and I pressed my forehead against the white blaze on hers, knowing the familiar hard warmth and the smell of her, hoping that she would not be afraid when the time came; hoping that I should not be afraid, either.

I mind Ceredig the Captain, once more in the roofless mess hall, with the troop leaders close about him.

Two who had been leaders all along, four who had stepped up to take the place of friends now fallen. Aneirin was there too, standing back a little from the rest, with the long folds of his cloak that was the colour of spilled wine gathered close about him.

The Captain spoke to us kindly, almost gently, that last time of all, making sure that even the least of us knew the plan for the night, and what was before us. He was like one or two generals, not many, who I have known since, merciless on the training ground but gentle before battle.

'The waiting time is over, and an hour after moonrise when the shadows are still long, we ride out. We shall charge at full gallop, remembering always that we come to kill Saxons, not to break through the siege-ring. They, not knowing that, will thicken their battle mass to hold us at the point of our attack, and to do that they must thin the shield-ring elsewhere. And that, Lord of the Harpers, will be your chance.' He turned a little to Aneirin, 'Garym the scout will have five horses waiting at the west gate where the moon shadows will be longest and most deep. Our last charge will cover you until you are clear of Catraeth. Sing us nobly in the King's Hall.'

'That I will do,' Aneirin said, 'though with a bitter heart.' He gathered the weatherworn folds of his cloak more closely round him, and half turned as though to be away, then checked and stood waiting till the Captain, who had turned back to us, should be done.

'There is one thing more,' the Fosterling said. 'In the year behind us we trained as Arrowheads. Here in Catraeth the fighting has been of another kind, and we have for the most part laid the Arrowhead aside; but

men's hearts are easiest and their weapon-hands most
sure when they follow the ways in which they were
first trained. Therefore tonight we shall return at least
in part to the old way, though since there are swords
enough for all who still live, we shall go armed alike
on this ride. Therefore let all shieldbearers whose lords
yet live go to them now; and let all Companions who
lack one shieldbearer or both, take from among the
lordless ones standing by.' He looked round at us with
a kindly eye. 'There is no more, my brothers.'

But Aneirin said, 'One thing more. A small thing.
Give me leave to speak, Fosterling.'

'Speak, then,' the Captain said.

The King's bard looked us over. 'When the choosing
is done with, let some among you bring me dry stuff,
anything to make a fire, up to the signal tower, and
above all, seven branches of the rowan tree that yet
stands at the south-western corner of the fort.'

There was a small surprised silence, and we waited
for more, but there was no more. And suddenly I was
remembering his words among the broom bushes
below Dyn Eidin; something about a fire of rowan
wood, and a mist all across Roscommon. I had
thought at the time that it was only a thing spoken in
jest. Now I was not so sure.

'Seven rowan branches you shall have,' someone
called out. I think it was Morien, rising as usual to
anything that had to do with fire.

It took a little while for Companions and shieldbearers to sort out their Arrowheads, and Faelinn and
I were still together and still unclaimed when Cynan
came by and stopped in front of us. 'Prosper, come
you.'

'I come, Lord,' I said, and stepped forward, and then as he would have turned away, 'Sir, Faelinn who was shieldbearer to Peredur is lordless, also.'

He checked and turned back and looked Faelinn up and down. 'Not any more. Come you also,' he said tersely.

I cast a hasty glance at Faelinn. The thing that had grown between us in those past few days was too shadowy and still too prickly to be called friendship, and I was afraid that maybe I had taken too much into my own hand; but I saw that he was glad, as I was, that we should make the last ride together.

'Now go, fetch Aneirin his rowan branches,' said our new lord. Several of us went down to the south-western corner of the fort together. The rowan tree which grew there was young and sappy, which was why it had not been cut long since, the leaf buds unfurling, feathering on the twigs. We hacked off seven branches and carried them back to the signal tower, where others of our kind had arrived before us with dead branches and brushwood that had been gathered for fires in earlier days. We carried it all up the narrow stone stairway that led round the inside wall, and dropped it on the half-rotten timber baulks that yet made a kind of floor; Aneirin, like some great brooding bird of prey in his weatherwarm cloak watching us the while. A flash of blue deeper than any kingfisher at the breast showed where under the dim folds he was wearing his singing-robe, and his harp in its mare-skin bag lay nearby; and we paused for a moment, all of us hoping there might be a song, though a small one.

'Shall we build you a hearth?' someone said.

He put out his hand to a big block of stone thrusting out from the wall just above floor level. 'I have my hearth already.'

'Then shall we make the fire?' Faelinn asked.

And someone else, 'Have you the means to light it?'

'Make us a good mist, harper dear,' I said.

He smiled in his ragged beard, 'Nay, children, I will build the fire, I have the means to light it. It may be that the gods will send us a mist. Now go your ways.'

Clearly what came after was not for our eyes, and if there was singing it would not be for us. We bowed our heads one by one to the old man who we should not see again, and went back down the stairway.

At the foot of the stair I checked and the others went on without me. There were house martins darting to and fro overhead, their shadows darting after them in the evening light, about the business of nest building in the wall holes where tie beams had rotted away. Presently there would be new life in the old dead signal tower. I found the thought vaguely comforting, though I was not sure why. And as I looked up at them, they brought the memory of other house martins in the doorway of the bath house at home, and with it the thought of Conn. Oh, I should see him when we gathered to eat, but I wanted something else, a few quiet moments for saying goodbye . . .

I had used my sword – Gorthyn's sword – to cut rowan branches, and the keenness might have suffered. A good blade should take such service without much harm, but it could maybe do with a few strokes of the whetstone; and that would make good enough reason for my absence if Cynan asked for me – I was no longer free and lordless as I had been since Gorthyn's death.

'Tell Cynan I have taken my sword to the smithy. Not long I'll be,' I called after Faelinn.

And sword in hand I took my way to the armourer's shop. Surprisingly, firelight met me on the threshold. Conn and his mates had got together the fuel for one last fire, and were working steadily, plunging weapons into the red heart of it. Mostly captured Saxon weapons, but any of our own that we should not be carrying with us tonight. Iron that is forged and tempered by fire can be made useless by fire also.

The boy looked up first and saw me in the doorway, and said something over his shoulder to Conn whose back was towards me. And Conn turned, flinging a ruined sword blade on to the pile in the corner.

'One less for the Sea-wolves' taking,' he said.

I held Gorthyn's sword out to him. 'Has the whetstone gone the same way yet? I have been cutting rowan branches –'

He took it from me and crossed into the furthest part of the smithy, and I heard the 'whet-whet-whet' of the sharpening stone. In a little he came back, feeling the edge with his thumb. 'That should serve its purpose well enough.'

I took it and slid it home into the wolfskin sheath.

Neither of us knew what to say to each other. But standing there in the smoke-blackened mouth of the smithy we put our arms round each other's shoulders and strained close. 'It is but five springs since my father gave us to each other,' I said after a few moments, 'yet it seems as though we came into life together.'

'And the grief is on me that we may not go out of it together also.'

I forced a kind of laugh, not a very good one for it cracked in my throat. 'Somebody has to get Aneirin back to the King, and it will take the four of you at least, for his heart is not in it.'

And he laughed also, and stepped back so that only the tips of our fingers rested on each other's shoulders.

'When you get back to Dyn Eidin –' I began.

'If I get back to Dyn Eidin.'

'You will.' I knew that, because suddenly I saw the pattern that was forming for Conn; and when the Fates set their pattern on your forehead it does not melt away. 'When you get back to Dyn Eidin, go you to Fercos – glad he will be to have you back – and work for him until you may call yourself a swordsmith; then go back to the valley.'

'No bondman may become a smith.'

'And you are a smith, and therefore no longer a bondman. If you are a swordsmith, then you will be able to take Loban's place when he is past swinging a hammer – which cannot be long now – seeing that he has no son to follow him. Meanwhile, carry my love back to Luned and Old Nurse, and anyone else who you think may care to have it, and rub Gelert behind the ears for me.'

'You were always one to make patterns of other people's lives for them,' Conn said.

'Can you think of any better pattern for the following?'

He shook his head. 'Not really, no – unless it be to ride with you an hour after moonrise.'

So we parted, and I went to find Cynan.

The light was beginning to thicken, and as I passed the foot of the old signal tower, a waft of wood smoke came trailing downward from its ragged crest, and I thought I caught the sound of singing. So faint that I was not really sure that I heard it at all; faint as the sea in a shell, but oddly potent. A high sweet singing, that had nothing human in it – and that seemed to be made by more than one voice.

And the hair lifted a little on the back of my neck.

# – 18 –
# The Shining Company

We ate meat that evening as men should do before battle, for there were a few more horses than there were men to ride them, and we ate with our war-harness – dead men's harness for the shieldbearers – already on, and dead men's weapons lying beside us. The other horses had already been watered and fed – with a mere handful of fodder each, the last scraping of the Saxon forage store. If any man had asked me a few days since if I could chew my way through half raw horseflesh and enjoy it, knowing that within an hour I should almost certainly be dead, I should have thought them mad; but a fierce lightness of heart was upon us, and we shared the half raw meat among us, aye, and the laughter, too, and only wished that we might have had harpsong for our feasting. But Aneirin had matters of his own to see to, and still the faint waft of burning rowan wood drifted across the fort from the crest of the old signal tower.

As we ate, beyond our firelight the dusk came down and deepened into the dark and the dark began to lighten as the cloud-swept eastern sky took on a faint silver wash. And suddenly the rim of the moon slid up over the black edge of the world beyond the woods and the Saxon watchfires. There began to be a silent coming and going as men left the firelight and slipped away towards the barrack-row where our wounded lay. It was time that those too sorely hurt to ride were sent on their way; for they could not be left to fall into the hands of the Sea-wolves. The last mercy, among fighting men, performed by brother for brother, friend for friend. I was thankful in the depths of my belly, even as I swallowed my last red rag of meat and turned to the mail coif that lay beside me, that both Gorthyn and Lleyn were beyond the need of that mercy from me.

I mind now the slippery fish-scale chill of the ring mail even through the woollen cap as I pulled it on; the unaccustomed weight on the crown of my head, the way it flattened my ears inward, and the way sound came through it well enough but with the edges slightly blurred. The fine unlined mask I left hanging open for the moment, but I put on my own iron rimmed war-cap and buckled the strap under my chin, as men were doing all round the fires. So we flung on the hairy wolfskin cloaks and broached them at the shoulder, hitched at swordbelts and gathered up bucklers and lances. The men who had been in the barrack-rows came back to gather their own war gear, no man remarking on their return as no man had remarked on their going. Madog, who was now our standard-bearer, brought the standard out from the little still-roofed inner room where we had lodged it, carrying the lance somewhat at the slant, to let the folds hang free, there being as yet no wind under that shining sky to set them flowing. The torches struck the blood-red colour of the dragon-coils, the only colour in a world that was becoming striped frost-grey and ink-pool black like a badger's mask as the moon rose higher.

'Time to saddle up,' said the Captain's voice with an oddly hollow note to it, and as he stepped out from the shadows into the torchlight beside the standard, an uncanny figure, half a head taller than his usual seeming, we saw that he had pulled on Aethelfrith's great wolf helmet with the gilded comb in place of his own war-cap that he had given to one of his shield-bearers.

Speaking for myself, it was in that moment that I noticed the mist. Scarcely more than a faint thickening and gilding of the air round the torches, but mist all the same.

It was thicker down at the picket lines, thin scarves of it lying along the ground, reaching halfway up the horses' legs and making the ruins at the far side seem to have no standing on firm ground, though if one looked upward all was clear as a crystal ball overhead.

Such mists are common enough after dark in low country. But they seldom carry, even as faintly as this one did, the scent of burning rowan wood.

We saddled up and slipped in the bits. I mind Shadow playing with hers delicately in the way she had, as I have seen a girl playing with a flower. I took a final look at her shoes, tested her girth again though I had but that moment buckled it, and swung into the saddle, men to the right and left, before and behind me, doing the same thing.

Last moment orders were passed back down the picket lines from where Ceredig Fosterling who was a king's son sat his horse under the dragon standard; no shouted commands that might reach to Saxon ears: speed was everything; we must be across the river before the sea-wolves had time to gather against us. (We saw the wisdom of this having no wish to meet a storm of spears and throwing axes as we scrambled up the further bank.) There would be no sounding the charge, no sounds of horn before we reached the further side, but we should ride full gallop from the moment that we were clear of the gates. We should kill – and kill – and kill.

'Kill, and kill, and kill! A red harvest before we ourselves go down,' said a hollow voice in the great wolf helmet.

I pulled the mail mask across my face and made it fast. I pulled out my dirk and leaning forward, cut Shadow's tether only a splinter of time behind Cynan; almost the instant Faelinn did the same, and the rest on beyond him, pulling clear as the picket line fell loose and lax.

The Captain wheeled his tall bay and headed for the gates and troop after troop we followed, heeling the horses into a canter as we went. Down the broad straight track that gashed like a blade through the midst of the fort; and out through the north facing gateway where the thorn-work had been pulled aside and rotten timbers and fallen stones heaved back to give us wide passage.

Outside, the mist that had been only a faint scarfing along the ground as we came down from the horse-lines, thickened and rose to meet us; a mist that smoked up from the marshy ground, lying in broad swathes and wafts of ghost-paleness that marked the course of the river, and glimmering in the light of the rising moon. But overhead the sky was still clear, and from the high ground at the gate we could still see the Saxon fires, before we dropped lower, and lost sight of them as the mist took us. Aneirin's mist that could cover an army . . .

Clear of the gates we quickened, troop after troop, from a canter into a gallop, heading down to the ford, past the dark shape of Gorthyn's horse still lying where it had fallen. The standard lifted and streamed out on the wind of our going, and my ears were full of the rolling thunder of hooves over the rough ground. I snatched one glance behind me. I do not know why; it is a stupid thing to do when riding full gallop among a smother of horsemen. Maybe it was something to do with knowing that Conn would be just about mounting with Aneirin's small band at the west gate.

So – I turned in the saddle and looked back. And I saw the Companions on their last ride. I have never forgotten that sight, nor, I am thinking, will any of the Saxon kind who saw them coming and lived beyond that night. I saw the Wild Hunt. I saw riders with black eyesockets in glimmering mail where their faces should have been, grey wolfskins catching a bloom of light from the mist and the moon; a shining company indeed, not quite mortal-seeming, but made of another kind that might dissolve at any moment into the mist that smoked about them. Only for that bright breath of time I saw them by the white levin-light of the moon, as something in which I had no part at all. Then I faced forward and settled down to ride; a part of them once more, in a oneness that was more potent than the oneness we had come to know on Dyn Eidin training grounds. The bloom of light was on my own wolfskin, and my own mailed face, faceless with the rest.

Faelinn was beside me, and Cynan's crouched shoulders loomed ahead; and up beyond, the great wolf helmet, scarfed as though with smoke, showed where Ceredig the Captain rode under the wind-lifted standard.

We took the river at the ford. The raids of earlier days had taught us where the shallows ran for a couple of spears' lengths on either side of the paved way, and we took to the water on a broad front, sending up sheets of spray and churning the shallows till they seemed to boil.

We reached the far side and plunged ashore with a slipping scramble that turned the bank into a quagmire before half of us were over, and among the ruins on the north bank swung left-hand on to the remains of the north road and went straight down it like a flight of arrows.

Our horn was sounding now, not the charge, but the hunting call that sicks on the hounds when the quarry is in view. Ahead of us in the mist was a sudden urgent springing into life and movement; men snatching up their weapons and running for the stockades, and from the midst of the camp the hollow bull-bellowing of the Saxon war-horn burst out, answered and slung back by the clear yelping of our own hunting horn. '*Tran ta ta ran tran tra . . .*'

If only we had the hounds with us, I thought, but the last of the mingled pack of war and hunting dogs that had feather-heeled out from Dyn Eidin with us were dead days ago. And then suddenly we were giving tongue ourselves, like a pack of hounds in full cry as we swept down upon the stockade.

Then happened a strange thing, a few moments of wavering, a loss of purpose, at the rough defences, as the men behind them seemed gripped by something that was almost like the beginning of panic. I have learned since that the Saxons also have their Wild Hunt, though for them it is Woden himself who hunts

his demon pack through the stormy skies. Maybe it
was that, something of that, that they saw coming for
them. A few moments more, and they had rallied and
came roaring against us, armed with their long knives
and the terrible swinging war-axes. But in those few
moments we were through and over the breastwork
and into the Saxon camp.

We charged through them to the farmost side, and
turned and charged back, leaving a red wake behind
us. 'Not to break through, but to kill Saxons,' the
Fosterling had said. 'Not to break through, but to
kill –' and, ah yes, we killed, that night, killed and
killed, while our own numbers also bled away.

They were coming in on us from all sides in yelling
waves out of the mist, men from the further reaches of
the siege-ring, crossing the river by the ford, and the
shallows above the broken water, swarming in to
answer the bellowing summons of the war-horn.
Faelinn and I were still together at Cynan's back,
thrusting after the standard and the hunting horns;
until the standard went down, until the horn fell silent
in mid call.

We were no longer one fighting force, but splitting into
smaller and smaller knots of desperate struggling men.
Faelinn was gone. I do not know how or when for I
never saw him go; and I was no longer at Cynan's back,
but stirrup to stirrup with him, as we plunged through
the red embers of a scattered fire, towards the upreared
horsetail standard that marked the heart of the Saxon
swarm. I do not know how many or how few we were
by then, but the dull thunder of hooves on soft ground
was still behind us as we crashed into the shield-mass,
tearing great gaps in it, hurling it aside. But it seemed

that fresh men sprang out of the ground like dragon's teeth, two where every one had fallen. A heavy throw-spear homed in on my shield, and stuck there, making it useless so that I flung it aside. My sword hilt was slippery with blood, but the blood was not mine. A man came running low with his axe angled for Shadow's belly. I managed to wrench her aside at the last instant, and cut him down and trampled him into the ground. She reared up with a scream of fury, her forehooves lashing, and a man with a beard the colour of hot coals went down to join him with his forehead smashed in. The last charge of the Companions had become an ugly swirling soup of fire and mist and moonlight and snarling faces, the cries of men and the screams of stricken horses, the smell of blood and filth.

The mist had got into my head, and when, some way ahead, I saw a battered and half-naked body wearing the great wolf helmet hoisted aloft on spear-shafts, it was a moment before I knew whether it was Aethelfrith or the Fosterling.

Indeed we never saw Aethelfrith, that night.

The pressure round us was beginning to slacken a little, but I was scarcely aware of that, my one clear thought was that I must keep with Cynan, keep with Cynan at all costs . . . A blue-eyed ox of a man made for me swinging a pole axe. The blow would have lopped off my sword arm if it had landed but it went astray – or I was not where I had been when the blow started – and met my blade instead, and my sword went spinning into the mist, leaving me with an arm numbed to the shoulder by the impact.

Cynan was half a length ahead of me. He raised the battle shout, and I took it up from him, fumbling with

still numbed fingers for my dirk, which was the only
weapon left to me. There was no war shout behind us,
no drum of hooves.

We were not far from the road where it came out
from among the ruined warehouses, and the wayside
gravestones were about us in the trampled grass. And
outlined against the mist a huge man stood straddle-
legged and howling on a half-fallen burial stone,
swinging a great iron-studded club two-handed above
his head. Cynan made for him, his sword upswung,
which would have been madness if he had been interested in living, and the Saxon dived in under the sweep
of the blade; and I heard the ringing crack as the iron
shod club took my lord on the side of the head, bursting his helmet strap and sending the warcap leaping
away. I caught the man off balance as he stumbled
down after his blow, and drove my dirk in under his
still up-flung arm, and left him coughing his heart's
blood up into the graveside grass as I went after
Cynan. He was shaking his head, then he straightened
in the saddle – only a glancing blow, then, after all –
and rode on as though he were quite unaware of it, and
of the battle raging round us, which was strange. But
stranger still, I realized slowly that there *was* no battle
raging round us. Maybe we had broken through the
fringe of it and come out on the far side. More likely, I
think looking back, that somehow in the mist and the
confusion, the last of the fighting had flowed over and
past us, leaving us behind.

Just the two of us.

I could hear scattered shouting in the distance; but
close at hand there was the kind of half quiet that
descends on a battle field when the fighting is done and

before the kites and ravens gather. Only a faint blur of brightness here and there in the mist told where the embers yet remained of cooking fires that we had scattered under our horses' hooves. There were bodies in the trampled grass, that cried out or writhed or lay still. Presently there would be torches moving over the river levels, as men went looking for their own wounded among the dead, stripping the gold and ring-mail and fine weapons from our dead, our wounded. It did not do to think of our wounded, so I did not think, not then. Presently the ravens would come, and wolves of the four-footed kind.

Cynan had let the reins fall on his horse's neck, and the poor beast had come to a weary halt. I thought that he was breathing him before he turned and rode back towards that distant shouting. But next instant, without a word, without a sound of any kind, he sagged forward across Anwar's neck. And almost at the same instant a wild-eyed riderless horse came plunging by and crashed into the big chestnut's rump.

Cynan's horse had had all that he could take of fire and shouting and weaponclash and the smell of blood; he was frightened already by the sudden bewildering change in his rider; and the crash of another horse unseen against his rump was too much for him. With a shrill neigh of terror he plunged away in full gallop.

I drove my heel into Shadow's flank and was away after him, coming up with him just as Cynan was beginning to slip sideways from the saddle. I slammed the bloody dirk back into my belt, and controlling the mare as best I could with my knees, got an arm round him before he could slip further, and caught up the reins from where they lay on the terrified horse's neck.

On the edge of a thicket of alder trees I got him reined to a halt at last, and he stood shivering and sweating, blowing distressfully through flared nostrils. I spoke his name softly, soothing him with hand and voice, bidding him stand; and dropped the reins over Shadow's head to keep the two of them together while I saw what was to be done about Cynan.

He was still living. I could hear his snoring breaths, and feel his heart beating when I got a hand under the folds of his cloak; but he gave no sign of hearing me when I spoke his name. Not such a glancing blow after all. My hand when I touched his head came away sticky; and when I craned over him I could see in the cobweb light the black ooze that would be crimson in daylight, seeping through the ringmail of his coif all up and down the right-hand side.

Far off behind me I could still hear the faint last sounds of battle. If I had been alone, I think I would have gone back, not out of any false heroics, but because it would have seemed the natural thing to do. But Cynan was with me, and the training of a year was with me, and I never thought of it. We had gone into battle as an Arrowhead; Faelinn was gone, but I had brought my lord off, and now it was for me to get him away, living, and into safety if that might be.

Which would seem to mean finding Conn and the rest and joining up with them – supposing that they also had got away.

Still sitting Shadow among the alder trees, I thought, quite clearly and coolly. The mist would give us cover, and there would be no hunt out after us, so there was time to think, though not too long. I dared not try to pull off Cynan's mail coif to see his hurt; I had a horrible fear that if I did that his head might fall to pieces; and in any case, if I got him off his horse to see it I should never get him mounted again. In the end I managed to get off his neck-cloth, and bound it round his head over the coif with some kind of crazy hope that it might help to stop the bleeding. I got him carefully balanced in the saddle, and dismounting myself, pulled off my own scarf and tore it lengthwise, and with one half lashed his wrists together under Anwar's neck and with the other bound his feet under the horse's belly.

When all was made safe as might be, I hauled myself back into my own saddle and gathered up both reins. And so rode away from the place where the last of the Shining Company were still dying.

I headed north, though keeping well away from the road. If I did not find the others, at least we were travelling in the right direction. There was no hunt on our tail, but I kept my ears turned behind me all the same, and held to the scrubby woods and off the cleared land as much as might be. Time and again Cynan began to slip sideways in the saddle, and I had to pause to get him righted again. But we came at last into thicker woodland fringing the true forest, and following the sound of quick water reached the bank of a burn coming down from the high moors to join the river which we had now left far behind. The moon was swinging over towards the dark mass of the Penuin, but a new light was waking in the east, and the mist still scarfing the river valley was turning milky. I paused to let the horses drink, keeping a careful eye on Cynan to see that he did not go off over Anwar's head, and when they had drunk their fill, dismounted to scoop up a few palmfuls of ice cold water for myself. I tried to give some in my cupped palms to Cynan, forgetting that there was no way that he could have drunk with his mask still across his face. But anyway, it seemed he was still out of his body. I did not let myself think about the time when he came back into it – if he did come back into it. I did not let myself think beyond the next thing at all; and the next thing was getting further into the safety of the forest.

I had just picked up Shadow's reins again when a little puff of air came down to us through the trees, and Anwar pricked his ears, then flung up his head and whinnied as a horse does in greeting to his own kind. And from somewhere upstream on the edge of hearing, a horse whinnied in reply.

# – 19 –
# The Road Back

When the blackness that had come rolling over me cleared away, I was lying in the long streamside grass of a woodland clearing. Staring up I could see trees arching over me, and beyond them a clear morning sky.

I heard movement and a murmur of voices and a horse ruckling down its nose. I got to my elbow and then sat up; and the world spun round me, then settled. Cynan lay close by, with Aneirin and the scout crouching over him. Conn and his mates had taken our horses down to the little willow-fringed pool that broke the fall of the stream just there, and were washing off their legs. The other beasts were tethered on the far side of the clearing. Having made sure that everybody was there, I got my knees under me and moved in for a closer look at Cynan.

They had got his mail coif off him, and his head had not fallen to pieces, but a horrible black and broken place led out from under the clotted hair on his temple and down to his jaw, like over-ripe fruit. Aneirin had swabbed away the worst of the blood with somebody else's neck-cloth, sopping from the stream, and was picking splinters of bone out of the pulpy mess where it crossed his cheek-bone, while Cynan lay seeming to feel nothing of what went on, his right eye not quite shut so that a thin line of white showed under the lid, the left too lost in swelling and broken bruises to be sure that there was an eye there at all.

'He has not come back to himself?' I croaked.

Aneirin looked up for a moment. 'No. But it seems that you have.'

'But he will come back?'

Aneirin went steadily on with his work. 'It is in my mind that he will come back, though something lacking in the beauty that set girls' hearts quickening. Lucky it is for him that the heaviest part of the blow landed where it did, and not a thumb's length further – this way, or his brains would have been like an addled egg within his skull. What was it? A club?'

'A club, with iron studs in it.' Vileness twisted in my belly and rushed up into my throat, and I rolled over hurriedly towards the burn, and threw up what little I had in me into the waterside bushes.

When I turned back, Cynan had not moved, but there was a kind of wincing in his face, and as we watched, his right eye opened. For a short while he lay staring straight upward, then forced his one-eyed gaze back from his private distance to buckle on to our faces, slowly, painfully, shifting from one to another of us. The other three had brought the horses up from the stream and we were all of us round him by that time. But the faces that he wanted were not there. He gave a long shuddering sigh, and closed his eye as though it was all too much for him, and sank away from us again.

I looked up at Aneirin in sudden fear, and Aneirin looking up also, caught the question that I could not quite speak. 'Na, na, did I not say? He will mend in time. The strength is in him, his body will mend in time.' He was making fast the makeshift bandage as he spoke. Then he added as though half to himself, 'But he needs rest. Several days of rest, and I can spare him only one. We must mount and ride at dusk, even if we bind him into the saddle again as you brought him here, and be far enough from Catraeth by tomorrow's dayspring.'

The guide put in, 'If we can keep him in the saddle through tonight, I can bring you by dayspring to a safe place where we can lie up for the needful days with no fear of Sea-wolves.'

So the thing was settled. Cynan seemed to have drifted into a kind of sleep.

'Sleep is what he needs, more than all else that we can give him,' Aneirin said. 'But not unwatched, lest he sleep too deeply and come to harm.'

'I will watch him,' I said.

Aneirin shook his head. 'You are in scarcely better shape than he is, and you also must sleep.'

'I will take the watch,' Conn said, close behind me.

I crouched closer to Cynan and glared up at them. 'No!'

Conn told me after, long after, that I looked like a falcon mantling over its kill, and just as crazy.

'You can trust me,' he said steadily. 'I'll not let harm come to him.'

'No!' I said again. 'I am his shieldbearer. I brought him off: he's mine!'

One of the others, I think it was the old scout, started to try to reason with me, but Aneirin held out a hand to halt him, and said quietly, 'Prosper takes the first watch.'

And against Aneirin's word there could be no protest.

'Wake him if his sleep becomes too deep,' he said to me. 'Rouse me if there is any change in him.'

So I took that first watch sitting beside Cynan with my arms crossed on my up-drawn knees, while the others got some sleep and the horses grazed the streamside grass. The light grew and warmed to full day and the last of the mist wisped away in the early sunlight; and it did not seem possible that only a few hours and a few miles away the whole of my world – it seemed like the whole of my world – had died in the marshes and the croplands before Catraeth. There was a waking of birdsong among the branches, and a yellow butterfly hovered across the clearing. Those few miles away the Saxons would be gathering up their slain and building their death-fires. There would be many death-fires for the Saxon kind, wolves and ravens for the Shining Company. But none of that seemed quite real, and what reality it had was going further and further away.

I do not think I slept on my watch, but certainly I was not aware of any movement behind me, before a hand came on my shoulder, and Conn's voice in my ear said, 'My turn now. Sleep you.'

We had made no outcry of joy at finding each other again, both living, but his arm catching me from a headlong fall was the last thing I remembered before the swimming darkness engulfed me on the edge of the clearing, and now, with the quiet feel of his hand on my shoulder, I toppled over beside Cynan and slept where I lay, leaving him to watch over both of us.

Twilight was gathering under the trees when I woke again. The evening ration of wheat cake from the saddlebags was given out, and I made a sort of gruel with Cynan's share, crushed and mixed with water on a dockleaf, and tried to spoon it in to him on the tip of my knife. He swallowed a little not really seeming aware that he did so, then turned his head away.

'Enough, for the time being. It will not harm him to starve for a while,' Aneirin said. 'Eat your own, now. We must saddle up and be on our way.'

So I pushed in my own few mouthfuls, and going down to the stream with the rest, drank, and dashed the cold water over my face and neck which made me feel somewhat less as though I was walking in a dream.

How we got Cynan on to the back of his sidling and snorting chestnut I have never been quite sure, save that at one point I was sitting behind the saddle myself while Conn and the bellows-boy heaved him up to me. But once in the saddle we did not after all need to tie him there. It had always been said of him and his brothers that they had been born on horseback and suckled by a mare, and certainly I have known him sleep on horseback without coming off. And once we had him astride Anwar he stayed there, as though his body knew the way of it, though I do not think his head knew night from day. But he made no move to pick up the reins; I did that, and as we headed out from the clearing, Conn and I rode close on either side.

By full dark we had left the woods behind us and were out on to open moors, climbing steadily towards what felt like the roof of the world; a world of little sky-reflecting tarns and great rolling hill shoulders and upland bog country in which we would have been lost save for the scout, the mealy tail of whose horse was our leading light. Once, for a while, our hooves rang hollow on the remains of a paved road, but soon we turned off it and were alone with the emptiness once more. There had begun to be a smell of rain in the wind, and the moon, when it rose, had an oily ring round it. But the wild weather that was assuredly coming was still holding off when we came down out of the emptiness again into a narrow wooded valley. The woods were hushing softly as we came down among them. We were all fairly spent by then; weary men on weary horses, and Cynan's strange empty strength had given out, so that Conn and I rode with our shoulders braced against his on either side to keep him still in the saddle.

Aneirin sniffed the wind like a hound and said, 'We had best be finding this refuge of yours soon, I am thinking.'

And the scout answered him, 'It is not lost. Did I not say by dayspring?'

And sure enough, a mile or so further down the valley, we found the hardness of a made road under the turf again, and not long after, with the grey light growing about us, and the pale gleam of running water showing through the trees on our left, we came to ruined walls again, and pavement under docks and brambles, and the feeling we were beginning to know well, of a place where men had lived but lived no longer.

'I am weary of ruins,' Credne grunted.

'They have their uses. Unless they have fallen since I was last here, there are still a few rags of thatch on some of the outbuildings,' the scout told him. 'Should help to keep the rain off; and the Saxons will not come this way, as I have said.'

'What is this place?'

'Once it was a Roman posting station. The road crosses the stream by a ford just yonder.'

'It seems you know the place well,' Aneirin said, faintly questioning.

'I was born and bred a mile or so down the valley.'

We rode in among the tangle of hazel and thorn scrub and the tumbled stone footings of walls, dropped the reins over our horses' ears and slid heavily to the ground. We found the stable block with the skeleton of half a roof still on the far end of it, and laid Cynan there; and still moving in a kind of dream I helped Aneirin re-dress his wound while the others saw to the horses.

Afterwards we ate what was left of the wheat cakes, and scattered in search of dry wood while there was still dry wood to be found, then lay down to get a little sleep, Aneirin himself this time keeping watch. Presently we must hunt, if we wished to eat; but sleep seemed more important just then. There was no knowing if Cynan was sleeping or waking. He had taken in a little of the wheaten mush that I had made for him, and I think that when we spoke to him he heard, but he made no answer, and seemed to take no heed of what went on about him, just lay there with his one serviceable eye not quite closed.

I lay close beside him so that if he moved I should know, and tried to sleep myself. But though I could not seem to be truly awake, I could not be truly asleep either, but skimmed along the surface like a mayfly on a stream, and every time I dipped below the surface, ugly dreams drove me up again to the awareness of Cynan beside me, and the rising wind and the hush of rain. I must have slept at last, more deeply than I knew, because when at last I woke with eyes that felt hot in my head and the half remembered wrack of evil

dreams still clinging to me, there was firelight and a
kind of shelter rigged up from branches with our
cloaks made fast over them, and the smell of food. I
suppose it was the smell of food that had roused me.
The scout was cooking a fine fat trout over the fire on
the point of his dagger.

'Did I not say that I knew this stream?' he said.

There were four trout among us; not enough, but
better than nothing. I took one between Cynan and me
and teased the worst of the bones out of Cynan's half,
then put it into his hand before falling to like a wolf on
my own. But when I looked round at him, it was still
there. I took it away again and began to put bits into
his mouth, and he chewed and swallowed like an
obedient child. And still I felt nothing, nothing at all
through the numbness that made all things seem a long
way off and not quite real.

The wind was going round to the east, driving the
rain straight up the valley, roaring and booming
through the trees on a new note. Then I heard it
coming, sweeping towards us from far down the
valley: the sound of hooves; a charging, a stampede,
sweeping nearer at a speed that was beyond the speed
of mortal horses even at full gallop. So must come the
Wild Hunt, skeining through the stormy skies and
followed by all the souls of the dead, only that yet
again it lacked the crying of hounds. I thought – I am
not sure what I thought – for those few moments as the
ghost-riders came roaring up through the trees it
seemed that I was hearing again the last ride of the
Shining Company. The earth-shaking thunder of
hooves was right upon us, filling all the space between
earth and sky; there was a great screaming inside my

head, a vortex of rolling manes and fire-filled nostrils, a crash of power and terror like a breaking wave that reared up and arched over us – and passed on, blending into the booming storm voice of the trees.

I saw startled faces round the wind-driven fire.

'Only a trick of the valley's shape,' the scout said. 'It makes some kind of horn to catch the wind when it blows hard from this quarter, and conjures it into the sound of galloping horses.'

'You could, maybe, have warned us,' Aneirin said with faint amusement.

The scout spread his hands, 'I did not think, having known the sound all my boyhood. But you will know now why, once having heard it, the sea-wolves leave this place alone.'

I heard them quite clearly, but there were matters of my own in those few moments that concerned me more. The wild stampede had caught me up and back into the company of my sword-brethren, before sweeping on to leave me behind. And in doing so had stripped from me the merciful numbness of the past two days, and left me awake once more, and stripped naked and raw to what had happened. I had known it with my mind, the thing that had happened at Catraeth between the river and the woods; but now for the first time I was knowing it in my heart's core.

I got to my feet, mumbling something about going to see that all was well with the horses, and blundered out into the dusk and the booming wind. (Three times more that night before the storm blew itself out, I heard the wind play that trick. But having done its work on me it remained only the wind playing at ghost-cavalry among the trees.) I went across to the place where we had picketed the horses in a sheltered angle where two walls met in a tangle of hazel scrub. Shadow swung her head towards me at sound of my coming, and snickered softly down her nose in greeting. And I put my arm over her neck and drove my face into the harsh live wetness of her mane, and cried as I had never cried before, and as I do not think that I have ever cried since; for the last ride of the Shining Company, for the death of my friends, for strength and beauty and brightness gone out of the world though we had not killed the white hart; cried, I think, for my own boyhood that I had thought myself grown out of years ago, but that in truth I had only lost at Catraeth two nights since; cried for Cynan of the Three Battle Horsemen of Dyn Eidin – for what was left of Cynan . . .

An arm came across my shoulders, and Conn's voice under the beating of the wind said, 'Easy now, easy, brother,' as I have heard him speak to a nervous horse at the shoeing, its upturned hoof between his leather-aproned knees.

He did not speak again for a while, only kept his arm there; and presently the quiet pressure of it began to steady me, though my grief remained the same. Bewilderment as well as grief. 'Why us?' I choked out. 'Why me and Cynan, of us all?'

'Maybe there are others,' Conn said.

I shook my head. There would be no others, and in his inmost heart he knew that as well as I did. He said, 'Maybe the Fates have marked their pattern on your forehead and on Cynan's as a while back you told me that they had marked it on mine. But among mortal men there can be no knowing why.'

I turned away from Shadow. I was in control again. 'Has he changed –' I began.

'No, no change. With a dent on the head like that, it takes time, I am thinking.'

'It is more than that,' I said, thinking the thing out as I went along, as I had not been able to do before. 'He lost both those mad brothers of his within days of each other. Cymran he killed himself as one puts a wounded horse out of its pain. I saw him do it – even when the Fosterling split the tribes up among different troops he never tried to split up those three. The Giant's Seat would have cracked apart . . .'

'He still needs you,' Conn said. 'Come – and maybe the Giant's Seat will yet hold together.'

We were back at the far end of the stable block, firelight jinking out between the freshly rigged cloaks of our shelter; and I ducked in out of the wind and the driving rain.

We lay in that place for several days, six maybe, or seven, while the strength came back into Cynan's body. Quite early in those days I said to Aneirin, 'Let you ride on. It is for you to reach the King as swiftly as maybe. Leave me Conn, if you will, and take the others, and we will follow you as soon as my Lord Cynan has strength for the journey.'

But he shook his head. 'Neither of you has even my small knowledge of the healer's art.'

'Tell me what must be done, and I can do it. It is for you to get the word back to Mynyddog, of how we carried out his orders, and what came of it.'

'The King will have other messengers in these parts – a man on a fast horse to carry the tidings; and he will know it soon enough. The thing that is mine to do and can be done by no other man is to make the Great Song of the Gododdin at Catraeth, and for that there is no hurry.' And he took his harp out of its bag and began to tune and cherish it as he did daily, though he had not woken it since that last night at Catraeth.

And I went on about my task of gathering firewood. But his words clung about the back of my mind. 'The King will have other messengers in these parts – a man on a fast horse –'

Did Mynyddog know already? Maybe he had known while there was still time – while relief could still have reached us. There was a bitter taste in my mouth.

We hunted, during those days. There was wild pig in the forest, so our guide said, but we had not the hounds nor the spears nor the heart within us for dealing with a boar at bay. Credne had a bow and a few precious arrows, and with that and what we could improvise from our own gear, we shot and trapped through the woods about us, and tickled for char and trout in the stream and ate whatever came our way. Once it was a vixen. Fox meat makes rank eating, but it holds off hunger well enough.

The wild weather died out, though the forest was sodden and the few tracks turned to quagmires when we rode out once more on our journey. We rode in daylight now, the need for darkness being passed, up into the high blunt hills of the Penuin that were like the roof of the world; and I mind once on that first day, turning in the saddle to look away over much of the countryside that had opened to us when we had come riding down from the high moors, nine hundred of us, with Catraeth still ahead. Mile after mile of rolling forest, greener now with occasional clearings in it showing like the rents in a shaggy cloak; and far off on the edge of the world the grey swordblade gleam of the sea. But the faint blur of hearth smoke that we had seen rising here and there among the nearer woods no longer lifted into the air. That told its own story of villages left without men of working age, and women gathering up the old and the children and heading back for the coastwise settlements, leaving cold hearths behind them. We had made our mark on the Saxon kind.

'If we got Aethelfrith –' I began, as Aneirin reined in his horse beside me, looking the same way.

'If we got Aethelfrith. Aye,' he said, his eyes narrowed as he also searched for hearth smoke among the low wooded hills. I mind the jagged shape that his face made, cut darkly out of the sky. 'If the Flame Bringer is gone, then the Saxon flood is stayed, here in the north, for another fifty years, as it was for Artos after Badon.'

'I never saw him, when we made the last charge. How if he was not there? How if he was clear, to lead them again on another day?'

Aneirin was silent for a moment, his gaze still narrowed into a distance, 'Two years, maybe three,' he said at last.

'So great a difference, hanging on one man's life?'

'I believe so,' he said briefly. 'The word will like enough have reached Dyn Eidin by now. We shall know soon enough.' And he touched his heel to his horse's flank and we rode on after the others.

At nightfall the scout brought us down into a stone-walled and heather-thatched settlement of our own

kind. People who had been of Bernicia before the
Saxons came spreading inland from the coast and
drove them up into the hills. We told them what they
asked, but they did not ask much, and truly I think
that they were beyond greatly caring what happened in
the world of men, so long as their own thatch was left
unburned and their sheep to graze on the lean hill
pasture. But they gave us what little food they could
spare, and the warmth of their fire to sit by.

We rode slowly for Cynan's sake, though indeed
after the days of rest and refuge in the old posting
station his wound was healing clearly under its crusted
mess. Both his eyes were open, though I was doubtful
of what, if anything, he saw through them. And something of his strength was returning to him. He
mounted and dismounted without much need of help,
and rode with the rest of us – we were careful to keep
him always in the midst of our little band, where
someone could instantly catch his rein. He ate the food
that was put before him, and lay down between me
and Conn to sleep. And indeed in his sleep, despite the
half-healed wound that marred his cheek and forehead, he looked almost to be himself again, but still
he seemed shut off from all that went on around him,
and he never spoke. He was like one of those terrible
slain warriors who, so the ancient stories tell, were
put into the great Cauldron of Anwn, and came out
seemingly restored to life but without the power of
speaking.

For Cynan's sake we rode slowly, as I have said. But
even so, on the fourth evening we struck the Legions'
road again, just south of Onnum on the Wall, and
passed through the fallen gateway.

We were back among the hills that we had ridden through on the long-distance patrols last autumn.

That night we sat by the fire of a one-valley chieftain, where some of our patrols, though none that Cynan or I were on, had sat before. And that night the scout said to Aneirin, 'From now on the way is plain for you among your own hills. Now, therefore, I turn south again to mine, in the morning.'

'Will you not ride on with us to Dyn Eidin? It is in my mind that there will be a golden reward for you from the King's hand.'

The scout shook his head. 'I am a man of Bernicia; I return now to my own people. Give me the horse in reward, if you will.'

Later that night, when we had eaten and drunk, and it was time for the asking and answering of questions, and when Cynan had lain down to sleep in the further shadows with his cloak over his head, the chieftain asked, staring into his mead cup, 'Are there more of you?'

And Aneirin asked, 'How many but ourselves have passed this way, coming from Catraeth?'

The chieftain shook his head. 'No others.'

'Then there are no more of us.'

There was silence for a short while, and the hound bitch at the chieftain's feet whimpered in her sleep.

Then it was Aneirin's turn at the questioning. 'A month – nigh on two months, since, did a rider bearing the Cran-Tara come to your rath?'

'One came,' said the chieftain. 'The word was for a hosting at Habitancum on the fifth day. One man in every three, as many horses as might be, beef on the hoof.'

'So few?' Aneirin said.

'One man in three,' the chieftain repeated. 'That was the summons of the Cran-Tara. My younger son went, fourteen spearmen from this rath, the flower of my stables and my cattle yard. They waited at the hosting place three days; then the King sent word dismissing the warhost, so they came home.'

There was silence again, and the chief stooped forward to fondle the bitch's fluttering ears; mainly, I think, that he might not have to look into our faces. 'The willingness was there; but the King – my Lord Mynyddog – dismissed them. Not upon us, the blame.'

The hound whimpered as he pulled too hard at her ears.

'Not upon you, the shame,' Aneirin said.


Next morning we set out on the last long stretch of our homeward ride. We did not claim guest right in any man's hall after that, but slept rough in the ruins of old forts and signal stations, hunting as we went, as though we were still in enemy territory.

On the fourth day, towards evening, we came in sight of Dyn Eidin.

# – 20 –
# Ghosts

Word of the end of the Companions had clearly reached Dyn Eidin days ago. And as we rode up from the Royal Farm we could smell the stunned grieving of the town all about us; and hear the silence. No town that is not dead can ever be completely quiet, but along Eidin Ridge there was no more the ready-making for the war-trail, the smoke and clangour of the armourers, the neigh of horses, the young men and the laughter and the snatches of song. There were people about. Women spinning in doorways looked up as we rode by, men dropped whatever they were doing and turned to watch us pass, children and dogs were playing in the dust beside the cobbled way. Several times girls called out to us, asking for this one or that one of the Companions, for Tydfwlch or Madog or Morien, twice girls came running to ask for Cynan, not recognizing him. Aneirin made them some kind of reply; I do not know what. There was no welcome. Later, there might be, but not now, the news and the loss was still too raw. Only we felt eyes following us after we had gone by; the eyes of the people of Eidin, wondering why we had come back, of all those who had ridden out, less than two moons ago.

We came up past the steep horse-paddock to the gate of the Dyn, and the men of the guard passed us through into the outer court. Word of our coming must have run on ahead, and men were gathered there

to draw us in; men whose faces we knew, it seemed
from another life. A knot of richer colour showed
where the women of the royal house stood clustered
together before the inner gate, and out of the midst of
them the Princess Niamh came running to catch the
reins of Cynan's horse. She checked there, looking up
at him – *she* knew him well enough – and I saw her
face puzzled for a moment, then white and stricken.
Cynan did not return her look, or seem to know that
she was there at all. One of the older women came and
pulled her away. Then the men of the Teulu were all
around us as we dropped from the saddle, and hands
came out of nowhere as it seemed, to take the reins and
lead our horses away. We were back where we had not
thought to be again, standing like ghosts in the outer
court of Dyn Eidin.

That night, our battle-stained rags replaced by decent
clothes, and the worst of our filth washed off, we sat
at supper once again in the King's Mead Hall. We
knew by then that Aethelfrith was still living. The
messengers had come in days ago, and the thing was
common knowledge through Dyn Eidin. And the food,
when it came, had a bitter taste to it.

Conn and his mates, who had not supped in Hall
before, sat on the guest bench just within the main
door. Aneirin was in his old place at the High Table.
Cynan sat among the warriors of the Teulu at one of
the long side tables – that also was his old place, but
before my time – they made him welcome there, but I
saw how they left a little space on either side of him,
as though no one cared to risk touching or being
touched; and I wondered if living men had left the

same gap between themselves and the silent warriors who had passed through the Cauldron of Anwn.

The horn sounded and the King was brought in, leaning on the shoulders of two of his household warriors, the Queen and the royal women following after, the Champion and the steward and others of the household; and among them, Phanes of Syracuse.

I had not known whether he was alive or dead, and a warmth woke in me at sight of him, though he looked ten years older than when I had seen him last, and walked stooping a little forward and to one side as I have seen men walk since, hunched over an old body wound.

They eased the King into his High Seat; the horn sounded again and the food was brought in. Food as fitting for a King's Hall as ever we had eaten there, and yellow mead with its faintly bitter after-taste that I had never noticed so strongly before. But no harpsong; not that night; and the Hall itself was half empty. I mind the bare benches in the lower Hall that had been built on to make room for the Three Hundred, and the great roof ties naked of the weapons and armour that had used to hang there.

Cynan seemed aware of the emptiness also, the first time that he had shown awareness of the world around him. More than once I saw him lift his head and look about him as though seeking the crowding faces that he had been used to find there. Then, failing in the search, he would sink away inside himself again, and return to playing with the food before him or watching the fire.

When the eating was done, and the royal women had gone back to their own place, leaving the task of keeping the mead cups filled to the armourbearers, the King stirred in his great chair and turned stiffly to Aneirin, seeming to nerve himself for what he knew must come.

'Now, Prince of Bards, let you tell me what there is for the telling.'

There was a sudden piercing silence all up and down the Hall. And in the silence, Aneirin told; all that there was for the telling, from the night attack on the royal steading, on through the taking over of the old fort, the raids on the gathering Saxon war hordes, the waiting for the men of Elmet and the other British kingdoms who never came.

I was watching the King's face, and I saw how it flinched and then set into a mask when Aneirin reached that part, and how his gaunt hands gripped on the foreposts of his chair until the knuckles were like bare bones, betraying all that the mask concealed. Aneirin never paused but told steadily on; of the tightening siege and the decision to make that last desperate charge. The decision also that he himself must return living to Dyn Eidin.

The silence that closed over his words was such that if a little pale moon-moth had fluttered through the Hall we would have heard the pulsing of its wings. And in the silence, Aneirin turned his head and looked down the warrior-benches to where I stood with the mead jar in my hands. 'There is no more that I can tell at this time,' he said. 'Prosper, son of Gerontius, shieldbearer to Cynan MacClydno, the rest of the telling is for you.'

I had not thought of that, though I might have done, and for a moment I felt the breath gone from me. I set the mead jar down slowly and with great care, as though a drop spilled on the trestle board would have been the end of the world. Mynyddog's gaze was upon me. I could feel it. I could feel the eyes of every man in the King's Hall save Cynan who sat still staring into the fire.

My breath came back to me, and I took up the story where Aneirin had laid it down. I told it as well as was in me, though stumblingly and with long gaps between, knowing that until – unless – Cynan came back to himself again, I was the only one who could tell it, just as Aneirin was the only one who could make the Great Song. I told of the last ride of the Shining Company. I told of the fighting between the river and the woods. I told of that last sight of our Captain who was the King's son, broken and hoisted aloft on the points of spears (I thought for a moment something moved behind the mask). I told of the end of the fighting, and how Cynan was wounded among the gravestones by the north road, and how I had killed the man with the club, and of what came after until with Cynan tied on to his horse's back, we came up with Aneirin and the others at the edge of dawn.

The story, my part of the story, was done, and I looked to give it back to Aneirin; but he left it lying, feeling I supposed that what was left did not need a King's bard for the telling. So I took it up again. It could be told briefly enough. 'We lay up for the daylight and rode through the night, and came down to a place that had once been a Roman posting station; a place our guide knew of, safe from the Saxon kind. We waited there several days, for my Lord Cynan to gather some strength. We rode on, by day for we were beyond the Saxons' reach by then. We came into Gododdin territory and our guide turned back to his own people. We lodged that night with a clan chieftain known to our patrols of last year. My Lord Aneirin asked him if the Cran-Tara had come to his rath. He said that it had come and that his younger son and fourteen warriors of the rath had gone to the hosting place and waited there for three days, and that then my Lord the King had bidden them back to their own hearths. He said "Not upon us, the blame."'

I heard what I had said. And I saw the King's face show for an instant behind the mask, and there was a coldness in my belly.

Then Aneirin spoke again, in that trained harper's voice of his that seemed to be pitched only for the King and yet carried the length of the half-empty Hall. 'So – we have told all that is ours for the telling. Now let Mynyddog the King tell in his turn, whatever is his.'

For the time that might cover three heartbeats, Mynyddog sat looking at his own skeleton hand on the forepost, turning it so that the taperlight woke the life and colour in the great ring he wore. Then he looked up and said straightly, 'Ask then, Prince of All Bards, and I will answer.'

Aneirin asked gently, 'My Lord the King, why did the warhost never come?'

And the King answered, 'Because no other of the northern kingdoms answered the call, having fears and frontiers of their own to spend their swords on; each one fearing what his neighbours would do if he sent his warriors out on such a war-trail.'

He was fighting that dry brittle cough. In the old days his son or his bard would have taken up the speaking for him; but his son was dead, and Aneirin could not speak for him in this.

'What of the Gododdin war-bands bound by the Cran-Tara?' Aneirin said.

The King's voice was straining in his chest, but he forced the words out. 'If I had sent my own warbands, their chance would have been small indeed, against the joined hosts of Deira and Bernicia. I judged that my shining and beloved Three Hundred were enough to lose. I judged also that in their going down, they would take such a Hero's Portion of the Saxons with them that they would come thrusting no further into our heartlands until they had done licking their wounds; a few years, the lifetime of a man . . .'

'Aye, we bought your time for you, a little —'

I thought for an instant of the sunlight lying across the schoolroom table at home, and the unrolled Herodotus with the mould spots on the parchment. 'Tell them in Sparta —'

'But after the time is up?'

'By then I may have found a way to bind my sticks into a faggot, after all,' said the King.

The shamed and angry silence of the Teulu was enough to set the roof beams afire, though in all the place no man moved.

'My Lord the King,' Aneirin said, 'could you not have trusted us with the truth?'

The King drew a long painful breath. 'No man should ride on such a trail altogether without hope. I was not quite without hope myself, at the outset.' He began to cough, arched over himself, making yellow flecks on the chequered silk at the breast of his mantle.

And while he still coughed, though the paroxysm was passing, Cynan who had sat unmoving and staring into the fire throughout, got to his feet and stood swaying, then with a terrible howling cry, pitched forward across the table, scattering the remnants of the meal and oversetting the mead jar in a yellow flood.

On the King's orders, when he could speak again, we bore Cynan to the inner palace. Word of what had happened must have run ahead of us, for the Queen herself with some of her women hovering behind her met us in the gateway to the inner court.

'Carry him up to the women's house,' she said. 'It will be easier for us to tend him there.'

So we carried him up to the women's house that clung like a cluster of lime-washed birds' nests to the highest point of the fortress rock and laid him on a bed-place spread with soft rugs and pillows of striped wool that showed as bright as flowers in the light of wax tapers that had already been brought in.

The Princess Niamh was there. She made a tiny whimpering sound, bending over him as we laid him down, and touched the broken side of his face as women do these things, very gently.

'That will not help,' said the Queen, and bade one of her women fetch hot water and clean linen, and certain herbs from her still-room, called for a brazier, and ordered the warriors who had come to help carry him, away back to their own place. I think the order was for me too, but I did not go with them. I could not help it that I was in the women's part of the palace. I belonged where Cynan was, and I think the Queen must have understood that, for she did not repeat the order.

For a moment, when the Princess touched him, his eyelids had begun to flicker, and I had thought that he was coming back to himself, but the flickering ceased, and he drifted from us again. By morning, despite the strange brews that the Queen trickled into him drop by drop, and the pungent smoke of the herbs burning on the charcoal brazier, he was in some kind of fever.

The King's own physician came up from the monastery and pronounced the wound clean, but shook his head and talked of bruising to the brains, also of possession by demons brought away from the battlefield. He shook his head at the Queen's remedies too, and ordered different ones of his own, their infusing to be timed with Paternosters. The Queen listened to him with courtesy, and when he was gone, threw out his remedies, and returned to her own, applied with older healing spells.

For three days the fever raged through him like a fire despite all the infusions of yarrow and black willow bark. The women of the Queen's household tended him through the days, while I caught a few hours sleep in the corner of the chamber; and at night I took over, watching through the dark. I do not easily forget those nights in the women's house; the long-fingered light and shadows of the small night-lamp on the wall and the heady smoke of herbs burning in the brazier, the faint scratch and rustle of birds nesting in the thatch, and from time to time, the sound of women's voices or a bubble of laughter. And always the low muttering of Cynan on the bed. For with the fever, maybe from that moment in the King's Hall, speech had come back to him, though so low and broken that at times there was no making sense of it. But at others, squatting close beside him, I knew that he was living again and again through the days of the siege, through the last charge of the Shining Company, through the deaths of his brothers.

In the midst of the fourth night, I must have drifted into a doze, my head propped on my updrawn knees. I woke with a start to an unusual quietness in the room. For a moment I wondered what sound was lacking, and then I realized that Cynan's low mutterings had ceased. I came to my knees and was leaning over him on the instant, fear knotting in my belly. He was breathing slowly and quietly, and the constant restless movement of his head on the pillow had ceased. I got up and took the lamp from its wall niche and brought it to the bed, shielding it with my hand so that the light should not fall into his eyes. The little flame flickered for a moment, then steadied, and I saw the sweat on his face and pooled in the creases of his neck, and when I put my hand on his forehead it was cool and wet.

The fever had broken, and he was lying in a pool of sweat.

Trying not to wake him I eased out the sodden bedding and flung it into a corner, replacing it with soft dry skins that lay ready and wiped him down with a linen cloth. I was just pulling up the coverlid when his eyes opened, and he lay frowning up at me, the first time in many days that I had seen him look at someone as though actually knowing that they were there. As though actually knowing who they were.

'Prosper. What in the name of the Black One do you think you're doing?' he said, and his voice was weak, but clear-cut as a whiplash.

'Nothing that need concern you,' I told him. 'Let you go back to sleep.'

When he woke again it was near sunrise, the first grey promise of daylight dimming the light of the lamp, and the sky beyond the high window barred with saffron.

He tried to sit up, then fell back, and lay looking at me, the frown deepening between his brows. 'Great Mother of Foals! My head's swimming – I feel like a half-drowned kitten. What's amiss with me?'

'You were wounded, and you have been ill,' I said. 'Lie still, and you'll mend.'

He fumbled up one hand and found the puckered scar and the changed and gouged-out shape of his cheek-bone. 'There were studs in that club. I saw them in the moonlight.'

'So did I,' I said.

'Yes, you were there.' The fumbling hand was across his eyes. 'I remember – but there's great holes in it – like a dream – there was a moon – and mist – blood everywhere – the horses –' his voice, which had begun to blur, cleared again with quick anxiety. 'Is it well with my horse?'

'All is well with your horse. He's in the stable here.'

'Here.'

'You are in Dyn Eidin: in the Women's House. Trust you! And the Queen and her women tending you.'

He let out a crack of what would have been laughter if it had not been so weak and had such a broken sound to it. But his mind had gone on to other things. 'So we got back to Dyn Eidin. All those empty benches in the Mead Hall last night – the King said – was it true? Not an evil dream?'

'Truth,' I said. 'But it was not last night. You have lain sick for four days.'

His arm was still across his face, as though for a shield. 'The King betrayed us,' he said through shut teeth.

'I think he was caught in a kind of web. It was the only thing he could do.'

'He could have broken the web.'

'How? He is not Artos.'

'He is not Artos, that is a true word.' He remained for a little, his arm shielding his face. Then he let it fall away, and reached out towards me, 'You brought me off.'

'I am your shieldbearer,' I said. 'I brought you off.'

'Why in Epona's name didn't you leave me to die with the rest?'

'Bringing you off seemed like a good idea at the time.'

'Maybe one day it will seem like that to me, too. Maybe one day I'll thank you for it.'

('Not you,' I thought. 'You are not one to thank anybody for anything.')

I do not think he knew that he was clinging to my hand like a drowning man, as he drifted off to sleep again.

# The Flower of an Emperor's Bodyguard

Cynan was indeed as weak as a half-drowned kitten, and lay for many days while the slow strength crept back into him, and for the most part the Princess Niamh and I nursed him between us under the direction of her mother the Queen. It seems an unlikely arrangement, looking back on it, but I had the strength and the Princess already had much of the skill, so there was good sense in it, after all.

In the chamber in the women's house high in the heart of Dyn Eidin, with its window looking out westward over the huddled roofs of the fortress to the distant hills, the long days of summer went by with an odd peacefulness like the spent quiet of weather after a tempest. Even Cynan felt a kind of breathing space; a time to be gathering himself together.

In a while he began to be able to leave his bed and waver across the room with my shoulder to steady him, and sit huddled in his cloak beside the brazier – even at midsummer the evenings have a chill to them so far north, and he seemed always cold just then. The brazier no longer gave out the pungent scents of medicine herbs but the fresh sweetness of burning pine or apple wood. The Princess Niamh still came often, usually with the little dog, Cannaid, pattering at her heels, and sat playing draughts with him, or trying to make him laugh with the gossip of the women's house. And when she was there I could leave him for a while and go about my own affairs, exercise the horses, talk with Conn who had gone back to Fercos' smithy as though he and his mates had never ridden south with the rest of us – the weapon-smiths were hard at work once more, in Dyn Eidin – even ride hunting with the men of the Teulu, though only once or twice for it meant being away from Cynan longer than I liked.

Others began to come, beside the Lady Niamh; men of the Teulu who would lounge down on the bed-place or beside the brazier, and talk of the things that are common to all men bound together in a sword-brotherhood – the Companions had shared much the same talk in the year that was past and I remembered with something of surprise, that this had been his brotherhood before ever the Companions came together. I got the feeling that he also was remembering it with the same surprise, maybe even trying to find his way back among them but not quite succeeding, because of the things that had happened since, and the things that must remain unspoken.

Aneirin came too, but not often, and then only to stand by the window looking out for a while, and then go away again, scarcely speaking. We knew the signs. A poet when his Arwel comes upon him is not as other men, he was lost in the making of his Great Song, and all living men were shadows to him just then.

One night Phanes the merchant came.

The evening meal was over in the Mead Hall, and Cynan should have been in his bed, but he was still sitting huddled in his cloak by the brazier. The Princess and I were both with him, trying to keep him amused, for he was like most sick men on the mend, thinking that he had more strength than he really had, and becoming bored and restless as a falcon kept too long mewed.

Phanes came in, still stooping over the wound, and settled himself on the stool I drew forward for him, sitting hunched, just as I remembered him in the Hall, that first evening of our return. His skin, that had been nut-brown, showed yellowish and oddly transparent in the light of the lamp. He asked after Cynan's wound, then fell to talking of this and that – I think the trade in wolfhounds from Eriu came into it somewhere. It was a driech and cheerless evening, the small mean wind billowing the leather curtain over the doorway, and outside, the hush of summer rain, and by and by he leaned forward, holding his hands to the warmth of the burning apple logs, and as he did so his cloak fell back from one shoulder, and the lamplight touched the dagger in his belt.

A silver hilted dagger, the hilt shaped like an arch-angel with folded wings.

Cynan flicked a finger at it. 'That is a strange dagger, friend.'

The merchant slipped it from the sheath, and held it out to him; and he took it, leaning sideways to catch the light on its curious workmanship.

'Strange, and beautiful. Is it a new treasure? I am thinking I have not seen you wear it before.'

'I seldom wear it.'

'I think if this were mine, I would not choose to wear any other,' Cynan said, turning the deadly toy between his fingers.

'But it is not mine. And not wishing to risk another man's treasure in the kind of life that I have been living of late years, I have left it until now with my Lord Mynyddog for safe keeping.'

Cynan handed the dagger back. 'Do I scent a story? A story for telling by firelight?'

'Nay, no story,' Phanes said, returning it to his belt. 'It is work of Constantinople. I bought it from a friend in the Emperor's bodyguard who was somewhat desperately short of cash at the time. It has always been in my mind to hold it safe and sell it back to him one day. That is all.'

And for the moment I was back five years, in the doorway of the smithy at home and Conn with me, watching old Loban at work in the dappled shade of alder trees.

'One day, when you go back to Constantinople and he has the gold to spare?'

The merchant shook his head. 'That was the general idea, once. Not now. I am old and sick beyond far-travelling. I shall not see the Golden Horn again. The King has given me guest-space for what length of life is left to me, and here I shall bide, seeking some other of my kind to carry Alexion's dagger back to him, as my gift.'

There was a rather painful silence which it seemed to me needed breaking.

I said, 'I have seen that dagger before; at the smithy of Loban my father's smith. It had a broken wire to be mended. You showed it to Conn and me, and the blade bewitched Conn so that he wanted nothing after, but to be a swordsmith and forge blades for heroes.'

'And he is on the way to gaining his wish,' Phanes said; and then, 'For you, I think, it was the hilt that held the magic.'

'For me, the hilt told of far countries. A world beyond my own hills. You told us of the wonders of the Golden City.'

'Travellers' tales. Travellers' tales, my children. As much a part of a merchant's stock in trade as the silk and sandalwood he carries in his bales.'

'Tell again,' Cynan said, slipping into an easier position and leaning his head on the striped cushion behind him. 'Good stories will always stand re-telling.'

So I put more apple wood on the brazier, and leaning forward, gazing into the new flames as they sprung up, as though he was seeing there the things he told of, Phanes began to spin his traveller's tale. He told of the Emperor's garden that had little trees in it whose leaves were all of beaten gold; of the great horse races, blue faction against green, on the race-track overlooked by four bronze horses half as large again as life; of sailors' fights down in the docks, and evil doings in back alleys; of the rose-flavoured jelly that could be bought in the street of the Golden Grasshopper; of hunting with leopards instead of hounds, and the deeds and misdeeds of the Emperor's bodyguard.

He was almost as good a storyteller in his way as Aneirin. He had me tasting the strange fruits and smelling the gutters of the Golden City; as to the others, I could not tell. Cynan was gazing into the heart of the brazier, but there was no knowing whether he saw the things of which the merchant told, or other things of his own, or only the darkness within himself. The Princess sat very still, and I think that she was listening, but her eyes kept going from the storyteller to Cynan's face, drawn and scar-pitted in the lamplight, as though she too was wondering what he saw, what was going on within him. She had grown much older in the year and more since I had first seen her, and I knew that he would only have to whistle and she would follow – as Dara had once said – to Constantinople, or the apple islands beyond the sunset. But I also knew that he would not whistle. Something in him was hurt beyond that. It might mend one day, but not yet, not for a long time. And my heart was sore within me for the Lady Niamh, and behind the coloured skylines of the Golden City, I heard the chilly hush and whisper of summer rain across the thatched roofs of Dyn Eidin.

A day came when Cynan flung on his good cloak that I got out for him from the kist in the chamber of the King's house where he had been moved as soon as he was well enough, and came out to share the feasting in the Mead Hall. It was Lammas, the start of harvest time, and the first sickle cut of barley had been brought into the Hall and set up on the great tie beam in the crown of the roof; and the Lammas torches had been lit and carried round the crop-lands; and when the feasting was done and the stories and the songs of lesser harpers fell silent (there had begun to be songs sung and stories told again in the King's Hall), the men of the Teulu began to call to Aneirin for a new song; for though as a king's bard he was, as I have said, above the rank of those who wake their harp after supper, yet on the great feast nights of the year he would sometimes take harp in hand himself; so now they begged for a song – a new song to speed the harvest.

'My song is not yet made perfect,' Aneirin told them.

But we all knew what song it would be, and voices called out that he had had three moons for the making of it, and that surely there must be something of it ready to be brought forth, for they – we – had been long waiting. And in the end he sent for his harp and his singing-robe, and when they were brought, rose and pulled the mantle over his shoulders and stood with the kingfisher folds hanging to his feet and the little bog-oak harp cradled in his arms. 'So be it. At least you shall be able to tell your grandsons that you heard, when it was still rough-hewn, some part of the Song of the Gododdin at Catraeth, and that Aneirin sang it for you.' We knew what that meant, for when the song was made whole, and polished and perfect, the poet's part in it would be over, and it would be for other men to sing. And Aneirin sat down on the singing stool, settling the harp between his knee and the curve of his shoulder.

So that night, sitting at the King's feet, Aneirin sang for us, and maybe for the ghosts of those others, too. And listening, I remembered the ruined fort on the night before we rode out for the last time, and looking at Cynan in his place on the warrior benches, I saw that he was remembering, too. Aneirin tuned his harp and began to play, striking out flights of notes like sparks from a windy fire; and against their bright background he flung up his head and in the half singing, half declaiming voice of his kind, began his song.

I have wondered since what they were like, those songs when their final burnish was upon them. They were rough-edged when we heard them, but already they shone.

'The men rode to Catraeth, jesting by the way
After the feasting, clad now in mail,
Strongly they went from us into the morning.
Deadly their spears, before death come to them,
Death before their hair could be touched with grey.
Of three hundred horsemen, Ochone! Ochone!
Only one rider returned from that fray.'

The harp rhythm changed as he sang of this man and
that – of Gwenabwy, how he had killed a wolf with his
bare hands. Of Morien and Madog and Llif from
beyond Bannog, of Tydfwlch the Tall and Cynri and
Peredur, and Gorthyn of the Battlecry. A score or
more; the men whose fame he sang for us that night.
And when he had done, and harp fell silent, there was
a stillness in the King's Hall.

And in the stillness, Cynan lifted his head and looked
across the fire with eyes that were at once weary and
over-bright, and asked, 'And what of the One?'

'The One?' Aneirin said.

'The one of all the three hundred, who came back.
What honour song will you make for him?'

There was a stirring in the Hall like a little wind
through standing barley.

'It is already made,' said Aneirin. 'This is the song
for the One who came back.'

And he drew his hand across the harpstrings and
sang again, for the last time that night.

'In battle-fury like a lion, Cynan the noble and most
     fair;
His war shout on the farthest wing, a rallying point
     for men.
The Sea-wolves fell like rushes before his blade,
His spears were as the lightning-strike,

And when they landed, no need for second blow.
Whole war hosts he burst through, with lime-white
    shield hacked small,
Swift was his horse, leading in the charge.
His blade bit deep when he broke forth
Not lacking honour, with the dawn.'

The last flight of notes thrummed away and Aneirin stopped the faint humming of the strings with the flat of his hand.

And Cynan said, 'That was a good singing, harper dear. Death denied me my place with the rest of our company, but the greatest of all bards has not denied me a place with them in the Song of the Gododdin.'

The King, who had sat listening without a move throughout, stirred inside his heavy mantle, and summoned in his harsh, broken voice, 'Cynan, son of Clydno, come you here to me.'

And Cynan got up and made his way, stepping over the sprawling hounds, to stand before the King at the High Table.

For a long-drawn breath of time Mynyddog lay back in his great chair looking up at him as though he were a book that he was trying to read, then he said, 'The Gododdin will have need of all its fighting men yet living. Your old place among my warriors waits for you.'

'But it is no longer mine,' Cynan said. 'My place was with another company, and without them it is not in my heart to bide here in Dyn Eidin. My Lord the King, give me leave to go.'

'You must give me better reasons than that.'

'I have several. Three at least,' Cynan said, and I thought for the moment that there was a flick of laughter in his tone, but I must have been wrong.

'So. Tell me the first,' said the King.

And Cynan said lightly, 'Maybe the hunger is on me to carry my sword in distant places.'

Mynyddog bowed his head. 'And the second?'

'I am not minded to live out my life in a place where I see it in men's eyes that I am the One who came back living from Catraeth.'

'Even after Aneirin's song?' said the King.

'Even after Aneirin's song.'

'And so you will run like a hunted deer?'

I saw Cynan's shoulder jerk, and he answered as one flicked on the raw, 'I would not have run for that alone.'

'There was a third reason. Let you tell it to me.'

Cynan said a little breathlessly, 'My Lord the King, do not ask me the third reason, for it is mine to me.'

There was a long, breath-caught silence between the two of them. The King lay back among his ramskins, looking up into Cynan's face, waiting. He did not ask again for the third reason, but I think the knowledge grew in him of what it was. Maybe he was remembering the first night of our return, and that terrible cry of Cynan's when the truth pierced through to him. He could not know as I did, of Cynan in the women's house, lying with his arm across his eyes as though to shut out something horrible, saying, 'The King betrayed us.'

But I saw him begin to understand the accusation and I was afraid. Yet when he answered (for it was an answer, though the thing had not been spoken), it was without anger.

'Do you think that it was an easy decision?'

'No,' said Cynan.

'But still you wish to go from Dyn Eidin?'

Cynan said, 'Yes,' and the word stood like a rock.

'So be it then. Go free of the Teulu, and the sun and the moon on your path. But be gone by the morn's morning, and do not come back,' said the King.

Cynan made him a kind of bow, then turned and strode away down the Mead Hall.

I got up from my place and went after him. Phanes of Syracuse sat on the guest bench near the door as he often did, there being more air there than at the upper end of the Hall, and Cynan checked for a moment in passing, setting a hand friendlywise on his shoulder. 'Will you trust the dagger to me, to get it safely back to its master?' he said, and we went out through the great foreporch into the night.

Outside in the dark and heading for our sleeping quarters I asked, 'When do we start?' I think I had some stupid idea that he might be about to walk out of Dyn Eidin there and then.

'The morn's morning, as the King said,' he answered me, as though it was the simplest and most ordinary of matters. 'I need a day to gather up what I can by way of journey gold, and see to the bestowal of my horses – and my brothers' horses. The King knows that.'

I also had matters of my own to see to. And next noon, having whistled Conn out from the smithy and told him what there was to tell, I was leaning with him on the fence of the horse-paddock, feeding Shadow with the honey-cake that I had brought for her.

'And you must go with him?' Conn asked.

I was still feeling winded by the speed with which a new and unthought of future had opened at my feet; but it was the first time that the question had come to me. It had seemed to me last night in the darkness outside the torchlight of the Mead Hall that my going was as a natural part of Cynan's going. It still did. I said, thinking the thing out as I went along, 'He is not fit yet to be setting off for the other end of the world alone; and he is my responsibility because I was the one who brought him off from Catraeth. And he barely notices I am there anyway, so he will not mind as he would if somebody else tried to go with him.'

'Not that anybody else has,' Conn said dryly.

'Not so far as I know.'

'You're a good friend, Prosper, I should know that,' he said, and there was a kind of ache in his tone that made something tighten in my own throat, so that I made a great thing of fondling Shadow's forelock for a moment.

'As I should know it of you,' I said. 'Therefore will you take Shadow for me?'

He looked round at me quickly. 'You are not taking her with you?'

I shook my head. 'I cannot be taking her to Constantinople, and I would not be selling her to strangers in Caerluil. Ride her back to the valley when the time comes.'

'You are still harping on that tune?'

'When you feel that you are enough of a swordsmith to satisfy Loban – and my father, if you want Luned.'

I felt him startle and then grow still beside me. 'If I want Luned?'

'You do, don't you?' I said.

'Luned is yours.'

'No.' I was sorting it out as I went along. 'Luned is nobody's until she chooses. There is love between Luned and me – once I thought . . . But it is more like brother and sister. There is love between Luned and you, and that, I am thinking, is of another kind.'

'Even if you speak truly as to that,' Conn said slowly, 'the chieftain your father would never give her to me. I have been a bondservant in his house.'

'We have had this conversation before,' I told him. 'You are not a bondservant now. Make him a serviceable blade or a set of shoes for his favourite horse, and I think he might. She has no dowry to make her easy to marry off, and a smith is worth having in any family.'

'Aye, still the great one for ordering other men's lives, you are,' Conn said, and I heard a certain wry amusement in his tone.

I pushed Shadow's muzzle aside and turned on him. 'Only when they need it. Take the mare and ride beyond the sunset with her for all I care. But, Conn, along the way, go back to the valley and see that all is well with Luned and rub Gelert behind the ears in my name, before you ride on. Will you do that for me?'

'I will do that for you,' Conn said. 'And if Luned will have me but your father will not, then I will take her up before me and Gelert shall run at our heels. It should not be so hard to take a horse – and a hound – and a woman – across the western water, and there would be room for another swordsmith in Eriu – even if there is none in the valley.'

Next morning Cynan and I rode down from Eidin Ridge and away westward through soft late-summer rain not heavy enough to havoc the harvest. We both rode good serviceable mounts to be sold off before we took ship; and I led a pack beast with all our goods

and gear and food for the journey baled on its back.
Cynan had the archangel dagger thrust into his belt
beneath his worn wolfskin cloak, and some writing on
tablets which Phanes had given us for showing to
certain merchant houses and ship masters along the
way. And we both had our swords, and light wicker
bucklers slung behind our saddles.

We rode down from the town ridge and out past the
Royal Farm, and nobody came to watch us go. Only a
farm dog ran a little way snapping at the horses' heels.

Where the road lifted, I looked back once, seeing
the Dyn on its great boss of rock, upreared dark
against a sky that was brightening over beyond the
Giant's Seat where a bar of daffodil light broke the
clouds. Then I turned face-forward again, and settled
into the saddle.

There was another gleam of daffodil colour in the
grey morning, where Cynan had let his cloak fall loose,
and I saw that he wore a wisp of yellow silk round his
neck, finely worked with coloured flowers in a foreign
fashion. I knew it well, for the Princess Niamh had
often worn it to bind up her hair when she wished to
keep the braids out of the way.

It was not the first time that I had seen him wearing
a girl's favour, and I guessed that it would not be the
last; but I was as glad as a sentimental old hen-wife
that he should wear the Princess's favour as he rode
away. Glad for her sake, and also, I think, for his . . .

So we settled down to ride. Behind us Catraeth and
all the life that we had known; and ahead Caer Luil
and some merchant ship that did not yet know she was
waiting for us, and unknown roads and strange lands
and whatever of good or ill was written on our

foreheads. The faint road lifted over a ridge and there was heather round our horses' feet. The west wind blew my hair across my face and the taste of it seemed already salt on my lips.

Beside me I heard Cynan laugh. He was riding head up into the wind. He glanced at me over his wolfskin shoulder easily as a man looks at a comrade in arms. 'We may not look like the flower of an emperor's bodyguard,' he said, 'but Constantinople, make ready for our coming!'

# Author's Note

About the year 600 AD, Mynyddog, King of the Gododdin, gathered three hundred warriors together to his tribal capital of Dyn Eidin, where Edinburgh now stands. He housed them for a year, during which they were trained and hammered into a fighting brotherhood, and loosed them against the invading Saxons of what is now Yorkshire and Northumberland. One of the few survivors was the poet Aneirin, who rode with them and recorded the whole epic tragedy of the raid in *The Gododdin*, the earliest surviving North British poem.

I have based *The Shining Company* on this poem; but since Aneirin was really more interested in producing a string of elegies for young men killed in battle than in telling us what actually happened, I have had to invent a good deal of the story-line for myself. In doing this I have tried always to keep as close as possible to the way a raid of that kind might in truth have worked out.

Except for Prosper, who tells the story and is not one of the three hundred but a shieldbearer – something very like a squire – all my warriors are to be found in the original poem. But in three cases I have combined the exploits of two men under the name of one of them; therefore three of the brotherhood have been left nameless, and for this I ask their forgiveness.